WHEN WE DECEIVE

CATHERINE YAFFE

First published in 2023
Copyright © Catherine Yaffe 2023

ISBN
978-1-8384486-1-5 (eBook)
978-1-8384486-2-2 (Paperback)

Cover by BookCovers Art

For Dad, always
11.4.43 – 20.12.21

PART I

1

Ziggy stopped abruptly in his tracks as a bolt of ice ran through his entire body. No, no, it couldn't be. He'd misheard, surely? Blood drained from his face, and a wave of nausea ran from the very pit of his stomach. He needed to hear it again, but at the same time, he wanted the name to change. From the look on the face of his boss, he knew it wouldn't.

'I'm sorry, what did you say?' Ziggy gasped, trying to replace the air that had left his lungs.

He watched through a fog of confusion as his boss, DCS Whitmore, pushed his chair back away from his desk and walked round to where Ziggy was standing. He felt a hand grasp his shoulder and he willed Whitmore to let go, fearing his legs were about to give way. Ziggy closed his eyes and took a few deep breaths. He was aware of Whitmore speaking, but he needed to shake his head several times before the words made any sense.

'I'm sorry, Andrew. It came in as a three-nine call about

thirty minutes ago. First responders confirmed the ID of the victim. It's Doctor Leila Turner. I'm so sorry.'

Ziggy stumbled backwards. 'Lolly? Where is she? I need to get there.'

Whitmore passed him a slip of paper with the details. Ziggy snatched the paper out of his hand, turned on his heel, and rushed into the main office. 'Take Bates with you!' Whitmore shouted after him, as he pushed open the doors to the exit, almost colliding with DS Sadie Bates. She grabbed his arm.

'What is it, Ziggy? You look like you've seen a ghost.'

He turned and stared at her, his brain refusing to form the words he needed. Saying nothing, he pushed her off and headed down the stairs.

Reaching his car, he started the engine, hit the accelerator and sped out of the car park. Briefly glancing in his rear-view mirror, he saw Sadie following him in her own vehicle. The address was Merchant Quay, the apartment of Frankie, Lolly's girlfriend of over two years. The apartment that Lolly was in the process of moving into. It was a ten-minute drive from Leeds District Police HQ. Ziggy ignored every red light as he headed out past Elland Road. As he hit the inner ring road, he screamed past the other cars, driving on the wrong side of the road when needed. He didn't care. His only goal was to get to Lolly.

As he turned into the gravelled courtyard, he was greeted by the flashing blue lights of the ambulance. He abandoned his car haphazardly, just vaguely in a parking space, and headed for the lobby. Anxiety and fear rose inside him like a tornado, and he was doing all he could to hold himself together. He heard a shout from behind and briefly glanced over his shoulder to see Sadie racing across to join him.

'Ziggy, wait,' she shouted again. 'Wait, let me go in with you.'

He marched on regardless, bolting up two flights of stairs as though they weren't there and ignoring calls from the crime scene manager. The last time he had been to Frankie's apartment was a month ago to help Lolly carry some of her books that he had been storing for her. He flinched at the memory. What the hell had happened?

A hand reached out and planted itself firmly in the centre of his chest as he reached the landing. 'Sorry, sir, but I need you to sign in and wear overshoes and forensic overalls. This is a crime scene.'

Ziggy looked questioningly at the young police constable. His brow creased. Crime scene? Until now, he had assumed whatever had happened must have been some kind of accident. But forensics? His nausea from earlier came rushing back, and he took a moment to steady himself.

Accepting the proffered PPE, he fumbled to pull himself into it but somehow managed a decent enough job to be allowed in. As he entered the front door, he looked down the long hallway and saw the various metal stepping plates that scenes of crime officers used to prevent contamination. Doors off the hallway lay open, with bright lights shining from what he knew to be the kitchen. The click of the mechanical shutter of a DSLR camera came from further down, towards the bathroom, which seemed to be where much of the forensic activity was taking place.

'Ziggy.'

He turned towards the voice calling his nickname. He saw Frankie, her tall, elegant figure, hunched over the breakfast bar, clutching a glass of water. They had met many times over since she and Lolly had been dating, but he didn't really know her well, Lolly being their only point of commonality. She slid off the stool and revealed her tear-stained face. Her usually carefully applied make-up had smudged and mascara covered her cheeks. Much to his surprise, she fell against him, and he had no choice but to place his arms around her as she sobbed into his shoulder.

He waited until she peeled herself away before speaking. His voice came out broken and coarse. He coughed and started his sentence again, trying to detach himself from the tsunami of emotion surging within him. He needed to apply his police officer mask. He couldn't be best friends with the victim right now. He had to put their intertwined past, their closeness, to one side, however incredibly difficult that would be.

He pulled himself up straight. 'What happened, Frankie?' He helped her retake the seat she had been sat on and grabbed a few sheets of kitchen roll, passing them over..

She noisily blew her nose and dabbed at her eyes before replying. As she spoke, a fresh batch of tears started coursing down her cheeks, and she had to keep stopping as her breath hiccupped its way out of her. 'I don't know. I wasn't here. When I got home, the lights were on and the door was open.' She paused to catch her breath and wipe her eyes again. 'I shouted, but there was no answer. I walked down the hallway and that's when I found her in the bath-room.' A flood of tears started again, along with guttural cries of grief and despair.

Ziggy couldn't stand it. Not when he was trying to keep his own emotions in check. He turned and indicated to the young uniformed constable to look after Frankie whilst he excused himself.

He walked back into the hallway where Sadie was still

struggling her way into a forensic suit as she called out to him. He stopped, closed his eyes, and took a deep breath.

'Boss, I'm so sorry.'

Ziggy looked at her and saw that she had been crying too. There were more than his feelings at play, he knew that. As a pathologist, Lolly had worked with the entire team and had formed many friendships outside of work. 'I know you mean well, but we have a job to do.' He stopped, thinking that they may be the coldest words he had ever said. 'Um, yes, we have a job to do, and we owe it to Lolly to do it properly.'

'Yes, yes, of course, but—'

He interrupted her. 'Let's see what we have, shall we?'

With much trepidation, he headed towards the bathroom. As he tried to process the scene visually, all pretence of being detached from emotion left him.

His friend, his best friend, the person he had grown up with, who knew him better than anyone else in the world, was lying naked in the bathtub, her face just visible above the bloody waterline.

2

Ziggy took a step into the bathroom. The lead forensic officer stopped what she was doing and turned to him.

'You can't be in here, DI Thornes.'

He heard the pity in her voice, but he was staring at the figure in the bath, trying to reconcile it with his whacky, hippy, fun-loving, very-much-alive friend. *Oh, Lolly.*

Bruising had developed around her eyes. Her lips had already darkened and her skin was mottled, discoloured, bloated. Glancing down at her thin body, he saw that it was covered in stab wounds. Too many to count. Her arms were above her head, and he could see defence wounds on her forearms.

My God, she fought back, was his only coherent thought.

He felt a hand on his shoulder and turned to see Sadie standing behind him. 'Ziggy, we need to let them get on with their work,' she said gently.

Stepping back from the horror in front of him, he realised that everyone had stopped what they were doing to give him some space. He wiped the tears that had formed in the corner of his eyes, apologised, but for what, he wasn't sure, and left the room.

'Whitmore's waiting downstairs for you. I think perhaps we should go find him.' Sadie was still at his side. He sensed she was reluctant to leave him, probably fearing how he would react to the whole situation.

Hard-wired to respond to any murder, he was suddenly filled with a sense of urgency. He grabbed Sadie's shoulder, ticking off a list on his fingers as he spoke. 'We need to start door-to-door, if it hasn't happened already.' He marched off, trotting down the stairs with a renewed sense of purpose. 'Does this place have CCTV? Where do the cameras point? Where's the building manager or caretaker? Have they been called?'

Sadie ran just to keep up with him. 'Andrew!' she shouted.

Ziggy stopped at the sound of his first name. Apart from Whitmore, no one at work called him Andrew.

'What?' he snapped at her.

'You need to go see Whitmore.' She was pointing at the exit, whereas Ziggy had been making his way towards the rear of the building and an office marked *Caretaker*.

He closed his eyes, always reluctant to do as he was told as opposed to what needed to be done. There was no getting out of it, though. He would have to speak to Whitmore at some point. Perhaps if he did it now, he wouldn't have to do it again later.

Sighing deeply, he headed outside. DCS Whitmore was standing with the other members of Ziggy's team: DS Nick Wilkinson and DC Angela Dove. As he approached, everyone peeled silently away.

'Sir?' asked Ziggy, impatiently tapping his foot.

'Yes, Andrew. First, I'm incredibly sorry for the loss of your friend. I know you were very close.'

'Thank you, sir,' Ziggy replied, in a deliberately dismissive tone. He couldn't cope with displays of sympathy. He had to keep up a professional front whilst he was still processing everything himself. He coughed. 'We need to start—'

Whitmore held his hand up, and Ziggy saw a look of trepidation on his face. 'Look, there's no easy way to put this.' Whitmore paused. 'I'm sorry, Andrew, but, you won't be able to work this case.'

Ziggy stopped mid-sentence and stared at his boss, incredulous. He couldn't believe his ears. 'What?'

'I said you can't work the case. You're too close to the victim— I mean Lolly, Doctor Turner. It's a conflict of interest. I'm sorry.'

The tsunami of grief that had been building turned into a roaring volcano of molten hot lava. Unable to form words, he stood to his full 6 feet 4 inch height, glowering down as Whitmore struggled to speak under Ziggy's intense stare.

'You know the protocol, Andrew ...'

Ziggy had stopped breathing. His head was screaming a multitude of profanities that he couldn't yet process. He spluttered, his words mashing together. Trying desperately to get a grip, he turned his back, inhaled and exhaled loudly several times. Though his face wasn't exactly a picture of calm when he turned back round, he had regained some sense of composure, and he'd vaguely controlled the urge to punch the object closest to him – that being his superior officer. Drawing on his every reserve, he spoke in a measured tone, trying to convey his true feelings.

'Sir, it's for those reasons that I *should* be SIO on this case. I need to find who did this and—'

'And it's those exact reasons that you won't be, Andrew. I understand your need for justice – honestly, I do – but we need a cool head and a sense of distance to solve this. And don't worry, we won't be handing over to another team. The assistant chief constable has approved me to be SIO, and DS Bates will be deputy.'

Ziggy felt as though the bottom had fallen out of his world. He was speechless. He continued to stare at Whitmore.

'Don't make this harder than it needs to be, Andrew.' Whitmore turned and went to address the crime scene manager who had been trying to get his attention. Ziggy stood stock-still, gobsmacked. Had that really just happened? What was Whitmore thinking?

'Ziggy, come and sit over here. I think you're in shock,' said Sadie, leading him over to a low wall. For once, he did as he was told and sat down. He leant forwards, his head in hands. The night air temperature had dropped, or maybe Sadie was right, and he was in shock. He'd seen it often enough with families who had lost loved ones to horrendous crimes. He had lost his own parents when he was just eight years old.

A stabbing ache pierced his stomach. 'Oh shit, I need to speak to Bill and Irene ... Oh my God, Rachel and Ben.' The foster parents he shared with Lolly, as well as his ex-wife and their son. They loved Lolly as much as him. They had to be told. He couldn't let anyone else break the news. He made to move, but his legs were like jelly. Sadie urged him to stay put whilst she went in search of a blanket and sweet tea.

As he hugged his knees to himself to generate warmth, his mind wandered back to the first time he had met Bill, Irene and Lolly, or Leila, as she was then.

.   .   .

Once the social worker had handed him over, Andrew looked at the kindly couple in front of him and felt tears building. He was sure they were very nice, but he just wanted his mum and dad. He wanted his Liverpool FC-themed bedroom and his brothers and sisters around him. All that was gone. It had been snatched away from him without warning and he had been thrown to the mercy of social services.

The couple introduced themselves as Bill and Irene and showed him where to put his small suitcase; at eight years old, he had little in the way of belongings. They left him to unpack, but instead he took the time alone to lie on the bed and let the tears fall.

Suddenly, the bedroom door burst open, and a girl marched in. 'I'm Leila. Who are you?' She stood directly in front of him with her hands on her hips.

Sniffing again, Andrew looked her up and down. She was a tiny thing, but Andrew thought she might be older than him. She had short, cropped hair and was wearing brightly coloured clothes that looked as though they'd come from a scarecrow.

'I'm Andrew.'

'Ah, so you're the one they've been talking about.' She was staring at him, clearly judging his size and weighing him up.

'Who's been talking about me?' he wanted to know.

'The olds. They've been in a tizzy all week waiting for your arrival.' She moved around the room. 'Bill's been decorating your room.'

Andrew wasn't sure what he was supposed to say. 'That was nice of him.'

'Yeah, they're not bad actually, and trust me, I've been in some right weird homes.'

'Yeah?' Andrew pushed himself into a sitting position.

'Oh yeah, been in the system for years. My dad was a right bastard, used to hit my mum. Anyway, she died, and he ended up in prison for her murder.'

It was said in such a matter-of-fact way that Andrew stared open-mouthed, lost for words. He felt uncomfortable and awkward at the bombshell she'd dropped. 'I'm sorry, that sounds rubbish,' he said finally, not sure where to go with the conversation. Was he supposed to tell her what happened to his parents? He didn't want to. He couldn't, it was too hard. Instead, he changed the subject. 'I need to put my stuff away,' he said, reaching for his bag.

He expected Leila to leave him to it, but she stood watching him as he self-consciously unzipped his bag and placed his underwear in a drawer next to his bed. Then he pulled out his much loved Liverpool football kit, and she snatched it off him.

'Cool, I'm not a fan myself, but this is cool.' She held it in front of her and turned it over. 'Is he your favourite player, then?'

His parents had bought him the latest Liverpool home shirt, and it had Hughes on the back. He knew it would have cost more than they could afford, so he cherished it for many reasons, not the just name.

'Yeah.' He took it back off her and carefully placed it in a drawer.

Leila seemed to realise that he had nothing else exciting in his bag, so she turned and left the room. Standing at the doorway, she looked him dead in the eye. 'I think I like you.'

He gave a slight smile. The first in weeks. Maybe this wasn't going to be so bad.

3

'Here.' Sadie nudged Ziggy's leg, snapping him back to reality.

'I managed to get a blanket for you.' She helped him wrap it around his shoulders and he was grateful for the sliver of warmth it gave. 'I've sent Angela in search of a hot drink. You know how resourceful she is.'

Ziggy was aware of Sadie waffling on but, 'Thanks,' was all he could mutter.

He watched as the private ambulance pulled into the car park, fighting every urge to go with her. He knew the procedure. Lolly would be removed to the morgue, the scene would be handed over, the post-mortem would take place and all the while, the investigation would accelerate with all their resources thrown at it. Whilst he would have to sit on the periphery. Twiddling his fucking thumbs. He wasn't sure he could bear it. His entire police career had been about seeking justice, providing closure for families – something that had never happened with his own parents' deaths. His thoughts circled back round to his foster parents.

'I need to go, Sadie. I need to see Bill and Irene.' He stood up, dropping the blanket to the ground.

'Wait, I'll get someone to drive you.'

'No, it's fine. I need some time on my own anyway. Can you let Whitmore know?'

Sadie agreed, and Ziggy headed to his car. He sat in the driver's seat, his hands shaking, willing them to stop. He glanced out of the window, to where Sadie had been joined by Whitmore. He gave them both a slight wave to reassure them he was OK to drive and started the engine.

Heading north, finally alone and in silence, the images of Lolly lying in the bath came surging back to him unbidden. Why such a brutal death? Who could do such a thing to his friend? Multiple frenzied stabbings indicated anger. Was it a burglary gone wrong?

Frustrated, he slammed the steering wheel and let out a growl of exasperation through gritted teeth. Not being involved would drive him insane. He had to find some way of knowing what was going on, what lines of enquiry they were following. Walking away just wasn't his style.

As he exited the roundabout and left the A64, he tried to work out what he was going to say to Bill and Irene. They were in their eighties now, though apart from the occasional aches and pains of old age, they were both well. He knew this would devastate them. They had fostered many children over the years, but Lolly had always been their great success story. No one had been more proud at Lolly's various graduations than Bill and Irene.

As he pulled up outside the home that he had shared with them until he had left at sixteen, he closed his car door quietly. It was after midnight and he didn't want to wake the whole neighbourhood. He tapped gently on the door and braced himself.

After a few minutes, he saw a figure wrapped in a dark-coloured dressing gown, cautiously edging his way downstairs, through the frosted glass.

'It's just me, Bill. Don't worry,' he assured the elderly man. He heard him fumbling with the locks and eventually, the door opened.

'Andrew, what are you doing here at this time of night?'

'Andrew, is that you? What on earth?' Irene had joined her husband. 'Is everything all right?' She was fiddling with the hairnet she always wore to bed.

He stepped inside the familiar hallway and took hold of Irene's hand. 'Sorry for the late-night visit, but I need you both to come and sit down.' He led the way through to the cosy living room and switched on the table lamp. The couple followed him, holding on to each other so they made a crocodile of hand holding that separated when they each took a seat.

'I have some dreadful news, I'm afraid.' He paused, having no idea how to continue. He swallowed, screwed his eyes closed, and when he spoke it came out as a whisper. 'It's about Leila.'

He opened his eyes and saw Bill glance at his wife. He moved to sit closer to her on the sofa and took her hand. Bill's anxiety was barely hidden in his forced chuckle. 'What's she done now, silly thing?'

'I don't think that's the case, Bill,' Irene, perceptive as always, leant forwards and tapped Ziggy's knee. 'What is it, son? Out with it.'

He swallowed. 'I'm sorry, I'm so sorry but ...' He couldn't say the words.

Silence filled the room. Ziggy looked at his foster parents, waiting for them to join their own dots. When neither spoke, he filled the silence. 'I've just come from

Frankie's apartment. It was an emergency call ... I can't work the case ... Conflict of interest, but Sadie, you know Sadie? She is deputy ...' He knew he was racing his words, waffling, barely making sense.

'Stop, Andrew, stop. What's happened to Leila? Was she in a car accident or something?' Bill spoke as Irene just stared at him.

'No. It wasn't an accident from the looks of things. She'd been ... she was stabbed.'

'Leila? Stabbed?' Irene spoke in a whisper. 'Stabbed? Is she?' She looked at him in disbelief and it broke his heart.

Ziggy left his seat and sat on the sofa next to her, taking her hand in his. He felt a huge sense of guilt for hurting them both. 'I'm so sorry.' The tears fell.

'Oh, sweetheart, I'm sorry. This must be so hard for you.' She stroked his face.

How like Irene to put my feelings first.

'And you can't work the case?' asked Bill, who was stoically holding on to his tears.

Ziggy looked up at him, realising for the first time how frail he looked. 'No, it's against policy because we're related, kind of. We're close, anyway, close enough to be a conflict of interest.'

'Oh, Andrew, I am sorry.'

'Irene, please stop apologising.'

The three of them fell into silence again. Ziggy offered to make tea, but Bill insisted on something stronger.

After a while, Ziggy moved to an armchair. 'The next step will be a post-mortem, then she will come back to you for burial.'

'Oh gosh, yes, there will be all that to organise. Do you know what she wanted?' Irene looked at Ziggy, and it was the catalyst they all needed to stop the brave-faced charade.

They all huddled together on the sofa, arms round each other, lost in their own grief.

Ziggy felt his heart breaking, for himself and for his foster parents. The numbness, the shock he had felt earlier had started to wear off and the gut-wrenching pain was all-consuming. Finally able to let tears fall unchecked, and placed his hands on Irene's, squeezing gently.

4

Sunday, 15th September 2002

It was four in the morning before Ziggy arrived at his own home. It made no sense to call Rachel this early. Besides, he was emotionally exhausted. He knew he should go to bed for a few hours, but he couldn't face closing his eyes. The images of Lolly were still too fresh. He wasn't sure they would ever go away.

Instead, he took a shower and changed into his trackies and a T-shirt. After making a cup of tea, he headed into his home office.

Slumping into his chair, he felt hollow, empty. Not being allowed to work Lolly's case was a huge mistake as far as he was concerned. He knew her better than anyone. He knew her life, her friends, where she spent her time. At the very least, he should be considered a witness, interviewed as part of the victimology process. He scratched his head and cleared his desk, drawing a blank notepad towards him. He started listing everything and everyone he knew that was connected to Lolly, starting with himself and working outwards – in truth, outside of himself, colleagues and Frankie, the list was quite short. He pushed himself back in the chair.

'How can someone who was so full of life have so few connections?' he wondered out loud. Or was it that he didn't know her as well as he believed? That searing pain jarred him again, taking his breath away. He leant forwards, dropped his pen and banged his forehead with both hands.

'C'mon, man, think. Focus.' Frustrated and restless, he marched around his makeshift incident room. Years of training that had carried him through the traumatic scene had left him. Without them, he felt adrift. He had to pull himself together.

Still pacing the floor, he forced himself to walk through the crime scene again mentally, pushing down all his emotions.

Was there anything out of place? He knew there was CCTV. He'd seen the cameras. How could he view that? Sitting back in the cheap faux-leather office chair, he picked up his pen and tapped it against his teeth. He was going to have to call in a few favours.

Checking the time, he saw it was just after seven. Bracing himself, he dialled Rachel's number.

'Hello?'

'Rach, hi, it's me. Sorry to wake you.'

A few seconds passed before Rachel replied. 'Hi, Ziggy. What time is it?'

'Just after seven, I thought you'd be up getting Ben ready for school.' He felt bad. He knew how much his ex-wife enjoyed her sleep.

'It's Sunday, Andrew.'

'Shit, sorry. Course it is. Sorry. Look, I was wondering if I could call round?'

'Erm, sure. When?'

'Now, if that's OK?'

He heard the ruffling of bedsheets and the squeak of the mattress as she sat up. 'Yeah sure. Do you want breakfast?'

He felt his stomach clench. The thought of food made him shudder. 'No, thank you.'

'Is everything OK?' Rachel sounded more alert, but he didn't want to tell her about Lolly over the phone.

'I'll be there soon,' he said, evading the question. In a vague attempt to sound more positive, he changed his tone. 'Get the kettle on and I'll see you shortly.' He ended the call before she could say anything else.

Heading to the bedroom to change into his work suit, he thought about Lolly and Rachel's friendship. He had introduced them to each other not long after he had begun dating Rachel. They had hit it off from the get-go, which Ziggy knew they would. When Ziggy told Lolly they were getting divorced three years later, she had tried to stage an intervention. Ziggy had been, as much now as he was then, more married to the job than to Rachel. He was glad the girls had remained close, and that Lolly's relationship with Ben hadn't been hugely affected either. They had all tried to ensure that, with Lolly forcing Ziggy to take time off whilst they went off on some adventure somewhere – something Rachel had never been able to do.

Ziggy adored his son, and in turn, his son adored him and Lolly equally. At the thought of having to break the news to the young boy, his stomach took a dive. *How do you talk to a seven-year-old about death?*

Shaking his head, unwilling to go back into the depths of despair he'd been swimming in since the night before, he headed into the kitchen. He'd regretted starting the refurbishment work, another of Lolly's plans, but thankfully, it was nearly finished. He smiled at the recollection of Lolly bollocking him for not sorting it out sooner.

He locked his front door and turned to face the day. The late-September weather held a chill that warned of colder months ahead. Across the fields next to his house, a thick mist rolled in. There was a threat of rain in the air, so he zipped his jacket closed and got into the car.

Rachel had moved house recently, after the catastrophe that had been her last relationship. Ziggy shuddered at the memory of how it had ended. There had been so much upset in Ben's life recently, and he was about to add to it. The wave of guilt almost consumed him, but he knew it was unavoidable.

As he pulled up outside their house, he saw Rachel peer through the living-room window. Shortly after, the front door flew open and Ben came running out in bare feet and just his pyjamas. Rachel came chasing after him.

'Put your slippers on at least.'

Ziggy laughed, opened his car door and scooped Ben into his arms, which wasn't easy as he was growing like a weed.

'Oof, big lad. Come on, let's get you inside.' The three of them headed into the kitchen, Ben chattering excitedly about his latest computer game.

'Bet you can't get to the next level?' Ziggy teased lightly.

'Bet I can!' With that, Ben shot upstairs.

Rachel laughed and grabbed two cups. 'Coffee?'

'Hell yes, please.'

He waited until she sat down before speaking. 'Rachel, I'm sorry but I have bad news.' His heart began beating outside his chest. He watched her face grow pale.

'Is it Irene? Bill?' Her hand went to her throat.

'No, love. It's Lolly.'

Silence descended. Ziggy waited and saw the dawning recognition grow on Rachel's face.

'Lolly? What's happened? Wait, no ... Is she ...?'

'I'm so sorry, yes.' Once again he was fighting back tears, not just for himself.

'But I don't understand. How? Why? Are you sure?' Her forehead creased as she screwed up her eyes, tears ran down her face.

He took a deep breath and ran through the events of the previous night. When he reached the end, she reached out to him. 'Oh Ziggy, I am so sorry. How are you?'

How was he? 'No idea. All I know is that I need to find whoever did this.'

Sniffing loudly, Rachel blew her nose on the tissue she had in her pocket. 'Oh, Andrew, what can I do? Are you sure it was murder?'

'It definitely looks that way.' He explained the conflict of interest and why he couldn't actively work on the case.

'Will you stay out of it, though?'

'I can't, Rachel, but I'll deal with that later. I just wanted to tell you and we need to tell Ben.'

Rachel ran her hands through her hair. 'Of course we do. Do you want me to do it?'

'I'll do whatever you think is best. I'm not sure what to say to him.'

Rachel called Ben downstairs, and when he eventually came into the kitchen, Ziggy looked into his little face. 'Come here, mate, come sit with me.' He lifted his son and placed him on the stool next to him. 'I have some really sad news to tell you.'

Ben's innocent face was wide-eyed and questioning, but he didn't speak. He just stared between Ziggy and his mum with a finger hanging out of one side of his mouth.

Ziggy looked pleadingly at Rachel and shook his head a fraction. Taking the hint, Rachel leant over the table.

'It's Aunt Lolly, sweetheart. I'm afraid she's died.'

Ben didn't move. He continued to stare, and Ziggy reached over and took the finger from his son's mouth. 'Do you know what that means?'

'Like when my goldfish died, and we flushed it down the toilet?'

Rachel chuckled softly. 'Kind of.'

'Are we flushing Aunt Lolly down the toilet?'

Ziggy smiled at the innocence of his son and ruffled his messy hair. 'No, mate.'

'How did she die?'

Ziggy scratched his own head, again unsure how much to tell him. 'It looks like some bad people did something to her.'

'Baddies?'

'Yes, you could say that.'

'Why didn't you stop them, then? Isn't that your job?'

It was like a sucker punch to Ziggy's gut. Why hadn't he stopped them? The guilt that he hadn't yet acknowledged came crashing down on him with full force. He couldn't find the words to answer and was grateful when Rachel tenderly sent Ben to his room.

'From the mouths of babes,' muttered Ziggy, as Rachel returned. She sat next to him and grabbed his hands.

'Do not blame yourself, Andrew.'

'He's right though, isn't he? Why didn't I stop it from happening?'

'Because you're not psychic. You can't have known what was going to happen. Did you even know what was really going on in her life?'

Ziggy looked at Rachel. 'I thought I did.'

'We can't know everything about everyone, Andrew.'

Rachel was right, but it didn't change the sickening sense of guilt he felt. He shrugged free from her hands and stood up.

'I need to go.' He had to get out of there before he was sick.

'Do you have to? Can't you stay with Ben? He might need you?'

'He won't, and you're much better with him. I have to go, Rachel.'

He shot out of the front door and threw himself into his car. He drove round the corner, opened his car door and emptied his stomach into the gutter with Ben's words echoing in his brain. 'Why didn't you stop them, then? Isn't that your job?'

5

___

Monday, 16th September 2002

Ben's words had stayed with Ziggy all night. The guilt that he hadn't been able to stop the baddies weighed heavily on his shoulders. He had to fight for Lolly. He had to bring closure, whatever the cost.

Tired, drained and running on caffeine, Ziggy splashed his face with cold water and used some blue paper towel to dry it. Nick Wilkinson had followed him into the gents at Leeds District Police HQ.

'How are you doing, mate?' asked Nick.

'Honestly? I don't know.' He shook his head and turned from the mirror. 'What time's the briefing?'

'In about five minutes.'

Ziggy threw the paper towel into the wastepaper basket and headed out of the door, Nick following.

As the pair entered the MIT office, the atmosphere was quiet, subdued. Everyone was busy with actions, but the usual chatter and banter had stopped. He saw a few of his colleagues glance in his direction and he acknowledged them with a small smile.

'Where's Sadie?' he asked.

'In with Whitmore.'

Ziggy headed to Whitmore's office. He entered without knocking and saw Sadie and Whitmore had their heads together. They looked up as he walked in.

'Andrew, I didn't expect to see you. How are you holding up?' asked Sadie.

'I'm fine. Just wanted to catch up with what's happening. Has Frankie been interviewed yet?'

The pair looked at each other. It was Whitmore that finally spoke whilst Sadie twisted uncomfortably in her seat.

'Ziggy, we'll be updating the team in a few minutes. Why don't you grab a coffee and we'll catch up afterwards?'

Ziggy stared at him. 'Afterwards? What?'

Sadie stood up. 'Please, Andrew, you know why.'

Ziggy was gobsmacked. Of course, he knew the protocol, but to hell with that. This was why he had joined the force. To uphold justice. He could feel his anger rising, and he had to leave before he did something he wouldn't be able to undo.

He made his feelings known by slamming the office door on his way out. He stormed over to his desk and threw himself into his chair. He sat swinging back on it, counting to ten and taking several deep breaths, but to no avail. A cup of tea appeared on his desk. He looked up.

'Thanks, Angela.'

'Figured you needed it, boss.'

Nick came over and joined them. The three of them sat in silence, not knowing what to say. Along with Sadie, they had worked as a team for over five years. Each team member complimented the other. Nick, or Wilko as he was frequently referred to, was somewhat set in his ways with an air of the TV character Taggart about him. He was rarely phased by anything. Sadie was hugely ambitious and had an infectious enthusiasm for every case. Angela was a whizz with anything technical, and the most organised of them all. She had a quick analytical brain that they all leaned on in any investigation.

Eventually, Nick broke the silence. 'I'm working on a case I could do with you taking a look at,' he offered tentatively.

'That's true,' echoed Angela, clearly eager to divert attention away from the elephant in the room.

Ziggy looked at his colleagues and appreciated what they were trying to do. He didn't have the energy to be ungracious and rebuff them, so he went along.

'Yeah? What is it?' He pushed himself upright and took a sip of his tea.

Nick pulled his chair over and dragged a file across the desk. 'Money laundering.'

Ziggy frowned. 'Really? Thought that was ECU?' The local economic crime unit would ordinarily deal with cases that involved fraud or money laundering.

'Yep, but this is bigger, and they believe it involves a criminal gang we've had contact with before.'

'Yeah? Who?' Ziggy's interest genuinely perked up.

'The O'Connors,' said Nick.

'No way? That group of clowns? They struggle to tie their own shoelaces. At least the youngest brother does.' The whole of the district team had, at some point, had a run in with the O'Connors. From age ten onwards, one or the other of them had been on the police radar for petty theft, noise abatement orders, antisocial behaviour, and as they grew older, their crimes had become more serious.

Flicking through the file Angela had passed to him, Ziggy thought back to his last contact with the youngest brother, Freddie. Ziggy had recruited him as his 'informer', or covert human intelligence source (CHIS) if you wanted to get fancy. Freddie would sell his own mother to buy his next fix. Most of the time, his information proved useful, leading to a few arrests, but hardly enough to bring down a cartel.

'And how are they involved?' It wasn't obvious from the file in front of him, though he could see numerous actions had been taken by other forces, including the Met.

'That's just it,' said Nick. 'It's proving hard to tie anything concrete back to them.'

Angela coughed and discretely nodded to Whitmore's office door. He and Sadie were just exiting. *Going to the team briefing, no doubt*, thought Ziggy, his earlier frustration returning. What he wouldn't give to be a fly on the wall.

Trying to get Ziggy's focus back, Nick spoke in a louder voice. 'There's a bloke, sorry, a detective from the Met heading up later today to share his intel and I'd really welcome your input, boss.'

Ziggy sighed, leant forwards on the desk and rubbed his face. He stayed quiet whilst he did some thinking. He still wanted to speak to Frankie, and he also wanted to go back to the apartments, take a look around, maybe speak to a few people. Turning to Nick, he gave a slight smile. 'Sure, what time is he expected?'

'Around three this afternoon,' said Angela.

Ziggy stood up. He had a few ideas of his own that he wanted to surreptitiously explore so he made what he thought was a plausible excuse. 'Great, I'll be back before then. I'm just going to head home and grab a couple of hours' kip and freshen up, I think.'

Nick and Angela collectively let go of their breath. 'Sure,' said Nick. 'I'll see you back here at three, then?'

Ziggy nodded his agreement and headed down the stairs. As he pushed the exit, a familiar yet unwelcome face appeared in front of him. He closed his eyes, hoping that when he opened them, she would have disappeared.

'Detective Inspector, what can you tell me about the murder of your good friend and colleague, Leila Turner?' Chrystal Mack smiled.

'It's *Doctor* Leila Turner, and I have nothing to say.'

'You don't deny murder, then?'

He looked at the reporter from the *Yorkshire Press* and felt his usual loathing for the media. 'You really are vultures, aren't you?'

He pushed past her and headed to his car.

'Just doing my job,' she shouted after him.

He slammed his car door. Chrystal Mack, or Mack the Knife as everyone on the force called her, had been a pain in his backside for years. He had no idea how she had managed to get hold of the details of Lolly's death, but then she always turned up like the proverbial bad penny at most crime scenes.

Thrown off balance, Ziggy took a moment to recall where he was going, and then set off, heading towards Frankie's apartment. He knew that Frankie wouldn't be there. It was still an active crime scene, but he wanted to take a look around in daylight.

Pulling into the courtyard car park, he acknowledged the young PC on duty and ducked underneath the crime scene tape. A couple of uniforms were hovering around the entrance.

'DI Thornes,' he said by way of introduction as he flashed his warrant card. 'Much been happening?'

The PCs looked at each other. The taller of the two spoke. 'House-to-house has been concluded, CCTV is being put on disk and we're just waiting for further instructions from MIT. I guess that's you?' The PC laughed awkwardly, keen to impress the detective inspector.

Without wishing to incriminate himself, Ziggy ignored the question and spoke with authority. 'I'll just head inside, if you two could wait here.' He left before they had a chance to speak.

Walking towards the building, Ziggy had to steel himself as memories from the previous night came back, threatening to break his composure. Keeping his game face intact, he realised that he hadn't, in fact, taken much notice of anything on Saturday night. He could see now that the entrance access was via the intercom only. He looked at the door plate and could see black dust where the fingerprints had been taken. The door was currently propped open to allow unfettered access, and he wondered if that was a common occurrence or just for crime scene purposes. He moved the block and let the door close behind him. After all, he didn't want anyone on the scene that shouldn't be there.

He made his way to the caretaker's office that he remembered briefly seeing and tapped on the door. After a minute, it was answered by a harassed-looking man.

'Yes?'

'DI Thornes, I'm here about—'

'Another one? Seriously, how many more of you are there going to be?'

Ziggy stared at the man. 'As many as it takes, sir. There's been a murder.' He couldn't keep the tone of disgust out of his voice. *Who is this idiot?*

The caretaker rolled his eyes. 'Yeah, one of your own and

you're all in. We have incidences every other week and not a word, not even a crime number.'

What an attitude. Pulling himself up to his full height, Ziggy took a breath before replying. 'I'd like to look at your CCTV from last night, please.' He emphasised the *please*.

'Your lot has already taken it.'

Ziggy thought perhaps he'd misheard. That wasn't what the PC had said. 'I'm sorry, taken it? Wasn't it being put on a disk?'

'Yes,' said the caretaker, his voice deep in sarcasm. 'Your lot has taken the disk. Took it earlier this morning. I wasn't here. It was the regional estate manager that was called to the scene last night, and he handed it over this morning.'

'Do you keep your own records, or at least a record of handing it over? Were you given a reference number by the officer who collected it?'

The man turned to the desk and grabbed a sheet of paper. 'Good job it wasn't me. I wouldn't have bothered, but the manager is a bit of a stickler for detail. Here.' He thrust a piece of paper in Ziggy's direction.

Fucking jobsworth. Ziggy snatched it off him. He glanced at the paper. It wasn't an official police document. It literally had *Disk taken* and two signatures he didn't recognise. Without another word, he stuffed the paper into his inside pocket and turned to leave.

'Charming. It's all the same with you lot – just take, take, take. We pay your bloody wages.'

Ziggy turned, marched over to Jobsworth, grabbing him by the scruff of his neck, and rammed him against a wall, pinning him there with an arm across his throat. 'How fucking dare you, you despicable piece of shit! A woman died last night,' he snarled, spitting with rage.

'DI Thornes!'

Ziggy let go of the man and watched as the idiot dropped to the floor. DCS Whitmore and Sadie were standing in the foyer behind him. Ziggy saw the look of shock on Sadie's face, whereas Whitmore looked incandescent with anger, his hands on his hips.

'I'll have your lot up for assault, bastards,' called the man, as Ziggy walked away.

'Get your arse back to the station now.' Whitmore spoke in a low, measured tone.

'Sir, I was just—'

'Save it, Thornes. Get back to the station and I will deal with you later.'

Figuring there wasn't much point in arguing, Ziggy walked sullenly to his car, ignoring the quizzical look from Sadie as he did.

6

Reluctantly returning to the station, Ziggy pulled his car into the car park and sat there for a minute. He really didn't want to go in, but he knew he had to. Taking a few moments to pull himself together, he retrieved his Nokia mobile phone. Figuring he couldn't possibly get into any more trouble, he dialled Frankie's mobile number. He didn't even know where she was staying. He let it ring, and when she didn't answer, he let it go to voicemail.

'Hi, Frankie, it's Ziggy. Just wanted to catch up with you, see how you're doing. Call me when you've got a minute.'

He ended the call, dropped the phone into his pocket, and headed inside. The office was fairly quiet, with everyone out on their various jobs and chasing up leads. Nick was nowhere to be seen, but Angela was at her desk and she looked up as Ziggy approached.

'All right?' she asked, biting her bottom lip.

Clearly the jungle drums have been beating. 'You've heard then?' There was little point in hiding from the gossip or denying it. It would be all over the station by now.

'Yeah,' replied Angela, uncertainly. 'Anything I can do?'

Ziggy smiled. 'No, don't think so, but thank you.' It was very much like Angela to offer to help him. He had a lot of time for her. She was an integral part of the team, the glue that held them all together during any investigation.

Nick came back just as Ziggy was logging in. 'Boss, you're back early.'

'You haven't heard then?'

Nick shook his head. 'Heard what?'

One thing he admired about Nick was his ability to isolate himself completely from the rest of the office, whilst still keeping up with the banter. He cherry-picked the office gossip he'd listen to but always remained on the periphery.

'Bit of a run-in with Whitmore,' said Ziggy.

'Whitmore? I thought you were going home.' Nick sat down, the penny dropping. 'Oh God, I should have known. You went to the scene, didn't you?' When Ziggy didn't reply, Nick just shook his head. 'Thin ice, mate, thin ice.'

'What was I supposed to do, Nick? It's not just another case, is it?'

'Not for you, but you know we have the best team. Let them get on with it.'

Angela nodded her head in agreement with Nick. 'He's right, boss, everyone is throwing their all at it.'

Ziggy wasn't sure if it was the pity in their voices or the frustration of not being included, but he suddenly couldn't be around them any more. He felt pressure building in his head, and not wanting to lose his composure so publicly, he stood and headed to the bathroom. Once in there, he locked himself in a cubicle and let the tears fall. He sat on the closed toilet seat and silently sobbed, releasing all the pent-up anger and misery. By the time he dried his face, he felt drained and empty. He unlocked the door, washed his face again, and braced himself to face his team.

'Where's Thornes?' were the first words he heard as he returned to the office.

'Great,' he muttered under his breath. 'Really don't need this.' He tried to make his way to the exit, but he'd been pointed out.

'Thornes! My office. Now!' Whitmore shouted the instruction across the heads of everyone, but there had been no need to as the whole office had fallen silent as they watched the floor show in front of them.

Ziggy rolled his eyes and turned round, making his way across the office floor to get to Whitmore. Sadie was standing just in front of the office.

'Ziggy, I just—'

'It's fine, don't worry.' Ziggy pushed past her and waited for his bollocking, slamming the door to Whitmore's office behind him.

'I don't really need to go over what happened today, do I, detective inspector?' said Whitmore.

Ziggy remained silent, squirming in his shoes, acutely aware that he had a potential lead inside his jacket.

'You were out of line. You impeded an active investigation, one that I explicitly told you not to get involved with.' Whitmore paused, but Ziggy still didn't speak. 'I was prepared to be flexible, Andrew. I understand this is personal for you. I was prepared to let a few things slide, but now? Well, now I strongly advise you to take the leave owed to you and return when you're in a better state of mind.'

Ziggy couldn't believe what he was hearing. Not only was he not allowed on the investigation, he was effectively being suspended. Did Whitmore truly expect him to stay out of it when so much was at stake? 'I don't think there's any need for that, sir.'

'You're not listening, Andrew. Take the leave, or I will

have no choice but to report today's incident. You have DS Bates to thank for the caretaker not pursuing assault charges. Take the leave, or face the consequences – your choice.'

Ziggy didn't think he'd ever seen Whitmore look so angry. Realising that this was one argument he would not win, Ziggy dropped his shoulders and pushed his hands into his pockets. 'I'll take the next couple of days, sir.'

'So help me, if I find you sniffing around anything to do with this case, I will have you hauled up in front of disciplinary in a heartbeat.'

Ziggy turned, about to leave, when Whitmore shouted, 'Not so fast, Andrew. The receipt for the CCTV, hand it over.'

7

Summer, 1965

Leila walked into the corner shop with all the confidence of an eighteen-year-old even though she had barely turned twelve. Andrew watched on from over the road as she disappeared from sight, his own heart thumping out of his chest. A couple of minutes later, Leila came flying out of the little shop with the owner hot on her heels. She was laughing, and her legs were pumping away as she bolted across the busy main road in his direction, causing cars to swerve and honk their horns.

'Run!' she shouted, as she vaulted the fence and took off over the playing field.

Andrew, caught up in the excitement, followed, not daring to glance over his shoulder to see if anyone was chasing them. He finally caught up with her as they rounded the cricket pavilion and tucked themselves away from sight under the stands.

He couldn't stop laughing. The dare had been to pinch one of the lollipops that always stood on the counter. Leila had somehow brought the complete stand with her.

'What happened?' Andrew asked, tears streaming down his face.

Leila tugged one of the lollies out of the stand and waved it in front of his face. 'They're all stuck in – look.' She tipped the domed unit upside down to show him the perforated plastic that held the lollipop in place. Between bursts of belly laughter, she explained how she'd gone to pull one out and found the whole thing coming with her.

Andrew clutched his aching sides. 'Stop it,' he said, when his own laughter allowed him to. 'I'll pee myself in a minute.'

Leila wiped her eyes and sweaty face with the back of her hand. She pulled off the jacket she was wearing and used the arms to tie it around her waist. Peeling the plastic wrapper from the lolly she was holding, she stuck it firmly in her mouth and exaggerated sucking noises. Pushing it into her cheek so she could speak, she said. 'I love lollipops.'

Andrew laughed. 'You love anything that you haven't paid for.' He took one of the lollies from the dome and followed Leila's example, shoving one into his cheek. 'What are we going to do with them?' He ran his fingers over the heads and counted. 'There's twenty of them left!'

Leila screwed her face up at him. 'We'll have to eat them, won't we?' she said, very matter-of-fact. She made a loud cracking sound as she crunched the sweet treat between her back teeth.

Andrew winced, fearing she might lose a filling. 'You'll look like a lolly by the time they're finished.'

'Better than looking like a pogo stick.' She stood up and started bouncing around, making boing noises.

He hated when she did this. For some reason, last week, she had told him he looked like a pogo stick because he had long legs. He couldn't help it if he was tall.

He stood up and chased after her. 'Yeah, well, it's better than looking like a lolly,' he called, as she continued to bounce over the *field. From that day onwards, he only referred to her as Lolly, and the nickname soon caught on with everyone else. She would return the favour in his teenage years when, after a disastrous haircut, he was left with haphazard zigzags cut into a shaved head. Though, if asked, he would say it was his love for David Bowie that had earned him his moniker.*

The rest of the afternoon was spent chomping on the lollipops and chasing each other around the cricket stand. As the sun started to set, they headed back to the home of their foster parents, wrapped in each other's arms like soldiers returning from battle.

Tuesday, 17th September 2002

Ziggy reached out as the figures faded in front of him. He called his best friend back to his side, but she was just out of reach. He was clutching thin air. The movement woke him and he sat bolt upright in his bed and felt his face. It was wet from tears. Much like every morning since her death, reality crept into his waking moments.
Defeated before the day had even started, he lay back down and pulled the covers over his head.
She was dead.
And he was clueless about how to catch her killer.
As he lay in bed, mulling over the scant information he had, he became aware of a knocking on his front door. Groaning, he pushed himself upright and swung his legs out of bed. He grabbed his dressing gown from the back of the bedroom door and shrugged into it. The knocking started again and, annoyed, he shouted downstairs.
'All right, already. I'm coming.' He stomped down to the

front door and snatched it open. 'What the hell? What are you doing here?'

'Charming, checking in on an old friend and that's the welcome I get.' Chrystal Mack placed a pointed high-heeled shoe over the doorstep. 'Aren't you going to invite me in?'

Ziggy ignored the question and stared at his visitor. 'How the hell did you get my home address?'

'Andrew, come on, I'm an investigative journalist. I have my ways.'

'What do you want?' He was tempted to push her back, but he feared she might fall, and he really couldn't do with the hassle.

'I have information for you.' She winked.

'You're a walking cliché, aren't you?'

'Come on, Ziggy, it's bloody freezing out here and I'm wet through, let me in. It won't take long.'

Ziggy shook his head at her rapid change in demeanour. He stepped back and allowed Chrystal to stand in the narrow hallway.

'I didn't mean to wake you,' she said, as she strode past him, eyeing up his dressing gown and walking into the kitchen. Suddenly feeling exposed, he excused himself whilst he dashed upstairs to throw some clothes on. After a quick change and face wash, he headed back down, listening to noises coming from the kitchen.

'One lump or two?' she asked, holding up the kettle, clearly having made herself at home. 'Having a bit of a makeover, are we?' She cast a glance around the unboxed goods piled up by the back door.

He stormed over, taking the kettle out of her hand and dumping it on the worktop. 'Cheeky sod, just tell me what you want.' He leant against the sink with his arms folded.

Chrystal mirrored his movement and leant against the counter.

'Haven't seen you round the station, just wanted to check you were OK,' she said.

'Bullshit. You said you had something to say. What is it?'

'Can we at least sit down?' She indicated to one of the stools under the breakfast island.

Reluctantly, Ziggy joined her. 'What is it?' His patience was wearing very thin.

'Are you OK? Genuinely, it can't have been easy losing Leila. You were close friends, weren't you?'

Ziggy closed his eyes. He should have known she was just fishing for a story.

Standing up, he grabbed hold of her arm and pulled her to her feet. He proceeded to drag her down the hallway towards the front door. 'Get out,' he spat as he pushed her towards the open door.

'No, wait. Andrew, honestly, I have information, really I do.'

'I don't believe you, get out!' He gave one final push and slammed the door. As he turned the lock, the letterbox snapped open.

'Ziggy, I have information on Lolly's case that I wanted to give to you.'

Tempted as he was to ignore her, his interest was piqued. He turned the lock back and slowly opened the door.

'No more of your bullshit. Just tell me what you know.'

'OK, I will, but it would be better if I came in, honestly.'

He stepped back and folded his arms, only allowing her as far as the welcome mat.

'Shoot,' he snapped, in no mood for games.

She shook the rain from her shoulders, leaving drips from her coat all over the hardwood floor. Pushing her blonde

hair back, she pulled her shoulder bag to the front and
unzipped it.

'As we don't seem to be doing common courtesy, I'll get to
the point, shall I?'

'That would be good, yes.'

She pulled out her notebook, dropped her bag to the floor,
and flicked through a few pages as she spoke. 'I've been
trying to contact Frankie, but no such luck.'

Frankie had returned none of Ziggy's calls either, so he
wasn't surprised. 'What does that have to do with me?'

Chrystal looked at him. 'Nothing, I haven't finished.'

'Get to the goddamn point then.'

'As I was trying to say, I couldn't get a hold of Frankie, and
you had gone AWOL, so I thought I'd see if I could contact
anyone she worked with. Bill and Irene refused to speak to
me, by the way.'

'My God, you really have no moral compass, do you?'

'Oh, get that look of scorn off your face, DI Thornes, you're
no better at times. If you'll let me finish, I might have found
out something useful.'

When Ziggy didn't respond, just looked at her with his arms
still folded, Chrystal took the hint and continued. 'Did you
know Doctor Turner had been suspended from her role as
Home Office pathologist?'

A bolt of lightning shot through him and it was a minute or
two before he could talk. 'Why?'

'Why was she suspended? I don't know, and clearly you
don't know anything about it either.'

He shifted uncomfortably, dropping his arms and heading
to the kitchen. He leant against the worktop to steady his
hands. *Suspended?*

He switched on the earlier abandoned kettle and waited for

the water to boil, giving himself time to think and frame his next question.

Chrystal had followed him and was again perched on the edge of the stool. 'I couldn't find anything beyond the fact that she wasn't working. No one would tell me more than that, and trust me, I tried.'

'Who told you she'd been suspended?' Ziggy passed Chrystal a mug of coffee.

'A woman called Rita, administrator for Leila's boss.'

'How did you get that out of her?'

'Probably best you don't ask. Let's just say it involved gin.'

Ziggy shook his head. He'd never met someone so unscrupulous, and he caught killers for a living. 'You have no shame. What does it have to do with her death, though?'

'That's where you come in. Did you have that as a lead?'

Ziggy wasn't about to confess he didn't have any leads aside from a scribbled signature on a piece of paper he'd copied before handing it over to his commanding officer. He ignored her question. 'It's not much, is it? Hardly a smoking gun?'

Chrystal had the audacity to look offended. 'You don't know that. It could be.'

Tired of listening to her now, he took her mug from her hand. 'I think it's time you left.'

Reluctantly, she stood up. 'Fine, it was a bit of a long shot, anyway.'

He indicated that she should walk down the hallway to the front door, and though she dragged her heels, she took the hint.

'Why aren't you at work by the way?' she asked. 'Twelve p.m. on a Tuesday and the great Ziggy Thornes is in bed? That's a story in itself.'

He opened the door, raised his eyebrows, and pointed outside. 'Leave.'

'Ever the gentleman. Maybe next time ...'

He slammed the door shut in her face, muttering, 'There won't be a bloody next time.'

8

After he had showered and shaved, Ziggy headed to his home office. Yesterday, he had started to work on his own case profile with the little information he had. He grabbed a Post-it Note and scribbled, *Suspended from work?* He stuck that to the wall he had now dedicated to the case. Torn out pages from his desk pad were taped up, alongside various Post-it Notes scattered around like bullet points waiting to be actioned. He'd detailed what he could remember from the apartment, but what he really needed was access to the case file.

He walked over to the spot where he had scribbled what he could remember from the receipt for the disk that had the CCTV footage on it. Most of it had been legible. It had the date and time the disk had been handed over (16 September 2002, 5.06 a.m.), along with the estate manager's name (Edward Brockhurst), and his signature, clear but scribbled underneath. Next to it, there was another signature that looked like E. Soh. It meant absolutely nothing to Ziggy. He did, however, know that it wasn't legit. Any evidence taken from the scene would have been placed directly into an evidence bag and labelled with an official reference number, not scrawled on a scrappy bit of paper.

Who the hell is E. Soh? he thought, tapping his pen against his teeth. Moving on to Mack the Knife's piece of news, he seemed to remember Lolly mentioning a Rita way back. Ziggy had no real need to visit Lolly's place of work at the coroner's office, but he felt sure he had met a Rita at one of Lolly's social events. He wracked his brains, but he couldn't quite place her. He turned to his computer, knowing there must be some way to search for her but uncertain how.

After a few failed attempts, he typed Lolly's full name into the search engine. He watched as several news articles loaded. He knew her death had caused a stir, for several reasons. When Lolly had qualified, she was one of the youngest Home Office pathologists in the country, graduating at the top of her class. She had been much sought after for her forward thinking, and her sometimes unorthodox approach to a challenge. She thought nothing of attending a crime scene, one of the first to do so, and long before such a thing became commonplace. Ziggy knew from speaking to her colleagues that she had breathed fresh life into a service that was continuously under threat as harsh budget cuts did the rounds in the public sector. Despite this, Lolly had remained loyal to her mentor, Professor Canter, and followed her into the Forensic Science Services laboratory in Wetherby. She had made many friends and was well respected both within the scientific community and the police service. The news articles all detailed her career history, with well-meaning quotes from ex-colleagues, friends and tutors.

Ziggy closed his eyes. He'd never felt so removed from everything. He felt as though he was trapped inside a bubble, seeing the world through a warped lens. He didn't like it. He felt out of control and he wasn't used to the sensation of feeling useless.

He had to get a grip. He had to make headway, with or without the support of the police service he had dedicated and sacrificed much of his life to. It seemed unfair to him that when he needed their support, they weren't there for him.

'Fuck protocol,' he said to the computer screen, turning it off and kicking his chair back. He needed to get out of the house.

Unlocking his car, he didn't really know where he was headed. Bill had phoned him regarding the funeral arrangements that he and Irene had made. It would take place at the local cemetery once Lolly was released back to the family. They had opted for a burial, unsure of what her wishes had been. It wasn't a conversation any of them had ever had, or felt the need to have.

Looking out of the window, he could see rain was now pouring down, no longer the drizzle that had soaked Chrystal. It was now big fat drops falling from a darkened sky that looked set for the day. He threw his heavy coat on and locked the door. He had no clear idea of where he was going, he just needed to get out. He processed the actions he would have taken had he been SIO, and frustration crept in. Irritated by a perceived lack of action, Ziggy punched Sadie's phone number into his mobile that was resting in the holder on the dashboard. As colleagues of five years, they were close and had an intuitive relationship. They thought similarly, rapidly reached the same conclusions and often socialised together with Lolly and Ziggy's ex-wife Rachel.

The sound of ringing echoed through the car. 'Ziggy?'

'Sadie, hi. How are you?'

'I'm good, thanks. Was going to call you later.' He could hear the office activity in the background. It faded as he heard her walking out of the noisy room.

'Oh yeah? What about?'

'Just to see how you're getting on.'

'I'm fine. Listen, have you spoken to Frankie yet?'

The line went quiet. 'As part of the investigation, yes. She's given us a statement.'

'And?'

'And what, Ziggy? You know I can't talk about it with you.'

He ignored her second sentence. 'And where was she? Did she give you any indication?'

'Ziggy, please. You are putting me in an awkward position.'

He silently cursed his directness. He attempted to soften her. 'Oh, come on, it's just between you and me.'

'No, Andrew, you're not being fair.'

Ziggy felt the heat rise in his face. 'Don't talk to me about fair,' he snapped. 'It's not fair—'

'I'm hanging up now, Ziggy, please only call me if you *don't* want to talk about the case.'

The line went dead. Ziggy stared at his handset. 'What the actual fuck?' He reached out, ready to redial but stopped. It was no use. He knew she wouldn't tell him anything.

Pushing thoughts of Sadie out of his head, he replayed the last time he had spent any time with Lolly. It was perhaps two weeks before her death. Though it had been raining, Ben had insisted they went to the park. He laughed as he thought about Lolly negotiating with Ben that it had to be Roundhay Park or nothing so she could get a hot chocolate from the mobile catering van. Ben had happily agreed as long as he could have one too.

As he drove round the back streets of Leeds, through Harehills and onto Scott Hall Road, he could feel the cold he'd felt that day and he shivered. Ah, Ben. He hadn't seen him since that first morning, though they had spoken on the phone twice. He carried a tremendous amount of guilt, as he still wasn't able to answer Ben's question. He didn't know why he hadn't been able to stop it, and that was the crux of his pain. Why hadn't he known? Why hadn't she confided in him about what was going on in her life?

His thoughts were interrupted by his phone ringing. He glanced at the screen and saw it was the police HQ. He jabbed accept. 'DI Thornes.'

'Ziggy, it's Nick.'

'Ah, all right, mate?'

'Yeah, not bad. Listen, I hear you had a bit of a tough time from Sadie.'

'Yeah, seems she forgets who her friends are when it suits her.'

Nick sucked in his breath. 'Bit harsh, Ziggy. You know she plays by the book.'

Ziggy relented slightly. Nick was right, really, he'd just let his frustration get in the way. 'I guess so,' he conceded.

'I, however, don't. Well, sometimes, but you owe me big time.'

Ziggy laughed, feeling grateful for having at least one ally. 'Nice one, mate, go on.'

Nick dived straight in. 'We've had a statement from Frankie. She's been cleared of involvement – has a solid alibi. There was very little in the way of forensic evidence at the scene. Some carpet fibres that couldn't be matched to the apartment ...'

'That's interesting, something at least, anyway. What about the CCTV?'

'I was coming to that. It's missing. Seems it was signed out by someone pretending to be one of us. Signature on a scrap of paper. Definitely not official.'

Nick clearly hadn't heard about Ziggy handing over the receipt. 'And has the paper been submitted to Forensics?'

'I believe so.'

Ziggy could hear papers being shuffled. 'Anything else?'

'We've discovered Lolly was suspended from work. Sadie's going to interview her boss later. Door-to-door was slow going and revealed little. Post-mortem confirmed she bled out due to multiple stab wounds.' Nick paused. 'Sorry, mate, that sounded harsh. You OK?'

'I'm good. Listen, thanks, Nick. It's much appreciated.'

'No bother, well it would be if you told anyone, so keep it on the low, pal, and don't do anything stupid.'

Ziggy ended the call, feeling a little shaken. It was hard enough listening to that kind of detail on a normal case, but for him, this was anything but normal. Determined to keep his emotions boxed up, he made a decision.

He stopped at traffic lights, got his bearings and drove out of Leeds city centre towards Cross Green. Nick's words reverberated in his mind. Mack the Knife had been right; Lolly had been suspended. He made a mental note of tasks he would pursue once he'd done Nick a favour – more to get it out of the way, then he could move onto other things

Ziggy vaguely recalled Nick mentioning something about the O'Connors in conjunction with the money-laundering case when he was last in the office. He could kill two birds with one stone whilst he was in the Cross Green area. He'd catch up with what was happening on the streets of Leeds and see if he could shed any light on Nick's case. Long shot, but he didn't exactly have a lot on right now.

As luck would have it, as he rounded onto the industrial estate, a forlorn, scruffy-looking man was hanging around the street corner. Ziggy flashed his lights and honked his horn. Freddie O'Connor lifted his head against the driving rain. Ziggy watched as recognition crossed Freddie's spaced out, pockmarked face. Pulling up to the kerb, Ziggy leant over and pushed the passenger door open. Freddie jumped in the car, and the stench of body odour and stale cigarette smoke filled Ziggy's nostrils. He lowered both of the front windows a touch, despite the rain.

'Now then, Mr O'Connor. How's you?'

'Am all right, Mr Forns.' Freddie made himself comfortable in the passenger seat, tugging his wet, oil-stained jeans out of his crotch and having a good scratch at his nether region.

'Been up too much?' asked Ziggy as he pulled away from the kerb.

'You know me, Mr Forns. Bit o' this, bit o' that.' He ran the back of his arm underneath his nose then reached forwards to open the glovebox. 'Got any grub?'

Ziggy made a mental note to disinfect the handle. He often kept snack bars in the glovebox and had once made the mistake of sharing them with Freddie, who now, like an eager child, expected them every time.

'Sure, help yourself,' he said, as Freddie pulled out a packet of energy bars. Waiting until Freddie had eaten two in quick succession, he started the conversation again.

'So, what do you know?'

'Heard Badger got sent down for a long stretch.' Badger had been a name that Freddie had passed over to Ziggy months earlier, which he had passed onto the drugs squad.

It had led to several high-profile arrests. Ziggy hadn't seen Freddie since.

'Yeah, I heard that too. What are those brothers of yours up to these days?' Ziggy took a left and pulled up in a dead-end street. He stopped the car and turned to face Freddie who was now ramming a third chocolate bar into his mouth.

Freddie had two brothers, Stephen the oldest and Robbie, who was the middle brother. As the youngest by some way, Freddie had been the runt of the litter and hadn't been blessed with either the business acumen or the street smarts of the other two. He was, however, somewhat loyal. Unless there was cash involved.

'Dunno, Mr Forns,' he said, uncertainly.

'No gossip for me, then?' he asked, removing his wallet from his inside pocket. He made a show of the twenties that were tucked into the back. He saw Freddie's head turn towards him, losing all interest in the food.

''pends what you mean by gossip.' Freddie's nose went up in the air as he craned his neck, trying to see what Ziggy had in his wallet.

'Something I don't know, perhaps.'

'Let me think,' said Freddie, as Ziggy removed five twenties from his wallet and counted them out onto the armrest between them. 'There was one thing.'

'Oh yeah.' Ziggy put his hand on top of the money to stop Freddie grabbing it.

'Been some bloke sniffing around, looked like a plod. Not you.'

Ziggy rolled his eyes. *No shit.* 'What made you think it was plo— police?'

'Looked like that bloke off of telly that me mam loves.'

Ziggy watched as Freddie screwed his face up in thought. He could practically see the cogs whirring.

'Taggart, that's it.' Freddie looked at Ziggy, grinning, clearly pleased with himself.

Nick, thought Ziggy. 'OK, and where has he been sniffing that he shouldn't?'

'Just around. Round shops and that.'

'Shops?'

Realising what he'd said, Freddie tried to backtrack. His hand reached out to take the money, but Ziggy snatched it away.

'Come on now, Freddie, half a story is no good to anyone.'

Freddie tutted and banged on the inside of the door. 'Pawnshops. But you can't say owt,' he implored.

'Now, Freddie, who would I say anything to?' said Ziggy, attempting to lull Freddie into a false sense of security. 'What's the big deal, anyway?'

Freddie stayed quiet, and Ziggy knew his mind would be running overtime to try to back out of the conversation. Ziggy opened his wallet and added a couple more twenties to the money.

Freddie was practically salivating. 'Just there's been a bit of bovver recently is all.'

God, it's like getting blood from a stone. Ziggy didn't even know if it would be information he could use, but he'd started down the road and didn't want to give Freddie a reason to back out. 'Bother? As in trouble? With what, and who?'

'Our Ste. He's been a bit stressed wi' our Rob. Dunno why. Summat to do wi' Robbie using that laptop our Ste carries round wi' 'im.'

Ziggy frowned. 'I'm not sure what you mean, Fred, tell me more.'

Freddie, realising he'd talked himself into a cul-de-sac

gave out a heavy sigh. 'I dunno how it all works, do I? But I overheard our Ste bollocking Rob for being careless, leaving shit behind or summat. Not finking about stuff, and he didn't know what he was going to say to the boss. Oh, and that he could do with that detective doing one.'

'I see. Can you get me more specifics?'

'Oh, I dunno about that, Mr Forns. It would mean taking risks. And they're my brothers, aren't they?'

Since when did that matter? 'I'll make it worth your time, Freddie.' Ziggy rubbed his fingers together in the international sign for money.

'You'll 'ave to give me some time, then.'

'A week, Fred. I'll be back next week, and I want all the details.'

Favour done, it was now time to track down Frankie.

9

Wednesday, 18th September 2002

'Angela, it's Ziggy.'

'Oh wow, Ziggy.'

He could hear Angela's hesitancy in speaking with him, but after yesterday and another sleepless night trying to work out how he was going to track Frankie down, he had gone to the only source he could trust – the ever resourceful, ultra-reliable Detective Constable Angela Dove.

'Please don't say anything, Ang, I just need a tiny bit of help.'

He heard a muffled noise as she switched the handset from one ear to the other. When she spoke, her voice was distinctly quieter and sounded infinitely closer.

'Will it get me into trouble?'

'No. I just need an address for Lolly's girlfriend, Frankie.'

Her tone brightened considerably. 'Oh, that's an easy one. Hold on.'

He heard the handset being placed on the desk and listened to the general bustle of the office in the background whilst he waited. A couple of minutes later, Angela came back on the line.

'I have a mobile number and an address in Holmfirth. Do you want me to text them to you?'

'You're a star, Angela. That would be perfect. Thank you.'

'You're welcome. Just don't tell anyone. When are you back in the office?'

'Monday. Meeting with Whitmore at nine.'

'Well, try to keep your nose clean until then, eh? Listen, I've spoken with the FLO for Bill and Irene this morning. Lolly is to be returned to her family shortly. I wasn't sure if you knew?'

Ziggy took a minute then replied. 'I didn't know, I haven't spoken to them to be honest. I wasn't expecting it so soon.'

'I know, the coroner expedited the PM and cause of death wasn't in question so he gave the go ahead. There will still be an inquest, of course.'

Ziggy didn't know what to say. 'Thanks for letting me know Ang, appreciate it.'

'No problem. I'll text you that info.'

Within minutes, his phone pinged with the details she had promised. He checked the mobile number against the one he already had, and it was a match. He made a mental note to check in with Bill and Irene, then switched his attention to Frankie. He had no idea who the address in Holmfirth belonged to, but then he knew very little about Frankie, other than what Lolly had told him. Which, when he had thought about it, wasn't very much at all. He dialled the mobile number again, still no answer. He reckoned it would take him around forty minutes to get to Holmfirth from Leeds. If he set off now, he'd be there by lunchtime.

The rain that had been falling for days was still

hammering down, and the going was slower than he thought. Just over an hour later, Ziggy pulled his car onto a sweeping gravel driveway and he was blown away by the opulent surroundings. 'Wow,' he said to himself as he took in the multiple garages and manicured lawns. He wasn't sure what he had been expecting, but this looked like something from that *Footballers' Wives* show everyone at the office had been talking about.

Suddenly feeling self-conscious, he felt a need to check his appearance and remind himself why he was there. He wanted answers. He wanted to talk to Frankie about the life she and Lolly had shared. He knew that they were moving in together. Lolly had been staying at Frankie's on the night of the murder, but a couple of questions niggled at him. Who had hated her so much that they would carry out such a vicious attack? Why had she been suspended from work? Were the two things connected? He also wanted to see if he could get a better understanding of his best friend's life. He had always thought that they shared everything, but he admitted to himself, of course, it was impossible, even unreasonable, for him to think that Lolly would bother him with the minutiae of her everyday life.

The big stuff, though, the important stuff, they didn't keep from each other, did they? And if something was massively going on with Lolly, she would have shared it with him, wouldn't she?

He had so many questions and he hoped that Frankie held at least some of the answers.

Taking a few deep breaths, he opened the car door and stepped out. The modern barn conversion was tucked away at the end of a long, leafy lane. It seemed to Ziggy on his drive up that Frankie really had stepped away from the hectic city centre lifestyle that Lolly had told him about She had frequently regaled him with stories of eating at Michelin-starred restaurants, tickets for highly sought-after theatre shows and, of course, the live music that Lolly had always loved. This house was a sharp contrast to apartment living.

As he approached the front door, it opened before he had a chance to knock. Frankie stood in front of him, barefoot, in an oversized hoodie and a pair of ripped jeans. She looked radically different from when he had last seen her on the night of Lolly's murder, and not just her clothes. Wearing little to no make-up, her face looked heavily lined, her skin almost translucent. She held out her hand by way of greeting and he took it, noticing the sallow skin, which felt like tissue paper.

'Andrew,' she said, unable to hide the astonishment on her face. 'What are you doing here?'

Even her voice sounded different, deeper, huskier, like she'd smoked copious amounts of cigarettes. 'I've been calling, but it kept going to voicemail,' he said. 'I hope you don't mind me just dropping by.'

'No, not at all. I've turned my phone off, to be honest. Please, come in.' Frankie stood to one side to allow Ziggy to pass.

He stepped into a huge open-plan hallway with chequered black-and-white floor tiles.

The sweeping, galleried staircase, with oak beams as thick as the tree they had been carved from, dominated the space. Frankie directed him through into a startling white, clinically clean kitchen.

'Tea? Coffee? Something herbal?'

'Tea is fine, thank you.'

She flicked the kettle on and directed Ziggy through to an adjacent conservatory. Whilst she pottered about making the tea, Ziggy looked through the huge panoramic windows and admired the extensive back lawn.

'Wow, this house and garden are stunning. Is it yours?' He stopped, felt himself blush at his clumsiness. 'Sorry, that was a bit personal. I just meant, well, after the apartment.' He was really struggling to justify himself.

Frankie didn't seem to mind. 'It's on the market. It was part of my divorce settlement. I don't know what I'm going to do now.' She headed over with a tea tray that was laden with tea paraphernalia and biscuits. He noticed that she drank camomile, a favourite of Lolly's.

'Thank you for seeing me, Frankie,' he said. 'I understand your need to step away from everything.'

'It's fine, I'm fine. How have you been?'

He paused, taking a sip of tea. 'Hard to say, if I'm honest.' He fiddled with a teaspoon.

'Has there been an advance in the case? Is that why you're here?'

Ziggy shifted. It wasn't just the narrow wicker chair that was making him uncomfortable. 'Well, first, this isn't an official visit. I'm actually not "allowed" to work on it. Conflict of interest.' He saw the disappointment on her face.

'Oh. That must be so hard for you?'

'It is, but I know my team, and I know they will turn over every stone and interrogate every lead. It's just a matter of time.'

A few minutes' silence developed, each lost in thought. It was Frankie that spoke first. 'Forgive me, Ziggy, but what is it you want from me?'

He replaced his cup on a coaster and leant forwards. 'If I'm completely honest with you, Frankie, I'm not sure. I just feel like I'm missing a link somewhere and I can't get my head around it.'

'What kind of link?'

'I know you've given an official statement, but would you share with me what happened that night?'

Frankie let out a massive sigh and placed her head in her hands, pulling at her hair. A short cry of anguish came from her lips. Ziggy was taken aback by the drama of it all. He didn't have Frankie down as dramatic. She always came across as calm, collected, aloof, even.

When she spoke, she sounded like a moody teenager. 'Do I really have to? It's horrible to have to keep going over it in my head, never mind saying it out loud. I walked into a living nightmare that is still with me every waking moment, and I can't escape it.' She broke down sobbing again.

Ziggy immediately felt guilty. *You insensitive bastard*, he thought, annoyed with himself.

'Frankie, I'm so sorry. Of course, I understand. I guess I'm just like you, trying to make sense of it all.'

Frankie stood up, still crying, and went through into the kitchen. She disappeared into a side room and moments later, Ziggy heard the sound of running water. Unsure what to do, he took a good look around. He noticed there was nothing personal on any of the walls, no photographs of happier times, or of Frankie with her family. He guessed that as the place was on the market, all that kinds of thing had been removed. It occurred to him that he hadn't seen a forsale board on his way up. Did houses like this display such things?

The bathroom door closed, and Frankie returned to the garden room. He watched as she crossed the floor and lit one of the floor standing incense towers that were scattered around. A waft of patchouli hit Ziggy, and he was instantly reminded of Lolly. It was a scent that he always associated with his hippy, laid-back friend.

'I talk to her all the time, you know,' she said, retaking her seat.

The smell had triggered so many memories that Ziggy had a catch in his throat when he spoke.

'I need to ask you this, Frankie.' He was hoping she wouldn't shut down on him or go all dramatic again.

She wafted the smoke from the incense burner so that it circulated the room. He was finding it a bit overpowering, his eyes stinging slightly. When Frankie didn't answer, he carried on.

'Had she upset someone? Was there a situation, a person or something that would have made them angry with her?'

Frankie looked at him, startled. 'No, not that I know of. Why?'

'The attack. It was so frenzied, angry. It just doesn't seem like a random assault.'

'You think someone did it on purpose? Your colleague said it could be a burglary gone wrong. Is that not the case?'

Frankie stood again, pacing the room. Ziggy stood as well, gently taking Frankie by the elbow and turning her to face him.

'No, not at all. I'm just batting ideas around, Frankie.' He guided her back to the chair she had been sitting in, hoping she would calm down. He passed her a cup of tea and saw her hand was shaking. He sat back in his own seat, keen to restore a calmer atmosphere.

When Frankie spoke, it was so quietly he had to lean forwards to hear her. 'My world ended the moment I saw her lying there and I don't know how to restart it. I've spent hours here, talking to her. I don't know if I will ever get over it.'

Ziggy couldn't think of anything to say that would help, so he remained silent, letting Frankie talk.

'You never know what you've lost until it's gone, do you?' She looked at him, but he didn't answer. 'I didn't realise how deeply connected we were until I didn't have her any more, you know?' She continued, still looking at Ziggy. 'I keep expecting my phone to ring with a crazy update from her. That someone could be angry with her, it never crossed my mind.'

Ziggy took a deep breath, almost choking on the intense fumes that now filled the air. 'I understand. I'm much the same. I can't bring myself to delete her number from my phone.'

'I'm lost, Ziggy. I don't know what to do.' She wiped her face again.

He didn't know what else to say. He was rubbish at the emotional stuff and had barely got a grip on his own feelings, let alone knowing how to comfort Frankie. He again shifted uncomfortably, wondering if he should offer a shoulder or a hand, but Frankie made the decision easy for him as she blew her nose and wiped away her tears.

'Have you heard about the funeral?' she asked.

'Not yet but she'll be returned to Bill and Irene shortly so I'm guessing it will be soon.'

Frankie shifted in her seat. She paused, twisting a tissue in her fingers. 'You didn't answer my earlier question. Are there any leads?'

'Some stuff around the CCTV, carpet fibres, but in truth, not a great deal. I'm beginning to realise that we weren't as close as I thought we were. I guess it was inevitable when she had you. You were building a life together.'

'She adored you, Ziggy. You were always her voice of reason, even as she and I grew closer. Few decisions were made between us that didn't get run past you first, even though she denied it.' Frankie laughed. 'I often felt there were three of us in the relationship in the early days. Once she'd explained your friendship to me, I understood.'

Ziggy felt comforted by her words. 'I know she loved you. She was prepared to change her entire life to be with you. You met at an industry event, right?'

'Yes. We met in the bar when we were both escaping a boring lecture.'

'You were married at the time?' asked Ziggy.

'Kind of. My marriage was hanging by a thread. We'd been childhood sweethearts, and we were going through the motions. He was having affairs all over the place, and I was a workaholic. Neither of us wanted children, just the finer things in life, and we were both prepared to work hard for it.'

'What was it about Lolly that changed all that?'

Frankie sighed and started pulling at a loose thread on her jeans. 'She was a breath of fresh air,' she said, and Ziggy noted the hint of wistfulness in her tone. 'I'd never met anyone like her. A true whirlwind. I loved spending time with her. My husband was away frequently, and even when he was here, he wasn't, if you know what I mean. The more time I spent with Lolly, the harder I fell until it became impossible to ignore my feelings.'

'So what happened then?' These are questions that he'd always meant to ask Lolly, but they always seemed to have so much to talk about, and he regretted never having the chance.

'I told my ex I'd had enough and wanted a divorce. He was happy to go along with it. He'd moved on years before, he just didn't have the balls to say it.'

'It was an amicable split then?'

'Eventually. He was a bit blown away when he realised I

was in love with a woman, but even he could see that Lolly and I gelled in a way we never had.'

Ziggy smiled. 'I'm glad she met you. I'm glad that the last couple of years of her life she'd found someone she could rely on, someone that made her happy.'

Silence settled between them as each was lost in their own thoughts. 'Just one final question, Frankie, then I'll go.'

Frankie looked at him questioningly. 'Go on.'

'Did you know she had been suspended from work?'

Frankie dismissed the question with a wave of her hand. 'Oh, that. She wasn't exactly suspended. She'd been put on leave whilst some investigation took place.'

Ziggy was surprised. 'So you knew about it?'

Frankie stood and together they walked to the front door. 'Yes, I knew, but Lolly said it was no big deal, a mix-up in results or something. It's unlikely to be anything to do with her murder, is it?' She reached forwards and opened the front door.

Ziggy stepped outside. 'Possibly not, but every avenue has to be investigated. Do you know what the investigation was about?'

Frankie shook her head. 'Not really. Lolly played it down, said it was a mistake and, to be honest, I was so busy with my work I didn't pay much attention.'

With little else to say or ask, Ziggy made his excuses and left, acutely aware that he had generated more questions and even fewer answers – legitimate ones, at least.

10

As Ziggy climbed back into his car, his mobile phone rang in his pocket. He pulled it out, connected it to the Bluetooth in the car, and plugged it into the dashboard holder.

'Rachel?'

'Ziggy, where are you? I need you over here now.'

He was taken aback by Rachel's tone. She sounded angry. It was so unlike Rachel to be so demanding. 'Holmfirth, why? What's wrong? Has something happened?'

'Just get here.'

The line went dead, leaving Ziggy none the wiser. He put his foot down and headed towards the local A roads, avoiding the congestion he had sat in on the way over. He joined the M1 at Denby Dale and floored it into Leeds, his heart racing the entire journey.

He pulled up outside Rachel's in record time and raced up the path.

'Rachel?' he shouted as he headed through the front door, not bothering to knock. She came out of the living room, ghostly white and looking very shaken. He immediately darted forwards and grabbed hold of her, taking her into a huge bear hug. 'What on earth has happened?' he asked as he stroked her hair. 'Where's Ben?' He pulled back at looked at her face.

She stepped away from him and headed into the kitchen. 'He's upstairs, he's fine. But' – she passed Ziggy Ben's backpack, holding it gingerly between her thumb and index finger – 'I found this when we got back from school.'

Ziggy couldn't immediately see anything wrong with the bag. 'What am I looking at?' He walked around the table to join her. She was pointing to a builders glove sticking out of the net side pocket. He looked at her. 'What is it?'

'It came with this.' She pointed to a piece of folded notepaper on the worktop.

'Have you opened it? What does it say?'

'It's a threat, Ziggy.'

He glanced between her, the glove and the paper. 'What? What kind of threat?'

'Read it.'

He had never seen her so angry. He checked his pockets for latex gloves to prevent further contamination, but he didn't have any to hand, so he ran to the car and retrieved a pair, instinctively grabbing an evidence bag as well. When he returned, Rachel had been joined by Ben. She was in the process of sending him back upstairs when he rejoined them.

'All right, buddy?' he asked.

'Dad! What are you doing here?' Ben threw himself around Ziggy's legs, causing him to almost fall over.

'Ben, please, go upstairs. Dad will be up in a minute.'

'Aww but, Mum ...'

'No, Ben! Do not make me tell you again.'

'Hey, Rach, calm down.' Ziggy had never seen Rachel

this worked up before. She never raised her voice, and certainly not at Ben.

When Ben was out of the room, he pulled on the gloves and walked over to the side. He carefully picked up the piece of paper by a corner and unfolded it. The message couldn't have been clearer.

TELL YOUR EX TO STAY AWAY FROM THE CASE OR PAY THE PRISE WITH BENS LIFE. DO NOT INVOLVE THE POLICE.

Ziggy had to read the message through a few times before it finally sank in.

'What the fuck?' he exclaimed, staring at the paper. He felt the blood drain from his face.

'What do we do?' Rachel was wringing her hands together.

'I ... Well ... I don't know,' Ziggy stammered, lost for words. He needed time to think.

Whoever this was, knew his son. They knew his school, his class, his name. Shivers ran down his spine.

'Tell me when you found it. Has Ben seen it?'

'No, I don't think so. I picked him up from school as usual. He came running out with his backpack and lunch box and passed them both to me as we headed to the car. He said goodbye to his friends, climbed onto his booster seat, and we came home.' As Rachel spoke she mirrored her actions, walking over to the kitchen sink. 'I took his backpack and started to empty it over the sink. There's usually a half-eaten apple and God knows what,' she pointed, 'and this piece of paper fell out of the side pocket. I opened the paper, as it could have been a note from his teacher. The glove that's still in the side pocket isn't Ben's or even mine.

Besides, look at the size of it. Neither of us have touched that, just the note.'

'You touched the note?'

'Briefly. I didn't know what they were and as soon as I did, I dropped them both and haven't touched either since.'

Ziggy looked closely at the glove, keeping his contact with it to a minimum. It was a coarse, knitted workman's glove. The kind used for heavy lifting. Certainly not something a seven-year-old would wear or likely even own.

'Have you spoken to Ben about it?'

'No. I was so angry, Ziggy, I haven't spoken to anyone but you.'

He realised her anger had been adrenaline fuelled, and it was starting to wear off. He clicked the kettle on, knowing that she would go into shock soon enough and sweet tea was the best remedy for when the insulin left her body.

'Let's sit down, think this through.'

She did as he asked, and he saw she was quietly crying. He sat next to her, pulling her against his chest.

'Our boy, Ziggy. They know all about him.'

'Shh, I know. I will find who sent this, I promise.'

'How, Ziggy? You're not even in the office.'

'I have my ways, Rachel. No one threatens my son and gets away with it.'

'But we can't involve the police. You read it.'

'We have to Rachel but it will be handled discretely, I know that much.' He took a photograph of the letter using his phone.

She suddenly pushed him away, her anger flaring up again. 'This is all your fault.' She jumped up and hit his arm with a closed fist. 'You and your bloody job.' She started pummelling him. It didn't hurt, and it wasn't hard, but he was still shocked. He'd never seen Rachel so overwrought.

'Rachel, Rach, love, calm down. I'll sort this, I promise.'

She looked up at him with steel in her eyes. 'You had better, Andrew. I've made many sacrifices for you and your job. Losing my son is not something I am prepared to do.'

Ziggy left Rachel's with an even stronger sense of purpose. He needed to work out who he could trust and rely on. Nick had already stepped up, and for that, Ziggy was grateful. He knew Angela would help him with tech stuff if he asked.

'Do not involve the police,' he muttered with scorn in his tone as he started his car. 'Too late, we're already involved.'

Being away from the office wasn't about to stop him from pulling in all the resources he needed to protect his son. Whoever sent the note had clearly undersestimated Rachel – a mistake he had only ever made once, that had resulted in their divorce. As he drove towards home, he dialled the office, Angela answered.

'Ang, I need a favour.' He then relayed all the relevant information to her knowing that she would expedite the next steps. She agreed to send someone to Rachel's immediately to take a statement, and officers would visit Ben's school; plain clothed and discreet.

Pulling onto his road, he let out a frustrated groan as he remembered that his home was upside down as the workmen finished tiling the kitchen and plumbing in the washing machine. The only place he could be on his own was in the car, and it was starting to show. He hadn't had a full night's sleep for the last four nights, and he knew he looked rough.

Despite his assurances that he would go to any lengths and do whatever was necessary to keep Ben safe, Rachel had phoned twice since he had left. He had suggested moving in with them, albeit temporarily, just until this was resolved. Rachel was considering it but he understood that she wanted to keep things as normal for Ben as they could. He would see them at the school gates, viewing from a distance.

All this was spinning through his mind as he headed home. As he pulled up outside his house, he saw the workmen packing up for the day. The foreman approached him as he locked his car.

'Oh, God, not more problems.' He briefly closed his eyes and rolled his shoulders. He was relieved to hear they only needed another day and the job would be complete. He thanked them and headed inside.

'You had a visitor today, by the way,' called the builder.

'Yeah?'

'A woman. All dolled up, she was. Can't remember her name, Chrystal something?'

Ziggy rolled his eyes and groaned. 'Right, thanks.' He waved them off and closed the front door.

A wave of tiredness washed over him, as if he needed reminding that he hadn't slept. He'd learnt over the years that he couldn't continually run on empty. He didn't work at his best when he was only functioning on twenty per cent. He threw his jacket over the banister and sloped into the living room, collapsing on the sofa. He closed his eyes and took a few steadying breaths whilst he processed everything. He was used to pressure. It was a daily state of being, but the mental stress of not being part of the investigation, the threat against Ben and the enormity of losing Lolly – he hadn't had a moment to process anything. He was living on his wits and his nerves were frazzled.Where the hell did he start? He raised his arm above his head and rubbed his forehead. It was no use. He wasn't going to sleep and he needed to empty his head.

Stretching, yawning, and standing up, he headed to his office. Grabbing a large sheet of paper, he pinned it to the wall and added the new information to it. He now knew for certain that Lolly had been suspended, but he didn't know why. He'd hardly even scratched the surface as far as he was concerned and already the stakes were sky high. He had the funeral to get through. He also wondered why Sadie or Whitmore hadn't wanted to speak to him about Lolly yet.

Perhaps he should start there.

Or maybe he should talk to Lolly's neighbours at the apartment. Would turning up at Ben's school, just to check around, be useful or should he let the team deal with it?

He let out a growl of frustration. He needed to be in the office. He needed to be closer to the action.

11

Friday 20th September 2002

Ziggy stood at the front of the church with a sheet of paper in his shaking hand, fighting back tears. He kept his eyes down, looking at the pulpit, not daring to catch the eye of anyone fearing it would tip him over the edge and he'd be unable to deliver his eulogy.

When Irene had first asked him to deliver a few words on their behalf, he had refused. He had no idea how he was supposed to stand in a packed church and talk about his best friend. What they shared, what they had meant to each other, couldn't be put into words. It transcended a friendship, it didn't have the complications sometimes found in blended families, and although they worked together from time to time, they were far more than colleagues. In the end, he'd sat with Bill and Irene and they had agreed to talk of Leila's love of the natural world, her one-woman-mission to rid the world of all its plights in her own small way. To share

Lolly's message that there is only one planet, and it needed protecting at all costs. That he could do. That seemed the right thing to say and he hoped she would have agreed.

Once the vicar had delivered the rest of the service, and the congregation had sung 'Morning Has Broken,' they left the church and headed to the graveyard to say their final goodbyes. The churchyard was packed with anyone whose life Lolly had touched. A fitting send off for a remarkable woman was the general consensus of opinion amongst mourners.

He waved Sadie off and wandered over to his foster parents. They climbed into Ziggy's car and headed back to their house. He made sure they were settled and had everything they needed before he headed off. Taking Sadie's advice, he put his foot down and headed for the Yorkshire Dales in the hope that the rolling hills and dark skies would help clear his head.

12

_____

Monday 22nd September 2002

As Ziggy drove to the office, he reflected on the weekend. After the blur of the funeral on Friday, and his all too brief trip to the Dales he had spent the rest of the weekend at Rachel's. He felt a need to be near to Ben, and Rachel had made up the spare room so he could stay as long as he wanted. Between gaming with Ben and long talks into the night with Rachel, he had enjoyed the familiar but distant feeling of belonging somewhere. One day, they'd wrapped up warm and taken a flask of hot chocolate to the local park. Whilst Ben played, he and Rachel had swapped stories of nights out with Lolly. They had laughed together, cried and although the experience had been cathartic, both continued to ask themselves why. Why Lolly?

There was only one way Ziggy was going to find out. He needed to get back to work.

Pulling into the car park, he braced himself for his meeting with Whitmore. In theory, Ziggy had just taken a few days' holiday, he wasn't 'in trouble', per se but he knew he'd pushed his luck with his senior officer, and now he had to at least be seen to be playing by the book.

He stepped out of his car and headed for the entrance, but was stopped in his tracks by Chrystal Mack. She slid in front of him, as if out of nowhere. He sighed, closed his eyes and took a deep breath.

'What do you want, Chrystal?'

'Pleased to see you too. I've been trying to get hold of you.'

'Most people just use this thing called a mobile phone. They don't doorstep people.' Ziggy made to move forwards, but Chrystal sidestepped into his path.

'I was in the area,' she said, with a smile.

'Course you were. Seriously, Ms Mack. I have to get to work. If you want updates on the case, wait for the press briefing.'

'That's just it though, isn't it? There hasn't been one.'

Ziggy was well aware of that, and it was one of the many questions he had for Sadie – or Whitmore, should he ever make it into the building.

'What do you want, Chrystal, seriously?'

He watched as she rummaged around in her bag and pulled out a piece of paper. 'This was sent to my personal email address. I received it late last night.'

Ziggy unfolded it with a sense of foreboding.

STAY AWAY FROM DR TURNER'S STORY OR PAY THE PRISE.

His hand started shaking, and his mouth went dry. The same threat, but without naming Ben this time.

'To your personal email?' was all Ziggy could think of to ask, as he tried to get his head around it. Two threats in a matter of days? What the hell was going on? He studied the printout. It had the sender's email address of joebloggs123; no clues there. At the bottom were some handwritten notes, a series of letters and numbers.

'What's this?' he asked, pointing to them.

'It's the IP address that it was sent from. I wondered if your tech guys could do a reverse search and see who had sent it?'

Ziggy shook his head, mulling over the questions that were forming. He probably could take it to Tech but did he trust Mack the Knife? Could she have somehow found out about the threat against Ben and duplicated a similar one to herself? Was she that desparate for a story? He didn't think so. They had a tempestuous relationship to say the least, but she seemed genuine about the note. He didn't doubt it was from whoever had sent the note with Ben, the misspelling of *prise* for a start.

'What story are you working on?'

'Local girl, done good, that kind of thing.'

'Why?'

'Lolly has an interesting background. I thought an in-depth piece might trigger some leads.' She shifted from foot to foot, clearly feeling the cold wind that had picked up since they had started talking. 'Can we sit in your car?'

'No. I have a meeting in' – he checked his watch – 'ten minutes. Look, meet me later today, text me with a time and place and I'll see what I can do.' He stuffed the paper into his inside pocket. 'Now, I really have to go.' He moved past her, reaching for the door handle.

'See you later then.' She winked.

He shook his head and stepped into the police station.

. . .

Not quite the start to the day that Ziggy had planned. The paper was burning a hole in his pocket, and he still wasn't sure who could help him with that just yet. More than likely Angela, but he had to get this meeting with Whitmore out of the way first.

As he walked into the Major Investigations' team office, the first person he saw was Sadie. They hadn't spoken since the funeral, and even then, it had only been pleasantries. He headed for his desk, taking off his jacket and pulling in his lanyard.

'Morning, boss.' Sadie came over to stand at the side of him.

'Morning, Sadie. How's everything?'

'I was going to ask the same of you. Beautiful service on Friday, I thought.'

'Yes, it was. I have a meeting with Whitmore, so if you'll excuse me. We can catch up later, if you have time?'

She reached out and touched his arm. 'Are you OK?'

He appreciated the gesture and turned to her. 'I'm fine, honestly.'

'Thornes!' Whitmore's voice echoed from his office, making everyone jump.

Sadie laughed. 'I think he's seen you.'

Ziggy smiled, glad that they seemed to be back on an even footing. 'Here, sir,' he called back, rolling his eyes at Sadie.

He turned round, and jumped, Whitmore was right on his ass. Ziggy took a step back. 'Uh, morning, sir.'

'Morning, Andrew, we have a meeting in the calendar.'

'Yes, I was just on my way.'

Whitmore turned and headed back towards his office. Ziggy started to follow, saying hello to Nick and Angela as they arrived for their shift.

'Come in, Andrew, take a seat.'

DCS Whitmore's office was small, with a large Formica desk in one corner and a faux-leather office chair tucked in behind it. There was paper everywhere, and the walls had charts and league tables pinned to them. Behind the desk was a dark wood bookcase that had a selection of legal and procedural books along with a full library of James Patterson thrillers.

They never moved, and Ziggy wondered if Whitmore had actually read any of them.

To one side of the small office was a coffee table and backless stools around it. It was rarely used, as Whitmore favoured sitting behind his desk. Ziggy took the seat opposite, an old office chair that had seen better days.

Whitmore had asked his assistant to bring coffee and they waited, both awkward; Ziggy not knowing if he was going to get a bollocking, Whitmore making uncomfortable small talk whilst they both danced around the inevitable upbraiding.

Mercifully, the coffee finally arrived, and Ziggy held his breath.

'I hope you took the time off to process your, erm, your thoughts, shall we say?' Whitmore wrapped his hands around his coffee cup, blew into it and took a sip.

'I did, sir.' Ziggy had already decided to play it straight, to at least be seen to be toeing the line. Ordinarily he wasn't a yes-man, but he would do whatever he needed to get closer to Lolly's investigation.

'My hope is that we can put last week's actions down to recent circumstances and move on?'

'Yes, sir, absolutely.' It was killing Ziggy to be so affable.

'Good. Good. I see no need for it to be referred to again, and I'm sure I can rely on you to let the team get on with the investigation. You understand that I still can't let you work the case?'

'I do, sir, I just ask that I am kept abreast of any new developments as we would in any other case?' Ziggy knew that Bill and Irene had had a family liaison officer assigned to them, but he also knew that their relaying of developments was often highly curated.

'Of course, of course. DS Bates will bring you up to date.'

So he wasn't going to be completely closed out then, he thought, which was surprising, given his behaviour. That was something, but he would still have to tread carefully. He took a sip of his coffee. 'Thank you, sir. Much appreciated.'

'In the meantime, there's another case that we need you on. I believe DS Wilkinson may have mentioned it to you. Money laundering.'

'Yes, we discussed it briefly last week. I'll catch up with him when we've finished here.'

Whitmore stood and Ziggy took this as his cue to leave. 'Please do, and I believe Bates wants to chat with you too.'

They walked to the office door, and Ziggy stepped out on his own. Whitmore closed the door, and Ziggy took a few seconds to take in the atmosphere and buzz of the busy environment. This was where he belonged. This was his lifeblood, the reason he breathed. Upholding justice, his life purpose – he'd be damned if he couldn't do that for Lolly.

13

'How'd it go?'

Ziggy turned and saw Sadie and Nick heading his way. He smiled. 'Yeah, it's all good.'

Together, the three of them walked over to their corner of the office, any earlier awkwardness forgotten. Angela was already on the phone, chasing up something for Nick. They sat down, and Sadie spoke first.

'Has Whitmore updated you on Lolly's case?'

'Not really, he gave me the impression that there wasn't much new information.' He was aware of Nick shifting in his seat, but he wasn't about to drop him in it.

'We're still speaking with witnesses, not that there are many. No one seems to have heard or seen anything. The CCTV is proving a mystery, and Mr Unhelpful that you ... well, you know, pinned against the wall.' Ziggy cringed at the memory, but he would absolutely do it again. 'Yeah, so him, absolute waste of time. Ang contacted the estate manager and apparently there are backup recordings, so we're hoping that will be with us soon and reveal something.'

'That's great news, great work. Any news on the signature?' asked Ziggy.

'No, not as yet. We've been round the houses with it. No fingerprints either. Whoever signed for it knew what they were doing. Same for the apartment. Some random fibres that we're analysing further but initial reports are that they are common nylon carpet fibres. Most significant is the colour – a garish orange – so that might be something, but only if ...'

Ziggy finished Sadie's sentence. 'We can find the house they came from.'

'Exactly. Look, Ziggy. I promise I'll keep you in the loop, but please don't put me in any awkward positions.'

He appreciated her honesty. 'I won't, Sadie, I promise. Besides, it seems Whitmore has me tagged to work on the money-laundering case.' He turned his chair to face Nick. 'So spill the beans, young man.'

They all laughed. Sadie left them to it whilst Angela returned to the phones.

'Have you eaten?' asked Nick, thinking with his stomach, as usual.

'Not yet, what you thinking?' Ziggy replied.

'Canteen. Need you to meet someone and it's best done on a full stomach.'

Ziggy laughed, pulled on his jacket. 'Sounds good to me. Can you just give me a minute and I'll see you down there?'

'Sure.'

Whilst Nick headed off, Ziggy turned to Angela and smiled.

'Oh no,' she said, pointing her finger at him. 'No, Ziggy. I know what you're up to.'

'What? I haven't said anything yet.'

'I've seen that look before, and you waited until

everyone had left. I'm a lot of things, Andrew, but I'm not daft.'

'Just a tiny favour. I swear it will take seconds.'

'Not if it's to do with Lolly's case.'

'It isn't. Well, it is, but in a roundabout kind of way.' He flashed her his best smile.

'Oh, you're a bugger,' she said, relenting as he knew she would. 'What is it? Make it quick.'

He pulled the email from his pocket. 'Any chance you can ask someone in Tech to see if they can find out where this IP address comes from?'

Angela took the paper from him, studying it. 'Flipping heck, Ziggy, this should be submitted as evidence. I can probably run the IP, to be honest, but I can ask Tech as well. I'm guessing there's no "official" requisition?'

Ziggy grimaced. 'No, not at the minute. If we could keep it between us for now, I promise I'll turn it over when the time is right.'

Angela sighed. 'Don't ask me for anything else.' She turned in her chair. 'Now go meet Inspector Stiles.'

Ziggy raised an eyebrow, thanked Angela profusely and headed downstairs.

In the canteen, he spotted Nick seated at a bench with a rather animated, well-dressed man. Nick looked bored to tears. He jumped up when he saw Ziggy approach. 'Ziggy, come and sit down, join us. Please.' Nick gathered him up and pushed him towards the bench. 'Let me introduce you.'

Ziggy staggered forwards with Nick's hand on his back and extended his hand, greeting the smart-suited man who now wore a stupid grin. 'DI Ziggy Thornes.'

The man shook Ziggy's hand rather overenthusiastically. 'Detective Inspector Peter Stiles. Metropolitan Police, Fraud division, at your service.' With that he stamped his foot and did a mock salute.

Oh, dear Lord, thought Ziggy, cringing along with Nick. They exchanged a knowing look. *We've got our hands full here.*

14

'Pleasure to meet you, Inspector Stiles. I'm sure you've been made to feel more than welcome.'

'Thanks, matey, I have. Feet firmly under the table here.' He stamped his feet below the table.

Matey? He glanced across at Nick, catching him stifling a grin. Ziggy looked back in Peter's direction, taking the southerner in. He was dressed sharply. His jacket was open, and Ziggy could tell from the lining it was expensive. The jet-black, slicked back hair wouldn't have looked out of place on the trading floor of the stock exchange. *Perhaps that was how he got into fraud and money laundering.* Ziggy smiled to himself and scolded his own judgemental thoughts.

Nick coughed, drawing Ziggy's attention back to the table. 'Why don't I go grab us a brew whilst you two get acquainted, eh?' he volunteered, leaving the bench.

Ziggy silently cursed Nick, but turned to his new colleague and gestured at the table. 'Do you want to bring me up to speed, Peter?'

Stiles pulled himself upright as he sat down, as if he was about to deliver the opening speech at the Oscars. He produced a pristine Moleskine notebook from his inside pocket and flipped over several pages. 'Right, it's a bit of a complicated one,' he said. 'How familiar are you with money laundering? The process, etcetera?'

Nick returned with three steaming mugs of tea. He handed them out and sat down next to Ziggy.

Stiles continued in an overly loud voice, not waiting for an answer. 'Placement, layering and integration. Usually a cash-based business – so, for example, the drugs industry is prime for it. Systems for cleaning cash can be ultra sophisticated and we've been surveying a network in London for quite some time.' He looked up. 'Still with me?'

A silent nod from Ziggy and a roll of the eyes from Nick.

'Anyhoo, whilst we've been tracking this organised crime gang – OCG – we stumbled across some new intel that suggests there is another operating base in your wonderful Yorkshire. Whilst it may not be connected to the OCG in London, it is ringing alarm bells and needs our attention.' Peter sat back and waited. No one was sure what for. When he didn't get a response, he looked rather wounded. Ziggy just wished he would get to the point.

'Moving on, are you familiar with squares or squaring?'

'Money mules?' said Ziggy.

'Yes, exactly. Well, not exactly. We have intel that there's a small group operating in Leeds at present who are befriending students, convincing them to share their bank account details then using them to pay ill-gotten gains into, withdrawing the money elsewhere via an ATM, or filtering it through a cash-based business which, of course, is then clean cash.'

'Where or what is generating the dirty money?' asked Ziggy.

'This is where you guys come into it. Truth be told, we're

not sure. There's intel that suggests some kind of email scam, but that's just one of a couple theories we've thrown around.'

'So what do you *actually* know?' asked Ziggy.

'I'm getting to that. There's been a distinct rise in the number of students at Leeds University that have been targeted by this gang. Students, of course, are invariably broke Adverts have appeared in local magazines for a low-risk, high-return job with minimal hours accompanied by a mobile telephone number that changes with each advert. Untraceable, before you ask.'

'Wait, students are simply contacting whoever and handing over their bank details? What do the students get out of it?' asked Ziggy.

'Not just their bank details but their bank cards, hence "squares", for at least a couple of weeks. They're told that a deposit will be made of anything from a thousand to thirty thousand pounds, which will then be withdrawn with the promise of an amount left behind as "commission". In some instances, there's been as much as ten grand "commission" left in the account.'

'How did this come to light?' asked Ziggy, his brain already whizzing through possibilities.

'A few things happened. HSBC contacted Fraud as the number of cases and transactions were peaking around September, January and April, which is when student loans are paid out. It's an ideal time for the gang to filter money into an account, as it's more likely to go unnoticed. Where they screwed up was with the withdrawals. A few hundred over a series of days may go unnoticed, but a few thousand transferred electronically, well that raises red flags.'

'It's not particularly sophisticated. I mean, it's no Bernie Madoff Ponzi Scheme,' commented Nick.

'Agreed, which is why we're fairly sure this is a local operation. Sometimes the scheme doesn't always need to be complex – it just needs to work.'

'Who's depositing the money? Where and how?' Ziggy asked.

'Money mules, basically. People that are paid or black-mailed to collect cash and move it from one place to the other. It's then deposited into the relevant bank account, withdrawn, electronically transferred offshore or filtered through a seemingly legitimate business.'

Ziggy sat back and folded his arms, processing what had been said. Stiles just looked smug.

'From what I can see,' said Ziggy, 'we need to target the weakest link in the chain. To me, that's the students. Do you have any student names or anyone who we can chat with?'

'Yes, I can get them for you. One poor lad had to go to his parents and confess his stupidity after the gang started getting heavy with him when he told them he didn't want to do it any more. The bank had closed his account and had questioned him about it. He'd tried to brazen it out, but when he learnt the offence carried a fourteen-year prison sentence, he had a massive meltdown.'

'Did he give many details? Say who had contacted him, or how?' asked Ziggy.

'He said it was some bloke in the Library pub who first mentioned it, then he saw an advert in one of the student magazines, so contacted them, met up with the guy and handed over his card. A couple of weeks later, he was cock-a-hoop when five grand landed in his account, and he was told via text message that it was his to keep. Unfortunately – or fortunately, depending on your view– the bank closed his account before he could do anything.'

'It would seem that we need to chat with the gullible

teen ourselves and see what we can uncover?' said Nick thoughtfully.

'I agree. What else do we know?' Ziggy asked, keen to get the ball rolling.

'We've spoken to the newspapers and magazines where the ads have been placed, but no traceable numbers. Adverts were paid over the phone with a student's account details so that avenue takes us nowhere.'

'Where is the student contact now? Is he still in Leeds?'

'No. He's back with his parents down south. I can arrange a video interview with him, though.'

'Great,' said Ziggy. 'Can you arrange that for ASAP?'

Peter scribbled it down on his pad. 'Sure thing.'

'Nick, you mentioned the O'Connors before. How are they relevant?'

Nick shifted in his seat, and Peter jumped in before he had a chance to answer.

'Pawnshops. We were looking at a specific transaction that had taken place and when we followed the paper trail, it led us to a pawnshop on Burley Road. A search of Companies House brought up the name O'Connor – Stephen O'Connor, to be precise.'

Nick jumped in. 'But we haven't been able to tie anything back to them. I've been down to the shop a few times, just to get a feel for the place.'

Ziggy nodded, remembering that Freddie O'Connor had mentioned someone resembling Taggart had been hanging around. Ziggy had guessed correctly that it was Nick. He finished his cup of tea and stood up. 'Sounds like we've got plenty to be cracking on with. Shall we head back upstairs?'

The others agreed and, after stacking their cups, Ziggy raced ahead as the other two headed off to the gents. He took the time before the others caught up to have a good look around the detailed boards. A single operation, even if it was only a splinter of a major op, generated so much paperwork that had to be meticulously logged and processed. Ziggy could see that the already logged information pretty much matched what Nick and Peter had told him. He flicked through a file that was on the desk. It was a transcript of the initial interview with the student. Ziggy grabbed a chair and sat down, speed-reading the transcript. It didn't really shed much more light than he already knew, leaving him keen to speak to the former student himself. He appreciated the temporary respite from worrying over Ben, though it never truly went away ...

Nick and Peter returned, and Ziggy waited until they were seated before speaking. 'Aside from speaking to' – Ziggy flipped to the student's statement to find his name – 'Daniel, what are the next actions?'

Peter stood and walked over to the board that displayed the money-laundering process. 'The team down south are working the email angle, and I'm just waiting for some updates from them. I think this O'Connor is something to be pursued, but we don't have a reason for bringing any of them in. Nick tells me there are three brothers, yes?'

Ziggy nodded. 'Yes, that's right, Freddie, Robbie and Stephen. I have an in with one of them.' He turned to Nick. 'I spoke to Freddie last week. He let slip that Stephen and Robbie were at loggerheads, but that's all he knew. I gave him a week to get me more intel.'

Nick nodded. 'I'm impressed, considering this is your first day back?'

Ziggy winked at Nick, avoiding Peter's bewildered stare.

'So, Peter, if you can get that interview set up, Nick and I will see if we can find a reason to bring one of the other O'Connors in, yeah?'

With agreement all round, the meeting broke up and Ziggy headed to his desk.

'Bloody hell, you did well there, boss,' said Nick, who had followed him.

Ziggy turned round. 'What do you mean?'

'I've had him up my arse since he arrived last week. I even had to take him home with me one night.'

Ziggy burst out laughing. 'I bet Lesley loved that.'

'She wasn't impressed, let's put it that way. The twins soon had him settled, colouring in.'

Angela came over to see what was amusing them. Nick told her, and she laughed. 'Poor Peter, I feel sorry for him.'

'You take him to dinner then,' Nick joked.

'Who's to say I haven't?' replied Angela, with a cheeky wink.

Nick stared. 'You haven't?'

Ziggy and Angela were still laughing when Sadie came over to join them.

'I turn my back for one minute and all hell breaks loose,' she said. 'What's so funny?'

Ziggy shook his head. 'It's too long to explain.' He was momentarily distracted as he felt his phone vibrate in his pocket. He fished it out just as Sadie spoke to him.

'Fair enough. Good to see you laughing anyway. Can I have a word when you've got a minute?'

His stomach took a dive at her serious tone. 'Yeah, sure. I'm free now if you want?'

'Great, shall we ...?' She pointed towards Whitmore's office.

Ziggy followed her, checking his message as he walked. It was from Rachel, just letting him know that she and Ben were fine. Relieved, he switched his attention back to Sadie. Whitmore wasn't in, but Sadie didn't take his seat behind the desk. Instead, she took one of the stools, so Ziggy followed suit.

'What's going on?' he asked.

'There's been a development that I think you should know about. I couldn't say anything this morning, as I was waiting for confirmation.'

Ziggy braced himself, making fists so hard that his nails were digging into his palms. 'Go on.'

'Lolly had been suspended from work, but I think you knew that?'

Ziggy couldn't remember if he knew legitimately, so he kept quiet.

Sadie carried on. 'Anyway, it would seem there was a dispute over the outcome of a post-mortem that she had done some time ago.'

Ziggy frowned. 'A dispute?' Lolly was absolutely meticulous in her work. This had to be some kind of mistake.

'I know, it seems unlikely, but the family were questioning the ruling. Lolly had drawn a suicide conclusion, but the family was convinced it was murder.'

Ziggy was confused. 'What? That's a pretty fucking huge mistake to make.'

Sadie agreed. 'Everyone who worked with her was as shocked as you. It's completely unlike her. There was a second post-mortem, and the result was murder.' She paused, and bit her bottom lip.

Ziggy was shocked. Lolly would never make such a massive mistake, surely? He thought back to his conversation with Frankie. She had dismissed the investigation into Lolly's work as nothing to worry about. Was it more than any of them had realised?

'Sadie, I don't know what to say. I had no idea about any of it.'

'I didn't think so, but I had to ask. We've spoken with the family concerned and we're following up on their alibis, but my guess is that we'll be ruling them out. That murder is being investigated by another unit.' She let out a long sigh and folded her arms. 'I'm just hoping that Forensics turn up something on the carpet fibre samples.'

He sensed Sadie was as frustrated as he was. 'Like you said, Sadie, we've got the best team. We'll get there.' Even though he didn't really feel it, they were still part of a team.

'Yes, absolutely we will,' she said, with more conviction. She stood up. 'How are you finding our Met colleague?'

Ziggy smiled and followed Sadie to the door, still trying to process the update. 'He's an interesting one, isn't he?'

'I'll say. Keen to make an impression, I think,' she laughed. He's harmless enough, I guess.'

Having reached the end of the corridor, Sadie turned to enter the ladies, and Ziggy headed back into the office. He mulled over Sadie's news. All it really did was confirm what he already knew, but with added detail.

It was how he was going to use it that mattered.

15

Ziggy checked the time – just after 2 p.m. He'd been covertly watching the school gates as Rachel collected Ben each day. He was aware that plain-clothed officers were doing the same, but he didn't care. He needed to see for himself that Ben was safe. The updates he'd had from the team assigned to Ben's case had gone some way to putting his mind at rest. No new faces had been seen hanging around or acting suspiciously close to the school gates.

He grabbed his car keys from his desk and shrugged into his coat. 'Just heading out, Nick.'

Nick looked up from his computer. 'Oh, where are you going?'

'Running an errand won't be too long.' Ziggy headed off before Nick had the chance to comment. As he climbed into his car, his phone vibrated. Pulling it out of his coat pocket, he saw it was a text from Chrystal Mack.

'Oh hell,' he said as he opened the little envelope image. He'd completely forgotten that he'd agreed to meet with her later once he'd handed the note over to Angela. She'd suggested a local wine bar later that evening, so he sent her a quick text back acknowledging the time then set off.

Ben attended Middleton Primary School, which was a fifteen-minute drive from Rachel's house. It faced a fairly busy main road, but the speed limit outside the school was restricted to twenty miles per hour. Ben had been there since he was three, and he enjoyed it, whereas Rachel and Ziggy had been impressed with the community feel to the school and the friendliness of the staff. There was always something going on, and recently an after-school club had been introduced, so should Rachel need to work late, Ben would simply pop along to the allocated classroom without having to leave the school grounds. For now, they had agreed with the investigating team that until the source of the threat was caught, Rachel or Ziggy would collect Ben every day, regardless. He would have much rather bundled the two of them off to Rachel's mum's in Harrogate but Rachel had said no, that Ben had had enough upset in his life and Ziggy had conceded that routine was the best thing for him. He had always admired Rachel's inner strength and resilience, though he had been grateful she had allowed him to stay over the weekend.

All this was going through Ziggy's mind as he pulled his car into the bus lay-by. It was just far enough away from the school to not stand out or be seen by Ben, but close enough to watch the gates. He messaged Rachel to let her know he was there, then took a good look around. Ziggy's stomach was churning and although he was unsure what he was looking for, he trusted his copper's instinct. He would know if something or someone were 'off'. Ben being threatened had put him on a constant alert, and he knew it would all catch up with him at some point. He figured there would be plenty of time for that later. His priority right now was keeping his son safe.

He was parked opposite the school, near a large open grassy area where community football teams would play every weekend, along with a park and a small skate park. It was all owned and maintained by Leeds City Council. The area was well lit, and though the evenings attracted a different kind of crowd, apart from the sometimes noisy youths, there was very little trouble.

He spotted Rachel waiting just inside the school gate at the edge of the playground. When the bell sounded, she stepped forwards and Ziggy's eyes scanned round, looking for anyone or anything that seemed out of place. Children had to be handed over to a parent or someone that the child and teacher knew. He spotted Ben as soon as his class arrived at the main doors. He watched as Rachel stepped forwards again to greet him. She took the lunch box and school bag that he thrust towards her, but, much to Ben's annoyance, she clutched his hand and stopped him from running off with his friends. Ziggy watched and smiled as his son pulled faces all the way to the school gates. Rachel's car was a two-minute walk up the road, so Ziggy kept a close eye on them and watched until they were safely in and had pulled away. Rachel flashed her lights as she went past, and Ziggy waved quickly before Ben saw him. He breathed a temporary sigh of relief, though the anxiety remained.

Figuring he still had a bit more time before he needed to head back to the office, Ziggy headed towards the centre of Leeds, to Frankie's flat. Pulling into a space, he checked around to make sure the building manager wasn't in sight and swiftly exited his car. Forensics were long gone. All that was left to indicate anything at all had happened was a torn section of the blue-and-white police cordon tape that was attached to a nearby bush, fluttering in the wind. A sadness passed over Ziggy. How could someone's life be taken so violently and so little remain? It wasn't the first time he had thought this. He just never expected to think it about Lolly. Pushing his emotions to one side, he walked over to the door access panel and pressed the buzzer that he estimated would be Lolly's neighbour.

No response. He tried another number.

On the third attempt, he finally connected with someone. 'What?'

Pleasant. In a commanding voice, he said, 'It's the police. Can you open the door, please?' After the terse greeting, he expected to be challenged but to his surprise, the door clicked and he pushed his way through.

He headed up the two flights of stairs, taking two steps at a time. Even though he knew he wasn't going to face the nightmare from when he was last here, his chest tightened and his palms were getting sweaty as he grabbed the handrail. He forced himself to ignore his mounting anxiety. When he reached the right floor, he paused to give himself a minute to recover his breath and his composure. He made sure not to look as he passed Lolly's door and continued to the adjacent flat. Before he had a chance to knock, the door opened and an unshaven, sleepy-looking man appeared in front of him, clad in a fetching pair of boxer shorts covered in Bart Simpson slogans.

'DI Thornes,' said Ziggy, flashing his warrant card.

The man briefly looked at it, then pushed the door open and let Ziggy past him, did an unflattering scratch and flicked the kettle on in the kitchen. 'Yeah, sorry, mate, first day off in over a month, so I was having a lie in,' he said. 'Coffee? Tea?' He took two mugs out of the cupboard.

'Oh, yeah, tea, please, white with one sugar. Thank you. Sorry to have disturbed you, Mr ...?'

'Lloyd, Chris Lloyd.'

'Yes, sorry, Mr Lloyd. I know how that feels. What is it you do?'

'I'm a paramedic, so shift work. It's been crazy of late. We're hugely understaffed and there's quite a few off sick with flu.'

'I know what you mean about shortages. It's the same with us.'

Drinks made, they both sat at the bar stools that lined the kitchen island, and for a split second, although the layout of the flat was reversed, Ziggy was transported back to that fateful night.

Giving his head a quick shake, he took his notebook from inside his jacket pocket and flipped to a clean page.

'So, detective inspector,' Chris Lloyd said, 'what can I do for you?'

'It's in relation to the incident that took place next door on the night of the fourteenth of September. We're just chasing up a few loose ends and I wondered if you had any more thoughts?'

'Not really. I mean, I've given a statement. Can't think of anything else I would add.'

'OK, Mr Lloyd, would you mind going over it with me again? Sometimes it can help trigger new memories.'

'If you think it would help and please, call me Chris.'

Ziggy smiled. 'Thanks, Chris. Going back to that night, can you remember your movements, in particular any noises that were out of the ordinary?'

Chris closed his eyes. 'I'd just finished a back shift, so I was ready for a beer and bed. I remember opening my door, and there seemed to be a dragging noise coming from number twenty-two. I assumed new tenants were moving in so ...' He tailed off with a shrug.

'What time would that have been?'

'After midnight, definitely. Maybe one or two in the morning? I mentioned this in the statement, though.'

'And after this "dragging" noise, did you hear anything else?'

'Just the door slamming.'

'When you walked past the door, on your way home, was it open or closed?'

Chris put his head down. 'I'm just thinking. I think it was closed.'

'Are you sure?'

'Yes. In fact, yes, it was closed, otherwise I would have seen more and I know I didn't.'

So far, everything he was saying made sense. Ziggy wasn't sure what he had expected, but nothing was standing out. Trying a different angle, Ziggy took a sip of his tea.

'In the days prior to the incident, did you see or notice anything unusual?'

'Next door?' asked Chris.

'Or in the building. Anyone you hadn't seen before, for example?'

Chris hesitated and screwed his face up. 'I'm not sure, man. I'm lucky if I remember what I've had for breakfast most days.'

'I'm guessing you would have had a really busy shift that night?'

'What makes you say that?'

'World Cup final. Brazil beat Germany.'

Ziggy watched as the dawning recognition crept into Chris's face. 'Yes, that's right. Bloody hell, how could I forget that? It was one hell of a shift. Can't tell you how many callouts we had. A few units ended up stationing themselves on Briggate. We had to pull St John's ambulance in to walk the streets. It was crazy. I was an emergency responder that night. Traffic was horrendous around the hospital.'

Certain that Chris was reliving the moment, Ziggy carried on probing. 'And during the build-up to the match, the city must have been busy most nights, right?'

'Oh yeah, for sure. Especially whenever England played as you can imagine. I shouldn't say it, but most of us were relieved we didn't get through to the final.'

'And your neighbours, are they football fans?'

'There's a couple of suits that live in twenty and twenty-six. They were partying hard most nights.'

'Plenty of people in and around the building, then?'

'Not really, just the usual faces. Funnily enough, though, there was a bloke that seemed to be hanging around the lobby a fair bit, now I think of it.'

Ziggy's interest was piqued, but he couldn't let himself get too excited yet. 'Any idea what he was doing?'

'Not really. I didn't recognise him, but he always had a fag hanging out of his gob, dressed in black, wearing a leather coat.'

'Did you ever speak to him?'

'No. He looked like he was waiting for someone and he seemed to be there quite regularly, as he was usually there when I started my shift around six p.m.'

'Would you be able to describe his face?'

'Maybe not in any great detail. About my height, five ten, perhaps a bit taller. Quite heavy stubble, from what I could see – it was dark. He was wearing black, so I couldn't make out much.'

'What did you think he was doing?' asked Ziggy as he scribbled notes on his pad.

'Like I said, he looked like he was waiting for someone. Maybe a taxi driver?' Chris stood up and emptied the dregs of his coffee in the sink.

'That's great. Anything else you can think of?'

Leaning against the worktop, he adjusted himself again. 'No, man, I mean I wouldn't have remembered that much if you hadn't jogged my memory.'

Ziggy closed his notebook and handed over his mug. 'You've been a massive help, thank you. And thanks for the brew.'

'You're welcome. I'm sorry I didn't remember that bloke before. I hope it hasn't had any impact on the case.'

'Don't worry. It might be something and nothing. Here's my card. If you think of anything else, just call me direct.'

Ziggy quickly exited the building, avoiding the manager, and headed for his car. His head was spinning. It had been one hell of a first day back, and he had yet to meet Chrystal Mack. Though physically exhausted, he had never felt more fired up. He would mull over the information from Chris, see where it could fit into the bigger picture. Right now, he needed to head into the office.

Between Lolly's murder and the two threats from the anonymous note writer, he didn't have a moment to lose.

If there was one thing he had learnt over his twenty-seven years in service, it was that sometimes the system he had lived and breathed wasn't always fit for purpose.

16

Arriving back at his desk, Ziggy looked around for Nick, but the main office was almost empty. As he headed to the kitchenette to grab a glass of water, Angela stepped out of the incident room that had been assigned for Lolly's murder.

'Oh, hi, wasn't expecting you back this late,' she said, tucking a bundle of papers under her arm.

Ziggy checked his watch. It was past six – shift change would be over, which explained the empty desks. 'Hadn't realised it was that late, to be honest. Where's Nick?'

'He's headed home. Lesley rang – one of the twins has a temperature.'

Ziggy followed as Angela headed back to the group of desks that acted as the hub for Ziggy's team.

'Hope it's nothing too serious. What about Stiles?'

'Not sure, he was heading out with a bunch of PCs when I last saw him.'

Ziggy rolled his eyes. He was yet to work their new colleague out, and from the look on Angela's face, she was thinking the same. The pair moved towards their own desks, which was just across the quadrant from each other but separated by a screen. Ziggy logged in and quickly glanced at his emails. Seeing nothing exciting, he wheeled his chair round to Angela's side of the desk.

'I don't suppose you've had a chance to look at that email, have you?' he asked, somewhat coyly.

'Ha. Was wondering how long it would take you to ask.' She rummaged through a tray on her desk and pulled a piece of paper towards her. 'The email address was too generic to trace, but the IP address originated in Bradford.'

'That's ... great?' Ziggy mentally made a note to book himself onto an IT course at some point. Whilst he knew what an IP address was, he had no idea what Angela actually meant.

Knowing he was a Luddite, she laughed. 'When I say originates, that means it shows the location of the server. It won't lead you to a particular user's front door, or even a street, just a general location.'

'So where does that leave us?'

'Not very far at all, I'm afraid. You could do a WHOIS search and hopefully pin down a few more details.'

Ziggy stared at her, open-mouthed. 'I'm sorry, a what now?'

'A Whois search. Might shed a bit more light on it, but I would recommend you hand it over to Tech if you want that done.' She passed the email back to him. 'Sorry it didn't bring up more.'

'No, don't worry. I'm grateful you did this, really I am.'

'No worries, Lolly was a mate, but I have to draw the line now, Ziggy. I can't risk losing my job.'

'Absolutely, and thank you. I really appreciate it.'

Angela stood and pulled her coat on. 'You're not staying late, are you?'

Ziggy stretched in his chair, suddenly realising how tired

he was. *Oh hell, I've still got Mack the Knife to meet,* he thought. 'No, not much longer.'

'Good, cos you look like you could do with a good night's sleep,' added Angela as she bolted for the door.

'Cheeky sod,' he said, throwing a paperclip towards her. 'Goodnight, Angela.'

'Night, boss.'

He hadn't been to a wine bar in Leeds city centre for a long time. When he and Rachel were dating, they were regulars on Greek Street, but it had been so long, he doubted any of the bars they used to visit were still there. He looked around at the early-evening crowd. It appeared that most of them were office workers, heading into the bar to 'take the edge off' as he heard one suited woman say to another as they walked past. He'd never been a massive drinker. He didn't like the taste. He'd have the occasional beer, often with a lime wedge squeezed through the top of the bottle, but he hated the feeling of not being in control, so he usually quit whilst he was ahead.

He looked up at the neon light above him, telling him he was about to enter the Yates wine bar. He pushed the door open and stepped in out of the mizzling rain and was hit with the warmth and smell of stale beer. Looking around, he could see no sign of Chrystal.

Stepping out of the way of the incoming crowd, he pulled his phone and checked his messages. There was nothing from Chrystal, and no missed calls either. He checked the earlier message to make sure he had the right bar and the right time. He was certain he was in the right place, so finding a quiet corner, he rang Chrystal's number. It rang a few times, but then went to voicemail.

'Chrystal, it's Ziggy. I thought we were supposed to meet this evening. I'm at Yates. I'll wait another five minutes then I'm off. Call me back, please.'

He ended the call and took a walk through the bar, glancing across the room as he went. He made a quick trip to the gents, took another look around as he left, then feeling somewhat relieved that she hadn't shown, he decided to cut his losses and head home. The day had been long enough already. He had a ton of stuff he needed to do, and if the information Mack the Knife wanted to share was that imperative, she'd call.

He pulled into his driveway and headed up the overgrown garden path. Something else he needed to tackle when the weather was better. He unlocked the front door and headed into the now completed kitchen. Clicking the kettle on, he made a cup of tea, and poured hot water over a chicken-curry noodle pot. He stirred in the flavour sachet, grabbed a fork and headed upstairs into his home office.

Sitting at the desk, he spun his chair around so he could take in what he had posted on the home-made incident wall. There wasn't much there, but as he chomped through the noodles, slurping the sauce as he went, his mind went over everything that had he learnt during the day. Standing up, he pulled out his pack of sticky notes and added them to the wall.

He now knew for sure that Lolly had been suspended. That in itself was so strange, and highly unusual. She was so meticulous, he just didn't understand it. He made a note to see if he could get hold of the post-mortem report, or a copy of the complaint. He added the neighbour's observation about a man wearing a leather coat. Who was this mysterious lurker? What had he been doing?

He was mulling all this over when his mobile phone started to ring, making him jump.

That's probably Chrystal Mack, he thought. Distracted, he pulled it out of his pocket and answered without looking at the screen.

'DI Thornes.'

'Very formal, it's Rachel.'

'Oh, sorry. I was miles away. Thought you were someone else. Everything all right?'

'Yes, we're both good. I was just calling to see if you had any updates?' Ziggy could hear the tension in her voice. Though she had played it cool on the numerous occasions they had spoken earlier, she was clearly on edge.

'Nothing as yet. It's been one hell of a day to be honest, Rach.'

'Oh, OK.'

She sounded upset, and he couldn't blame her. Of course, Ben took priority, but he was being pulled in all different directions. 'I know you're upset, but I swear I'm on it. I'm just waiting for the forensic results.'

'I'm not upset, a bit disappointed maybe. I just hoped you would have something.'

'Whitmore's put me on some other case with a guy from the Met, but it's a priority first thing tomorrow, I promise.' Once again guilt washed over him.

'I'll see you outside the school gates tomorrow then?' she asked.

'Yes, of course. I'm sorry, Rachel.' The line went dead before he had a chance to finish his sentence.

He pulled copies of the two threatening notes from his

inside pocket. They had been burning a hole there all day, and particularly the one aimed at Ben. He had played mental tennis with it pretty much constantly since Rachel had handed it to him. Did he genuinely believe Ben's life was at risk? It wasn't something he was prepared to take a chance with.

Who did he trust in Forensics that he could ask a massive favour of? Joanna had helped him in the past, but he wasn't sure if she was back from maternity leave yet. He had pushed his luck with Angela, and in truth, he was reluctant to badger members of his team. Sometimes life sucked when you were juggling being a dad and being a detective. Feeling completely useless and exhausted, he called it a night and headed to bed, with what felt like the sword of Damocles hanging over his head.

17

Summer, 1965

Andrew pulled his pillow tighter and buried his face deep within the polyester filling. He had been crying until his eyes were sore and he could no longer breathe through his nose. He kicked off the Liverpool FC cover that his foster mum, Irene, had placed on his bed and was now shivering with cold, but he couldn't be bothered to pull it back over himself.

He heard a creak as his bedroom door opened.

'Go away,' he said, not wanting to talk to anyone.

'It's only me,' came back the little voice of his friend Leila.

She was the last person he wanted to see. Little Miss Popular. Little Miss Never-Puts-A-Foot-Wrong, or should that be Little Miss Never-Gets-Caught?

The floorboards creaked as she crept forwards.

'I said go away.' He turned his face in the opposite direction so she wouldn't see how blotchy and red it was.

'Everyone's left. I thought you might like some cake.' She placed a paper plate on his bed. Irene would go mad – they weren't allowed food in the bedrooms.

'It's not the end of the world, Andrew, even though I know it feels like that right now.'

It was his tenth birthday, and Irene and Bill had said he could have a party. They hoped it would help seal the tentative new friendships Andrew had made since moving in with them. He had heard them say on more than one occasion that Lolly wasn't a great influence, just because they had both broken curfew a few times. At least Lolly knew how to have a laugh, he had thought in his angry, resentful mind.

The party had been Liverpool themed, with everything from the napkins to the cake being either red or carrying the Liverpool FC emblem. Everyone he had invited from school had turned up, and he was relieved; he didn't think he could bear the humiliation of no one arriving. He was especially looking forwards to seeing his sister and cousins, who he hadn't seen since the day of their parents' funeral. His older sister, Elaine, had sent a Christmas card and a long letter letting him know that they all missed him, and they would come and see him as soon as they could, but they had moved away to Scotland.

Andrew missed his family desperately. Irene had told him that she had found a phone number for Elaine and had rung her a few weeks before the birthday party. She had even offered to pay for the trip and put them up. They had all gathered around the phone, waiting with bated breath for the reply. When she had replied with a grateful yes, everyone had been over the moon. They would arrive by coach on the morning of the party and stay for two days so they could have a proper catch-up.

Bill had headed to the Wellington Street Bus Station to collect them. He had waited for the Glasgow to Leeds coach, but when everyone had disembarked, there was no sign of Elaine. Worried, he rang Irene and asked her if Elaine had called to say she'd missed the coach. Irene rang the number she had, but it gave the unobtainable tone.

Flummoxed, she told Bill to come home and they would try again later. In the meantime, she rang British Telecom and asked them to test the line. It had been disconnected. She had waited until Bill came home before telling Andrew, and he was devastated. He felt like he had been punched in the gut. It was like losing his parents all over again. He had secretly harboured a wish that Elaine would let him return to Scotland with them, and he would have his family once more. That dream had been shattered, along with a thousand others.

He'd managed to brazen it out and had kept a brave face until it came time to blow the candles out on the cake. Then the emotion had caught up with him and he broke down. His friends had been confused but carried on eating and drinking, unaware of their friend's true anguish. He had stayed out of the way until their parents came to collect them.

Lolly sat on the edge of the bed. 'It was a stupid idea, anyway.' She picked at the icing as she spoke.

Andrew was confused. 'What was?'

'Inviting family. They always let you down.'

'Not true.'

'Really? Trust me, you have a lot to learn.'

'Oh, Little Miss Know-It-All now, are you?' He turned over onto his back, sniffed loudly and using the sleeve of his Liverpool goalkeeper's top, he wiped his nose and eyes.

'Nope. Just know how these things work. Everyone lets you down in the end. It's not their fault really, just that everyone is selfish in their own way.'

Andrew wasn't sure he believed her, but he did think Elaine had been selfish. She could have let him know she wasn't coming.

'They're not worth it. Best to learn that now than to be let down again and again.'

Andrew sighed and placed his arms behind his head.

'I'll never let you down, though,' she said, punching him play-fully on his arm. He pushed her back, and she tumbled off the bed onto the floor. Fifteen minutes later, hot and sweaty from wrestling each other, they ran downstairs laughing to finish the party food and watch his beloved team on the television.

18

Tuesday, 24th September 2002

Ziggy didn't think there was enough coffee in the world to carry him through the next twenty-four hours. Dreaming of Lolly again had added to his already busy mind, and if he was to make any progress, he needed a clear head. As he sat on the edge of the bed, he checked his phone. No word from Chrystal, and no missed calls. Stretching, he very briefly considered going for a run but settled on a cold shower to rinse away the crappy night's sleep.

Once dressed, he headed straight to the forensics lab in Wakefield. A couple of quick calls had confirmed that Joanna was back from maternity leave, and he hoped she might be able to help to speed up the results. Pulling into the huge, mostly empty car park, he parked up and waited. It was just after 7 a.m., so with any luck, he would catch her before she started work.

Much to his pleasant surprise, he saw her pulling into the car park shortly after him. He flashed his lights and got out of the car, wandering over to where she parked her car.

'Good morning,' he said, holding the car door for her whilst she gathered her bag from the front seat.

'Morning, early bird. To what do we owe the pleasure?'

'I was just passing,' said Ziggy with a shrug of his shoulders.

Joanna slammed the car door shut and clicked the remote button to lock it. 'Sure you were, Ziggy. What do you need?' She looked up at him, smiling.

'Is it that obvious?'

'We never get visits from your lot unless it's urgent, or you need a favour.'

'Fancy a coffee?' he offered, tilting his head towards the Costa that was on the industrial estate. 'You can tell me all about motherhood.'

Joanna laughed. 'Go on then, but I have a meeting at eight, so I can't be too long.'

As they crossed the car park and navigated their way over the busy road, Joanna told Ziggy all about her new arrival, a baby boy who had been two weeks early.

'I've only been back at work a couple of weeks, and I'm only part-time. Have no idea how those mothers do it whilst working full-time. It's exhausting.'

'I remember when Ben was born, Rachel and I seemed to walk round in a sleep-deprived state for much of the first year.'

Ziggy pushed open the coffee-shop door to allow Joanna past.

'Oh, God, don't say that. I don't think I can do a year with no sleep.' They ordered their drinks and took a table in the corner.

As Joanna stirred sugar into her cup, she said, 'I was sorry to hear about Lolly. You must have been devastated.'

Ziggy shifted in his seat. 'Yes, that's one word for it.

Don't think it's really sunk in yet.' He took a sip of his espresso, flinching as the scolding hot liquid burnt his mouth.

'Do you have any suspects yet?'

'That was one of the reasons I wanted to see you.' He pulled the note relating to Ben out of his pocket and laid it on the table. He turned it round so Joanna could read it.

'Jesus, Ziggy. When did you get this?'

'No, no don't worry. This is just a copy, the original was submitted the other day but I wondered if you could give it the hurry-up for me? Rachel found it in Ben's backpack last week.' He closed his eyes and scratched his head as he watched Joanna thinking the implications through

'I can't make any promises but I can see why you need answers. I'll see what I can do.'

Ziggy smiled. 'Thank you. There's something else as well. There was a glove with it, a workmans glove. Could you check and see if anything has been found on that?'

'They left a glove?'

'Not on purpose. My guess is whoever tried to leave the note wore gloves, and that it got left behind when they removed their hand from the side pocket.'

'Christ, Ziggy, you leave me speechless sometimes.'

'I know, I'm sorry, but I have to take the threat seriously. I really need to solve this. Is there anything at all that you can do?'

Joanna sighed, and he felt momentarily guilty for the position he had placed her in. 'I'll take a look, but seriously, mate, that's all I can do.'

Ziggy let go of his breath loudly. 'You're a star, thank you.'

'Don't worry about it. Lolly was a friend, and I don't want anything happening to that little boy of yours. Leave it with me. I'll see what I can do.' She glanced at her watch. 'I have to go. I'll call you later today.'

'I can't thank you enough, Jo, honestly.'

Delighted, but with a huge dose of guilt, he rose and uncharacteristically kissed Joanna on her cheek. Blushing, they laughed and parted ways. Watching her hurry across the car park, he felt grateful that Lolly was so highly thought of. Not for one minute did he think Joanna was doing the favour for him.

With the most important item ticked off his list, he headed towards the office via the primary school, just in time to see Rachel waving to Ben at the school entrance. He didn't stop, instead he dialled her number on his mobile. She answered straight away.

'Morning,' she said. 'We're fine.'

'Morning. I know, I've just seen you, but I didn't have time to stop.'

He thought she sounded quite terse, and he couldn't blame her. He listened as she walked back to her car and switched to hands-free.

'I wanted to let you know that I've chased the note and glove results directly with Joanna at Forensics. I'm sorry I didn't do it earlier, it's just with—'

'It's fine, Ziggy I get it.'

Definitely terse. He couldn't think of anything else to say. His guilt at not putting Ben first was already off the scale and he was certain it would take more than a few clumsy words of apology, however sincere they were. He said goodbye and ended the call.

Cutting through traffic and heading into the back roads of Leeds, he made it to the office twenty minutes later. He had half an hour before he was due in the morning team briefing. He pushed open the main office door, and let the atmosphere wash over him as everyone logged into their computers, chatted about last night's TV or just gossiped about some poor sod. Nick and Angela were sitting in the usual corner, with Sadie laughing about something.

'Morning,' he said in what he hoped was a more jovial tone than he felt. He needed another coffee. 'Anyone up for breakfast?'

At that, all three stood up. 'If you're paying,' said Nick.

'How's the little one?' asked Ziggy.

'Ear infection, he'll live. Bit of Calpol and ear drops. Missus always panics.'

Angela, herself a mother of a toddler, punched him gently on the arm. 'You can never be too cautious with a temperature, you patronising bugger.'

'Now, now, you two, no fighting,' said Sadie.

The foursome headed to the canteen, continuing the mickey-taking as they walked. As they stood in the queue, Sadie gently pulled Ziggy back.

'I've a couple of updates for you, if you've got five minutes before you head off?'

'Yes, absolutely. Any hints?'

'It's the carpet fibres. Not huge, but could lead somewhere. I'll tell you more later. The team is being updated in the briefing. I just wanted to keep you in the loop.'

'Appreciated, Sadie. Thank you.' He felt the hairs on his arms stand on end. *Please let it be a breakthrough*, he thought.

'Oh, and also, we're getting nowhere with the E. Soh signature on the CCTV receipt either.'

'Hmm, that's a mystery still, isn't it? Worth staying on it, though. How about a handwriting analysis?' he asked, handing over the cash for everyone's breakfast.

'With our budgets? Whitmore said no.' Sadie sighed as she filed past him.

'Why am I not surprised?' he muttered, suddenly losing his appetite. Decisions based on budget only served his disillusionment with the service.

Whilst the other three tucked into a hearty breakfast, Ziggy nibbled on toast and gulped his coffee as he half listened to them talk about the fallout from Sharon and Phil in last night's *Eastenders* episode. He wasn't a soap fan at the best of times, so he had zoned out, until Nick nudged him.

'Briefing in twenty minutes, yeah?'

'Sorry, Nick, was miles away. Yeah, no problem.'

Returning their dirty plates and cups, they headed back to the office, Sadie and Ziggy diverting into a side room.

'What's the deal with the carpet fibres then?' asked Ziggy, impatient to get the information out of Sadie.

She took a deep breath. 'Firstly, I've cleared it with Whitmore to tell you this, just so you know. Anyway, we've had an expert looking at what we found, and he's come back to us to say that although it's a mainstream acrylic fibre used in ninety-nine per cent of household carpets, the colour is unusual. It's known as ochre, like a mustard yellow, and it was bought in bulk in the 1990s via a contract with Leeds City Council to furnish council-owned property.'

'Really?' asked Ziggy, incredulous.

'Yeah, I know. We have narrowed it down to several housing estates in Leeds, and unless someone comes up with a better plan, it will be a case of door-knocking to see who still has that carpet down or remnants of it.'

'Damn, that could take weeks.' Ziggy felt his frustration rise. 'It's like one step forwards and ten back.'

'It might feel that way, but despite the whole budget

issue, we have thrown a huge amount of time and resources at it, Ziggy. We will get there, I promise.'

'I know. I just get frustrated but I appreciate the update. Is there anything I can do?'

'Not really. We've got uniform doing the house-to-house, speaking of which, did you go somewhere you weren't supposed to yesterday?'

Ziggy felt his face flush. He wasn't sure what Sadie was getting at, bearing in mind all his illicit 'errands' of late, so kept quiet, putting what he hoped was a confused look on his face. Sadie's expression showed it wasn't.

'Thankfully, I took the call this morning, but Mr Lloyd wanted to confirm that it was, and I quote "a long leather coat like that Matrix guy wears".' She raised her eyebrows and looked questioningly at him.

'Don't know what you mean, DS Bates.' He stood upright from the wall he had been leaning against and reached for the door handle.

'Hmm, I bet. As a result of this new information, we have requested the CCTV from the entrance that dates even further back than where we previously looked.'

'Well, that's something then, isn't it?'

'Absolutely, but talk to me first in future, eh, mate?'

He opened the door, did a mock salute, and turned to face the office. He heard Sadie tut and watched as she headed to see Whitmore for the team briefing. What he wouldn't give to be a fly on that wall, he thought, instead of having to deal with some student money scam.

19

With the others in the meeting, Ziggy pulled his chair forwards and joined Nick around his side of the desk. Stiles was waffling on to the local street team about something and nothing to do with his time in the Met, whilst Nick and Ziggy just stared on, shaking their heads.

'Showboating,' whispered Nick, tilting his head in Stiles's direction.

'Doesn't he get bored of the sound of his own voice?' questioned Ziggy. Deciding he'd waited long enough, he called out. 'Come on, Peter, we haven't got all day.'

Stiles looked up from his chat with a female police constable, who hadn't been as quick as the other uniforms to beat a retreat, and headed in Ziggy's direction.

'Sorry, chaps, just getting to know the locals.'

Ziggy cringed. 'I'm sure they were delighted, but where are we with everything? Have you arranged that interview yet?'

Finally taking the hint, he pulled up a chair and joined Ziggy and Nick. He opened his notebook. 'Updates so far.

I've arranged the interview with Daniel. It's in the meeting room in' – he checked his watch – 'ten minutes.'

'Just enough time for you to tell us a bit about him then,' Ziggy said, suppressing an eye-roll as they stood in unison and made their way to the allocated meeting room. 'I have read his statement, but what do you know of his background?'

'The young man's name is Daniel Kimble,' said Peter. 'He's twenty years old now, but was nineteen when the fraud happened. He was in his first year, taking an undergraduate degree in criminal psychology – oh, the irony – but he deferred his studies for twelve months when all this came to light.'

They sat around the conference table, and Ziggy spread out the papers that Peter passed over and found a picture of Daniel. He looked like a typical student; overly long, straggly hair, all limbs and acne, wearing baggy jeans and an old band T-shirt – Foo Fighters, if Ziggy wasn't mistaken.

'How has it all been left with him? Presumably the bank has decided not to press individual charges?' asked Nick.

'That's right. Daniel's statement will be used as part of a joint prosecution case alongside the bank as and when the fraudsters are caught.'

Nick pulled out Daniel's statement and read through it. When he'd finished, he turned to Peter. 'It's clever isn't it? You can see why a cash-strapped student would fall for it?'

'Oh, for sure. I mean, they're young, naive, maybe holding down a weekend job whilst managing on the finances of the state or bank of Mum and Dad. Chance to make a few quid, no risk and with no strings attached? Why wouldn't you?'

It was the first statement Peter had made that Ziggy agreed with. He also noticed that much of the show-off attitude had dropped now. Ziggy wondered how insecure someone had to be to make them behave like a prick the rest of the time. He turned to Nick.

'I guess our purpose today is to ask how Daniel got involved with the scammer. Perhaps with local knowledge, we can pick up on something that may have been missed? What do you think, Nick?' Peter said.

'I agree. Let's pin him down on the finer details, see what he has to say.'

'Let's find out, shall we? How do you turn this thing on?' Ziggy was waving the remote control aimlessly. Nick took it out of his hand, clicked the on button and the screen in front of them flickered into action.

Daniel Kimble appeared on the big screen, pushing his hair out of his eyes and looking nervous. No, he looked terrified. A man, who Ziggy assumed was either Daniel's father or a solicitor, sat on the sofa at the side of him. They were in a soft interview room at their local police station, the design of which was meant to create a calming atmosphere, all muted colours and vague undertones of Scandinavian simplicity. A small coffee table sat in front of them, with a jug of water and two glasses.

'Good afternoon, Daniel,' said Peter. 'We haven't met before, but my name is Peter, and these are my colleagues Ziggy and Nick from Major Investigations here in Leeds.'

Daniel mumbled a 'hello' and the man next to him spoke. 'Afternoon, officers, I'm Daniel's father, John.'

With the pleasantries out of the way, Ziggy began. 'Daniel, I'm sure you've had this explained to you, but you're not in any trouble. You're here to help us with our enquiries, and some information has come to light that you could help with. I've read your statement, and I'd like to ask you a few questions. Is that OK with you?'

Daniel nodded.

'I'm going to have to ask you to answer verbally, Daniel, just so we're clear.' Ziggy watched as Daniel nodded again until his dad nudged him.

'Sorry. Yes, that's fine,' he said.

'Great. I'd like to take you back to when you first met the friend who asked you to take part in the bank fraud. Talk me through what happened.'

Daniel took a deep breath. His body language showed that the young man was probably sick of going through it, reliving the embarrassment. He was slouched in his seat, feet kicked out in front of him, arms folded and left foot twitching wildly. He let out an audible sigh and began his story.

'I started Leeds Uni in autumn 2000 to study as an undergrad in criminal psychology. My parents paid for accommodation. I worked on a weekend in a bar to pay for food and shit—' His father thumped him with his elbow. 'Sorry, *stuff*, but it wasn't enough.' He stopped to pour a glass of water and took a sip. 'One night, I was hanging out at the Student Union bar and I noticed this kid was buying everyone drinks. I wondered how he could afford it if he was a student, so I kept an eye on him. Every Friday and Saturday night, he was either in the bar buying drinks or sat outside in a flashy BMW. I never saw him in any lectures or anything. Course, now I know why.'

'How was he paying for the drinks?' asked Ziggy, though he suspected he already knew the answer.

'Cash, and not just the occasional note but wads of cash, like a bundle. I'd never seen so much money.'

'How did you get talking to him?'

'I didn't. Well, obviously I did in the end, but at first I just watched him. I asked around to see if anyone knew who he was.'

'Did they give you a name?' Ziggy knew this question had been asked extensively both during Daniel's initial and subsequent interview, but he had to try.

'He's known as Esso, as in the petrol company. Don't know why, I never found out his proper name.' Daniel sighed. 'I'm sorry, going over it all again is so embarrassing.' He shifted in his chair, and Ziggy noticed beads of sweat on his top lip.

Esso. Ziggy kept his mouth shut and parked that titbit of info for later.

'It's OK, I get it. What did Esso look like?'

'Normal, I suppose. Not overly tall, not short. White, pale skin, short cropped hair. He wore some bling, but not too much. Looked about twenty-five or something.'

'How were you introduced?'

'One of my mates, Jordan, who was working at the same bar as me, met up with Esso one night after our shift and I was there. Earlier that night, Jordan, or JP as we know him, had told me it was his last shift. He'd found an easier way to make money, and he'd show me if I was interested.'

'And obviously you were?'

'Who wouldn't be? Leeds isn't a cheap place to live or eat, and the wages are shit. I was sick of asking Mum and Dad for money so I was up for anything.'

Mr Kimble senior eyebrow's raised, and he shifted himself in his seat.

'What happened next?' asked Peter.

'We finished our shift. JP went out front for a fag and I followed him. We were standing waiting when Esso pulled up in his BMW. JP jumped in the front and told me to get in the back, so I did. Esso didn't drive off straight away. Instead, he asked JP for his "square", which is basically his bank card.'

'Had you heard of squaring before then?' Ziggy asked.

'Nope. It wasn't described to me as that, though. Esso said it was "refunded payments", all totally legit and above board. JP opened the glovebox and Esso had bundles of fifty-pound notes, I mean, like, the glovebox was stacked with them.'

'Where did you think the money had come from?'

'To be honest, I had no idea. I guessed it was from some drug dealing or something, but as long as I wasn't involved with that, what could go wrong? Esso told me that a friend of his would put money into JP's bank account and JP wouldn't use his card or bank for a couple of weeks until he'd heard from Esso when he'd get his commission.'

'How much "commission"?'

'Ha, well, that's where I thought I was being clever. I thought, no way am I handing my bank card to anyone without knowing how it works, so I held off. Made out like I was well up for it when I was just killing time to see what happened to JP. Three weeks later, JP turns up at the bar, tells me we're going out, shows me an ATM receipt for thirty grand. I couldn't believe it. The zeros just kept going.' Daniel became agitated as he spoke, clearly still visibly shaken by the whole event. He was wringing his hands, rubbing them on his jeans. He pushed his straggly hair back from his forehead again and wiped the sweat away with the back of his hand.

'Then you decided you wanted in?' It was Peter that spoke.

'I'd already decided I wanted in, but I made JP go to the nearest cash machine and show me it for real.'

'Your statement says that after you'd seen the money in

JP's account, you asked him to contact Esso and find out what you needed to do?'

'Yeah. What was the worst that could happen? I figured the gain was greater than the risk, so why the hell not?'

Daniel's dad crossed one leg over the other, tutted and sighed. Daniel threw him such a look that if it could kill, he'd be dead. Ziggy felt for the lad's father, hoping Ben was never daft enough to get himself into such a situation.

'OK. Tell me about the time you met Esso on his own.'

'Huh, that's where shit gets weird.'

Even though they'd all read the statement, they still leant forwards, keen to pick up on any new details.

'Go on,' said Ziggy.

'JP tells me that Esso will be passing by the Library pub on a particular night, Wednesday, I think it was.'

Ziggy shuffled through the statement. 'Yep, Wednesday.'

'I head out to meet him, and sure enough he pulls up in a brand new BMW, a different one to what I'd seen him drive before. This was bigger. Anyway, I get in the back seat and the car stinks of weed, and he passes me a joint.' He glanced over at his dad. 'I didn't have any,' he clarifies defensively.

'A few puffs of a joint are the least of our problems, son,' said Mr Kimble, through gritted teeth. Ziggy guessed he'd have more to say when they left the station.

Ignoring the rising tension between father and son, Ziggy urged Daniel to carry on. 'What happened then?'

'He drives off, he calls at McDonalds in Oakwood, gets a Coke, then we stop at Roundhay Park.'

'Whereabouts?'

'Near the flat where that weird DJ bloke lives.'

Jimmy Savile. Ziggy knew exactly where Daniel meant.

It was considered the 'top end' of Roundhay Park and featured several large mansions.

'So anyway, we pull up, and Esso tells me to get out, which I do. I stand there for a bit. He gets out, looks me up and down then tells me to get back in the car and we go back to Leeds. Weird.'

Ziggy imagined that Esso was showing the latest recruit to someone higher up the food chain. 'In your statement, you mention a description of Esso, and you mention a black coat?'

'Yeah, he was wearing one of those long black leather coats like Keanu Reeves. Thought that was odd too – no one wears those any more. Was some really weird shit, man. I didn't want to get involved after that, but I didn't have a choice. Apparently, I'd passed some kind of test and had to go ahead with it. I handed Esso my bank card along with my account details and the rest is history.'

'Do you think you'd recognise this Esso if you saw him again?' asked Ziggy.

'I dunno, yeah probably, but I hope I never do.'

Glancing at Peter and Nick, Ziggy concluded the interview and ended the call.

'Didn't really add anything, did he?' commented Peter as they gathered together all the paperwork.

'Oh, but he did, Inspector Stiles,' replied Ziggy, feeling a surge of adrenaline as he headed out of the room. 'He really did.'

Bewildered, Nick and Peter followed in Ziggy's wake as he marched into the incident room for Lolly's case. Despite a young detective constable's protestations, Ziggy frantically scoured all the updates, the pictures, the writing, the timeline. His hands were shaking as he moved from one display board to the next.

'What are you looking for?' asked Nick.

Ziggy didn't answer directly, completely caught up in a world of his own.

'I need to speak to Sadie,' he said as he left the incident room and headed for the Major Investigations' team office. He glanced around, his heart racing, but he couldn't see her. *Whitmore's office.* Without knocking, he barged his way in, taking Whitmore by surprise.

Nick and Peter had again followed him, completely baffled.

'What the hell, Thornes? Haven't you heard of knocking?' blasted Whitmore, rising from his desk at the unexpected intrusion.

'I need to speak to Sadie. Where is she?' demanded Ziggy.

'She's out, and you need to watch your tone. What on earth has got into you?'

'Ziggy, what's going on, mate?' asked Nick, hoping to get some sense out of his boss.

'It's connected, all of it. The money scam, the signature, Lolly's death. Can't you see it? It's all connected.'

20

'The leather coat, the signature – E. Soh, Esso. It's got to be the same person.' Ziggy looked between the faces of his boss and his team, all of which were looking at him nonplussed.

Nick spoke first, frowning his way through Ziggy's logic. 'What leather coat?'

Ziggy strode over to Nick, glad that at least Nick wasn't dismissing his claim, as he feared Whitmore was about to do.

'Lolly's next-door neighbour claimed to have seen a man hanging around the apartment block in the weeks leading up to the ... incident.' He still couldn't bring himself to use the word *murder*. 'Daniel Kimble – the witness in the money-laundering case, sir – just said a man in a long leather coat. It *must* be the same person.'

'That's a wild assumption, Thornes, and at best, only circumstantial.'

Ziggy ignored Whitmore and continued to address Nick. 'And the signature of the person who collected the CCTV? It was signed E. Soh, Esso.'

'I get what you're saying but it doesn't really take us any further forwards, does it?' said Nick.

Whitmore talked over him, his voice gradually getting louder. 'So now we've got a money-laundering murderer on our hands, have we? With no DNA, no fingerprints, no identity or any of what's commonly known as *evidence*?' yelled Whitmore. 'Get out of my office. Add your findings to the incident team and don't ever interrupt me like that again.'

Ziggy stared at Whitmore, took a deep breath, turned and left before he said something he regretted. He vaguely heard Stiles apologising on Ziggy's behalf, which sent him apoplectic. He couldn't be in the company of such idiots any longer.

Seething, he stormed out of the MIT office and headed for his car.

The cold air hit him as he pushed open the exit door. He was breathing erratically, trying to calm down, but all he really wanted to do was punch something, or someone.

'Evidence? You want fucking evidence, I'll get you evidence,' Ziggy muttered as he slammed his car door. He checked the time. It was almost time to head to Ben's school, so after clicking his phone into the hands-free holder, he headed in that direction. His mind was working overtime, trying to work out the connection. He needed to calm down. As he drove, some of the anger dissipated and he tried to think logically.

Occam's razor. The simplest explanation is likely to be the most correct explanation, he thought. He didn't have all the pieces; he knew that and reluctantly admitted to himself that Whitmore was right. He didn't have hard evidence. But he would get it. He slammed the steering wheel just as his mobile phone started to ring. He glanced at the screen. Unknown number.

'DI Thornes,' he snapped.

'Oh, hello. My name is Katie, and I'm calling from the *Yorkshire Press*.'

Oh for fuck's sake, this is the last thing I need, he thought as he considered cutting the call, then remembered he hadn't heard back from Chrystal. 'What can I do for you?'

'I'm Miss Mack's assistant and, well, it's just that we were wondering if you had seen anything of Chrystal recently?'

He hadn't been expecting that, and he gave a quizzical look at his phone, frowning as he replied. 'No, I haven't. Why?'

'Well, you were the last person she was meeting last night at Yates, but no one has seen or heard from her since teatime yesterday.'

'Right, well, she didn't turn up for our meeting. I did call her but it went to voicemail, so I left a message.'

'Ah, I see. I'll pass it on, but I think we might need to report her as a missing person. She always answers her phone, and she always checks in with me every morning, without fail, but ...'

Ziggy heard the young woman's tears. 'I'm sure she'll be fine, but check the usual places, call the local hospitals and if you get nowhere, it wouldn't harm to file a missing persons report,' he said by way of conciliation.

'OK, if you do hear anything, will you let me know?'

'Yes, yes, of course,' he said distractedly.

The call ended, and Ziggy was even more perplexed.

He pulled up outside Ben's school, waited until Ben and Rachel were both safe, then set off. He pulled up Sadie's number and hit the green button.

'Come on, answer,' he muttered to himself as he negotiated the dense traffic. She answered on the third ring.

'Who have you been upsetting now?'

'Don't, Sadie. I'm not sure how I kept it together. Has Nick told you what we've discovered?'

'Yes, but we need—'

'Evidence, yes, I know, and I will get you some.'

'Ziggy, Whitmore is furious with you. You were skating on extremely thin ice already.'

As much as he respected Sadie as his colleague and loved her as a friend, her insistence on playing by the rules sometimes drove him round the bend. He tried to not let his frustration come across in his tone, forcing himself to smile as he spoke, albeit through gritted teeth. She was going to love what he was about to tell her.

'Listen, I've just had a call from Mack the Knife's assistant at the *Yorkshire Press*. She's gone missing by all accounts.'

'OK, and what has that got to do with anything?'

'I didn't say anything at the time, but she approached me last week. She had been writing a story about Lolly, but she was warned off.'

'Warned off? How?'

'An email threat. It might be worth sending a uniform to check her flat.' Even as Ziggy spoke, he could picture Sadie closing her eyes and shaking her head.

'Ziggy, you are unreal ...'

'I know, I know, I've been an idiot,' he said.

Silence.

He heard Sadie draw in a deep breath, and he cut in before she had a chance to bollock him.

'I'm heading back in. I'll update everyone as soon as I get there.' He ended the call abruptly.

He did intend to head into the office, he just had a point to prove first.

Ziggy parked his car in the disused car park of the Cross Keys pub in Cross Green. He knew Freddie O'Connor would be surfacing soon for his evening pick-me-up. All he had to do was wait. Sure enough, at exactly 6 p.m., Ziggy spotted him leaving his mother's house. Ziggy flashed his lights, and he watched as Freddie peered out from the hood of his coat. He raised his hand in recognition and headed towards the car. Ziggy took in how worn his clothes looked, how his trainers slapped against the ground as the heels had been trodden down. He felt sorry for Freddie, but he had given him more than one opportunity over the years to escape this life, only for Freddie to once again return to his brothers' fold.

Ziggy unlocked the central locking, and Freddie climbed into the front seat. The familiar smell washed over him, and he lowered a window.

'Any news?'

'Yeah, I think you're gonna like this.'

Ziggy waited, leaning towards the open window for clean air before he gagged. 'Go on then.'

''Ow much?'

'Enough.'

'Nah, man, this is good shizzle. I want at least a grand.'

'Five hundred max.'

'Five fifty,' said Freddie.

'Done,' said Ziggy, knowing full well he would have given more than a grand if the information was worth it.

Seemingly satisfied, Freddie began. Ziggy knew better than to interrupt, no matter how quickly he wanted Freddie to get to the point. Freddie would lose his chain of thought and start the whole tale again, like some elongated weird stutter. 'It were to do wi' some emails that our Rob sent, warning someone or summat like that.' Warming to his theme, Freddie talked faster, almost spitting the words out. 'I was at our kids' shop and made out I needed a piss, but went to his office in the back instead.'

Ziggy stared at Freddie, reluctant to speak but willing him to get on with it.

'And?'

Freddie tapped the side of his nose. 'I could tell ye what I found, but then I'd have to kill ye.' At that he let out a guttural laugh.

Ziggy smiled, playing along.

Freddie stopped laughing and started fiddling with the inside of his coat. After what felt to Ziggy like an age, he pulled out some crumpled and creased papers. He put them on his lap and tried to smooth them out. Impatiently, Ziggy snatched them off him.

'Oi, gimme chance.'

Ziggy looked at what he had in his hands. Copies of the email threats to MTK and Ben. Printed on headed stock. *Cohen & Co.* He looked at the foot of the page: *Proprietors: H and F Cohen.*

Cohen, where had he heard that name before?

Hurriedly, he took his wallet out of his jacket pocket and gave Freddie the notes he had.

'That's not five hundred quid,' said Freddie as he counted it.

'You'll get the rest if anything comes of the info, you know that.'

'But it will, I swear down.'

'So you'll get paid then.' Ziggy leant across Freddie. 'Go on, before anyone spots you.' He pushed the door open for him.

Freddie got out reluctantly. 'Don't drop me in it.'

'As if,' said Ziggy, accelerating away.

The first person Ziggy bumped into as he entered the Major Investigations' office was Sadie, who had a face like thunder.

'Oh, decided to join us, have you?'

'Don't be like that, Sadie. I've been chasing up leads.'

'Into which case, or are you still convinced they're connected?'

He was taken back with her tone and attitude. 'What's wrong?'

'You, Ziggy, you're what's wrong. You're a loose cannon, forever going off on your own and jeopardising the case. Whitmore wants to see you.'

He closed his eyes. 'What's happened?'

'I'll let Whitmore tell you.'

She marched off, and he followed her. She knocked at Whitmore's door and they entered together.

'Ah, the Lone Ranger returns.' Whitmore's voice was dripping sarcasm, and there was an acrimonious atmosphere that could boil over any second.

'I was following up on leads, sir.'

'I know, in Wakefield. At the forensics lab.'

Oh shit. 'In fairness, sir, I didn't find anything out..'

'Really? That's not like you.' Whitmore's face was puce. 'I've already had to put you on leave once, Andrew. I thought you had learnt your lesson, but it seems not.'

'If you'll just hear me out, sir.'

'Take this as your final warning, inspector. Hand over everything – and I mean *everything* – to DS Bates that relates to the murder of Leila Turner, then get out of my sight.'

Whitmore spoke very softly in a controlled anger that Ziggy had never seen before.

Knowing he had pushed his luck as far as he could, Ziggy made to leave, then turned to face Whitmore. 'It's Doctor. Doctor Leila Turner. Sir.'

PART II

LOLLY'S STORY

21

Bramley, Leeds, 1959

Leila pulled the threads of the cardigan closer to her and shivered. The holes in the soles of her shoes were allowing the rainwater to seep through, soaking her bare feet, all adding to her misery. She waited around the corner from the local shop until someone left before ducking in through the entrance, avoiding the beady eye of the shopkeeper. Leila scuttled to the reduced-items shelf in the back corner, where the produce was just about to or had already gone out of date. Grabbing a sandwich and a packet of biscuits, she hastily shoved them back inside her cardigan and darted out in record time.

Leila didn't stop running until she was in the church-yard, hiding in the bin store at the rear of the church. Ripping open the wrapper on the sandwich, she ate it so quickly she gave herself hiccups. With no drink, she scooped some water in her hand from the outside tap. Having demolished the sarnie, she tore open the top of the biscuits packet more carefully, knowing that she would have to make these last. She had taken a packet of ginger biscuits, and eating them without a drink turned her mouth dry. A crumb caught in the back of her throat and she fell into a coughing fit. Tears were streaming down her face as she struggled to catch her breath. As she frantically clutched at her throat, a face appeared around the side of her hiding place.

'You all right in there? Oh, it's you. What have I told you about sleeping here?' The groundskeeper had become Leila's nemesis in recent weeks. One night, when she couldn't get into the house, not knowing where else to go, she'd retreated to her favourite spot under the shelter in the churchyard, only to have a rude awakening as he opened the gates at 5 a.m. Leila tried to explain that she hadn't slept there, but all she could do was point to her throat and cough. He reached in and grabbed her by the arm, dragging her out into the open.

'Come with me,' he said as he pulled her along the path.

Leila had built up enough saliva to at least calm down her coughing, but not stop it all together. He led her into a little shed, where he grabbed a tumbler and filled it with water from an outside tap.

'Drink this,' he demanded.

Leila gratefully took the cup from him and gulped the water down, feeling instant relief. She wiped her face on the sleeve of her cardigan and passed the cup back, thanking the groundskeeper as she did. He offered her a little stool, which she sat on whilst he leant against the workbench.

'Now then, we keep running into each other, don't we?' he said, leaning down, so they were at the same level.

'I'm not sleeping here,' said Leila defiantly. 'Well, I did that once, but I mean, not permanently like. I've got a home, with a mum and stepdad and everything.'

The groundskeeper laughed. 'I'm sure you have, young lady. How old are you?'

'I'm six but I'll be seven soon.'

'And you live close by, do you?'

'Why do you want to know?' asked Leila, instantly wary.

The groundskeeper reached forwards and placed his hand on her leg. Leila froze. 'Now that's not a very nice way to speak to me when all I've done is help you.' As he spoke, his hand ventured higher up her leg and his fingers slipped onto the inside of her thigh. Leila flinched, and didn't need to hang around to know where this was going, thanks to her stepdad. She swiftly raised her right leg and kicked the groundskeeper in the stomach with all her six-year-old might. Startled, he took a step back, and Leila saw her chance to escape. Ducking underneath his arm as he reached out to grab her, she set off at a pace that even a top athlete would have struggled to keep up with.

She looked over her shoulder and saw that he wasn't even about to give chase.

'Pervert!' she yelled and continued to run towards home.

Leila had been born in St. James's Hospital and raised in Leeds, West Yorkshire. Her mum said that she had been born kicking and screaming and hadn't stopped since. They had moved to Bramley, West Leeds, not long after Leila turned one, renting a council house in the east of the suburb. Soon after moving in, Leila's mum had met Jake, and he had moved in with them.

Leila detested Jake with a passion. Before he came along, Leila and her mum had been fine. There was always food on the table, a warm bath, and hugs in bed at night after story time. All that had changed when he pitched up. Now, she was lucky if there was any food in the cupboards. She had a permanent hole in her stomach that was never filled. Her mum, the fun-loving, outgoing person she had been, had disappeared and instead there was a ghost. It was the only way Leila could think of to describe her, not that anyone had ever asked. Her mum's vibrant red hair had faded to a dull copper with streaks of grey. Her teeth that used to be like little pearls were now blackened and one of her front ones was missing completely (thanks to Jake's temper, though her mum never said outright). At one time, she used to take a pride in both their appearances. 'Charity shop clothes are just clothes that people have fallen out of love with' was her mum's mantra, and she could have picked out a whole new wardrobe of clothes for just a few pounds. That was before.

Leila had no idea where her grandparents were. She didn't really remember them. They were a hazy memory and had never been spoken about since around the time that Jake moved in.

She really hated Jake. She knew she wasn't supposed to use the word *hate*, but she couldn't think of a better word. The thought of him made her feel sick, especially when he'd been drinking, which was every day. He would shout and scream at her and Mum for no reason.

Recently, when he had started hitting Mum, Leila had jumped in and kicked him really hard as well as biting him on the leg. He had tried to give her a backhander, but she was too quick for him, and she'd stayed out of his way ever since.

As she approached home, she spotted Mrs Dunn from over the road. She was nice. Leila liked it when Mrs Dunn baked. She would always save a little treat for Leila, and her house was always clean, warm and felt like a home.

Leila waved and reluctantly headed down the path to her own house. She stopped on the doorstep to see if she could hear any shouting. It was unusually quiet, which made her even more wary. She pulled the key from the chain around her waist and slipped it into the lock. Carefully, she pushed open the door and tiptoed across the threshold. The house was a three-bedroomed suburban semi-detached with a decent-sized front garden and a smaller garden to the rear. Her mum used to keep the gardens looking smart, with lots of colourful flowers and the lawns were always neatly cut, but after Jake sold the lawnmower and most of the gardening tools from the shed, both gardens had become overgrown with long grass and weeds. There was also an armchair, which used to be in the front room, sitting outside. Her mum had said it was for Jake to sit in the sun, but Leila wasn't stupid. There was a huge burn hole in the seat, and she knew Jake had fallen asleep with a cigarette in his hand. He did it all the time, but most of the time Leila caught it before it could do any harm.

'Mum?' she shouted, poking her head around the living-room door. Her mum was laid on the sofa, the TV blaring *This Morning* in the background. She appeared to be asleep as she was still in her nightie and dressing gown, and her head was back with her eyes closed.

Then Leila spotted the empty vodka bottle on the floor at her side. Leila entered the room and checked her mum hadn't been sick, then tidied up around her. Collecting as many cups and plates as she could carry, she took them into the kitchen at the rear of the house and placed them on the side.

'Fuck do you want?' snarled Jake, as he sat at the kitchen table, rolling a fag.

'Nowt. Just cleaning up.' If she'd have known Jake was in there, she would have headed straight upstairs.

'Be quick about it, then. Should have let fucking school take care of you. That was a mistake.'

Leila couldn't remember the last time she'd been to school. She'd joined the local junior school when she had turned five, and she loved it. She couldn't believe you could read books, learn to sing songs and play all day long. Her halcyon days had ended abruptly when one of her teachers had called round to the house to see her. Leila had been delighted to see Miss Henshaw, but Jake had been really rude and told Miss Henshaw that she had to mind her own business and that Leila was going to be homeschooled after the half-term holidays.

Jake had lied. She'd had no books or learning since then. If she knew how to get to the school, she'd walk herself, but Jake had made it clear to her what would happen if she did. Instead, Leila spent her days mooching around the local parks, along the canal banks and hiding out in the church-yard, but that was off the list now.

She ignored Jake's question and started running the hot tap. She waited for a while, but it didn't get warm.

'Why is there no hot water?' It was a question mostly to herself, but Jake heard her.

'Why do you think? Fucking boilers fucked, innit. That's your fault. All them baths you keep taking. You used it up and broke the boiler. What you gonna do about it?'

Leila felt like crying, but refused to let Jake see that he had upset her. She was pretty certain she wasn't responsible for the boiler breaking, so defiant as ever, she pushed out her chest and stuck her tongue out at him.

That sent Jake into a rage, and he lunged forwards for her. She ducked under his arm and dived for the front door.

Just as she reached it, her mum appeared from out of the living room, rubbing her face. 'What's going on?' She snatched hold of Leila and tugged her back into the hallway.

'Little bitch, give her to me.' Jake snarled.

Leila's mum pushed Leila behind her. 'What's going on?'

'Little cow stuck her tongue out at me, and she's broken the boiler.'

Leila's mum turned round and grabbed Leila by the shoulders. 'Did you stick your tongue out?'

Leila had started crying now. 'Yes, but he was being mean.'

'What have I told you about that? I'm not surprised Jake is mad at you. Now get to your room before I lose my temper with you.' She pushed Leila past Jake and sent her scurrying upstairs.

Leila had seen the way her mum had looked at her, and when Jake wasn't looking, she had winked at her too, a silent signal that Mum knew she had done nothing wrong. She sat at the top of the stairs, out of sight, listening to the ensuing argument.

'You're too soft with that little cow. She needs a good hiding.'

'And what would that solve exactly? Just get the police round here, probably.'

'Yeah well, you need to get tougher with her.'

'I will, I promise.'

Leila heard their voices fade as her mum led Jake into the kitchen. 'Come on, forget about her. Let's have some fun.'

'Yeah, all right then.'

Leila took this as her cue to disappear, and she headed out of the front door.

22

Mrs Dunn wiped her hands on her apron after closing the oven door. Not every day was baking day. Just Mondays and Thursdays. Of course, she didn't have the family to bake for now, so she would head out later and drop it at the church. She'd keep some for herself and the wee lassie up the road. As she moved the tray of scones from the baking tray to the cooling rack, there was a light knock on the front door.

'Ha, speak of the devil. That girl must have some sense of smell,' Mrs Dunn muttered to herself as she put the tin down and shuffled over to the door.

'Now then, hen, how are you?' Mrs Dunn had a lovely Scottish lilt to her Yorkshire accent that Leila found fascinating.

'I'm all right, thank you, Mrs Dunn. Can I come in?'

Mrs Dunn stepped back and let Leila through. 'Of course you can. I've just made some scones. How about I make us a wee cup of tea and we have a bite to eat?'

Mrs Dunn settled Leila on the sofa whilst she went into the kitchen to sort out the tea.

She had a soft spot for the young girl. Leila had a hard

life these days, and Mrs Dunn wasn't sure what, if anything, she could do about it. She had considered contacting the authorities, but she didn't like the thought of the wee lassie going into the care system. Who would keep an eye out for her then? The only other thing she could think of was contacting the local school. She knew that Leila had been going at some point, as she had seen her in the uniform.

It was all that good-for-nothing Jake's fault. Leila and her mum seemed to be getting on with things until he came along. Now she never saw Leila's mum sober, and she was regularly spotted getting thrown out of the local pub, or the local off-licence.

She carried the tea tray and scones through to the living room.

'Here you go, dearie, tuck in. Don't be shy,' Mrs Dunn encouraged, though she hadn't finished her sentence before Leila had crammed a scone into her mouth. 'My goodness, you're a hungry one. When did you last eat, Leila?'

She watched as Leila chewed and swallowed the scone. 'This morning,' she said through a mouthful of crumbs.

'Don't talk with your mouth full. What did you have?'

Leila went red and hesitated before answering. 'A sandwich,' she whispered, looking down at her hands.

Mrs Dunn knew from Leila's reaction that the sandwich had more than likely been stolen. She couldn't bring herself to reprimand the poor girl, so she just reiterated that she could always come to her house if she needed anything. Leila nodded, but the atmosphere had changed, and Mrs Dunn feared that she had scared Leila away.

Sure enough, as soon as Leila had finished her mouthful, she made her excuses and left. Mrs Dunn was reluctant to let her leave, and she made Leila promise that she would call around again tomorrow. As the little girl disappeared around the corner, Mrs Dunn decided it was time to make the phone call.

Leila waved as she turned the corner, but when she was sure Mrs Dunn could no longer see her, she burst into tears. She was embarrassed that her friend knew she had had to steal food, and she felt uncomfortable staying after that. She enjoyed going to Mrs Dunn's for more than just tea and scones. Mrs Dunn always had stories to share, and they would watch old films together with her head on Mrs Dunn's lap. Leila sniffed and wiped her tears away. At least she'd had something to eat. She kicked her way along the road, wondering what to do next. She wasn't far from Bramley Shopping Centre, so she made her way there, hoping she could sneak into the cafe and get warm. The owner was really nice, and he used to give Leila broken biscuits if ever she called in with her mum.

She wandered down to the shopping centre and kicked about the entrance for a while before deciding to head into Boots. She wasn't sure what had made her go in there. Perhaps it was the thought of the lovely fragrances, or the chance to browse the bubble baths and dream. She didn't even realise she'd slipped the lipstick into her pocket until she felt a hand on her shoulder.

'Turn your pockets out,' demanded the voice. She turned round to see the security guard she had passed minutes earlier staring down at her.

'I haven't got owt,' Leila replied defensively, trying to pull away.

'I saw you. Come with me.' He promptly frogmarched her into the manager's office. 'Got a smart one here, boss.'

The figure behind the desk looked up. 'You're a bit

young, aren't you, nipper?' was the first thing the manager said.

Leila didn't answer. She just glared at him.

'I saw her put a lipstick into her pocket, and now she won't turn her pockets out.'

The manager left his seat and came round to the front of the desk and perched on the edge. Leila looked up at him and hoped he wouldn't yell. Her heart was beating out of chest, and she was convinced she was going to wet herself. She crossed her legs.

'Show me your pockets, please,' he asked.

Leila bit her lip and shook her head. She was only wearing her cardigan and an old school shirt, so it wasn't like she had many places to hide anything. The manager stood up and made a call. A few minutes a later, a female colleague entered and asked Leila if she minded being searched.

Leila was aghast. What did she mean, searched? She'd seen that stuff on TV. No way was she letting this woman search her. Leila kicked out and hit the woman on the shin. A yell was heard, and the security guard wasn't taking any more. He called centre security and asked them to send the local police unit. Leila was kept in the manager's office until two police officers arrived.

'Hello, young lady, you've been causing quite the stir, haven't you?' said the female officer.

Leila just stared and shook her head. The seriousness of the situation slowly dawned on her, and she felt tears building. 'I ... I'm sorry,' she stammered.

'Did you take the lipstick?'

Leila unfurled her clenched fists and pulled the lipstick from where she'd been hiding it in her sleeve. The police officer picked it up and showed it to the manager.

'Will you be pressing charges?'

The manager looked at Leila, then at the police. 'No, not on this occasion, but she's banned from the shop.'

The officer asked Leila to apologise, then escorted her to the waiting police car. At first, Leila thought she was being taken to the police station, but they explained that she would be driven home so they could speak to her mum and dad, which was even worse.

'It's just my mum, and Jake,' gulped Leila, absolutely dreading what Jake's reaction would be.

The lady officer turned around in her seat and spoke to Leila. 'Is everything OK at home, Leila?'

Leila nodded, not wanting to draw any more attention to herself. 'It's fine, thank you.'

'Why aren't you in school?'

'I learn at home with my mum,' which is what she had been told to say.

'How old are you?'

'I'm six but I'll be seven soon.'

Leila directed them to the street where she lived, and hoped they would just drop her at the top of the road, but they insisted that they walk her down the path and knock on the front door. It was Jake that yanked it open.

Leila watched him do a double take before glaring at her. When he finally spoke, Lolly was surprised at how polite he was.

'Officers, everything all right?'

'Not really. Is Mrs Turner home?'

'Not at the moment, I'm sorry. I'm Leila's stepdad so I can deal with anything you might have to say.'

The two officers looked at each other, and Leila looked at Jake in amazement. 'Can we come in?'

Jake stood back and let the police enter. Leila thought

they looked out of place in the untidy living room, but they didn't seem to mind the mess as they sat on the sofa.

'Leila, go to your room, sweetheart,' said Jake, placing his hand on her shoulder. She glanced at the officers.

'She can stay if she likes, it does concern her,' said the female that had spoken before.

He tilted his head, raising his chin upwards. 'What has she done?'

'She was caught stealing a lipstick from the shopping centre.'

Leila watched Jake's reaction. His face went red, and she saw him clench and unclench his fists. 'Has she now?'

'Yes, but the shop is not pressing charges.'

'Well, that's lucky for you, then, isn't it?' said Jake, unable to keep the sneer out of his voice.

The female officer raised an eyebrow.

'That's not the main reason we're here.'

'Oh, right?'

Leila was confused now. She pulled the sleeves of her cardigan over her hands, intrigued to know what was going to be said next.

'No, the main reason we're here is that it's noon on a Thursday, but Leila isn't in school. Why is that?'

'Oh, I see. She's homeschooled by her mum.' Jake seemed relieved.

'Really? But her mum isn't here?'

'No, well it's in the mornings, isn't it? That's when you have your lessons, isn't it?' Jake glowered at Leila with venom in his eyes.

Knowing what she was supposed to say, she hesitated fleetingly, wondering if she dare go against Jake. Deciding that she needed to protect her mother more, Leila backed down. 'She's at the library getting some new books.'

The two police officers looked at each other. 'Are you sure?' asked the nice female officer.

Leila pressed her lips together and nodded as earnestly as she could. She stood to one side to let the officers leave, and as soon as they had driven off, Jake went ballistic.

23

Leila crouched in the corner of the living room, hoping Jake's rage would wear out so she could escape upstairs.

'This is all your lazy-arsed mother's fault. If she'd discipline you like I told her, you wouldn't be a thieving little bastard.' He swung out with the rolled-up newspaper he had in his hand. She ducked, but it glanced off the side of her head, causing her to yelp. She dived behind the chair, but he was on her too quickly, and raining blow after blow on her head as she tried to protect herself.

'Stop it, please stop. You're hurting me.'

'You have no fucking idea what I'm capable of, you little shit.'

Leila had had enough. She wriggled backwards and pushed herself up from the floor. She sprang to her feet and thundered up the stairs. She made it to her bedroom just in time to hear Jake pounding up the stairs after her.

'And you can stay in there, you little bitch.' He battered her door, and using all the strength she could muster, she pushed against it, praying to whoever that it would hold.

Eventually, she heard his footsteps retreating. With any

luck, he'd go to the off-licence and drink himself into oblivion. Leila laid on her bed until she heard the front door slam.

Slowly opening the bedroom door to double check the coast was clear, she sneaked across the landing into the bathroom. She rubbed her head where the newspaper had caught her and saw that her face was also scratched and red. She rinsed a flannel under the tap and washed her face, tears mingling with the cold water.

Her entire body jumped when she heard raised voices from downstairs. Her mum's voice drifted up the stairs. It hadn't been Jake going out, but her mum coming home. She locked the door, sat on the closed toilet seat and pulled her knees up so that her chin was resting on them. She placed her hands over her ears and scrunched up her eyes. She could hear thudding and banging about. It sounded like furniture being thrown. She prayed it would stop, as she fought the urge to protect her mum. After what felt like an age, the front door slammed shut again, shaking the whole house. Leila stayed where she was, not knowing if one or both of them had left. Minutes passed by, and there was a gentle knocking on the door.

'Leila, sweetheart. It's Mum. Open the door baby, please?'

Leila slipped off her seat and pulled back the lock. She peeped around the door and saw her mum's face.

'Mummy!" she cried, throwing herself against her mother's legs.

'Ouch, careful, sweetheart. Are you all right?'

Leila looked up at her mum and saw that she had a red face too, but it wasn't scratches that made it red. It was blood. Both her eyes were bruised and almost closed.

Leila started crying. 'What did he do to you?'

Her mum staggered into the bathroom and sat on the edge of the bath. 'Come here, baby.'

Leila took the flannel from the sink and dampened it before passing it to her mum.

'That's really kind, thank you, sweetheart. I just want you to do exactly as Jake asks. Try to keep him in a good mood, yeah?'

Leila didn't know what to say. She wanted to grab their things and run away to anywhere he wasn't. She was trying her best not to cry, but she couldn't help it.

'I don't want Jake to live with us, Mum.'

'I know, but he does and there isn't anything we can do about it, so we have to make the best of it.'

Leila took the flannel from her mum and started gently dabbing the areas where the blood had congealed around her mum's mouth and lips.

Much later, they lay down together on Leila's bed and fell asleep, holding on to each other as though their lives depended on it.

It was the front door being hammered that woke them both. Leila was lying on her side, tucked into her mum's back. She enjoyed the warmth for a couple of seconds more before sitting up.

'Who's that?' she asked, bleary-eyed.

'No idea,' said her mum. It can't be Jake. He'd use his key. I'll go see.'

Leila watched as her mum struggled to get to her feet. She could tell from her movements that she was hurting from the blows she had taken from Jake the day before, and it brought everything flooding back.

The banging went again.

'I'll go, Mum,' she said. She cautiously edged herself off the bed and tiptoed downstairs. She had no idea if Jake had returned when they were both asleep. He could be passed out on the sofa, and she didn't want to wake him.

She turned the Yale lock and opened the door to see the police officers from the previous day stood there.

'Hello, Leila, do you remember me?'

Leila nodded, and her heart began beating wildly. They'd come back for her. 'Is your mum home?'

Leila nodded again and stood back to let the officers in. She saw that they were also accompanied by another lady, who reached out to take Leila's hand.

'Hello, Leila, my name is Claire. Why don't you and I see if we can find some juice or something?'

Unsure and not knowing what else to do in response to the kind voice, Leila took Claire's hand and went into the kitchen. She hadn't had a chance to clean up recently, so there were cups and plates everywhere, and Leila felt embarrassed as she saw a mouse scurry across the floor.

Claire either didn't see it, or ignored it as she pulled out one of the kitchen chairs and sat down. 'Leila, do you know who I am?'

She shook her head.

'I work with the council, and it's my job to make sure children, like yourself, are being looked after properly by their mummies and daddies.'

'I am,' stated Leila. 'My mummy looks after me and I look after her. We look after each other.'

Claire smiled. 'I know that your mummy tries her best, sweetheart, and she does a great job, but do you think perhaps she might need a rest and a bit of help?'

Leila eyed up Claire warily. 'What kind of help?' She stuck her chin in the air, her mouth forming a grim line of determination.

Seemingly sensing Leila's reluctance, Claire lowered her

voice and leant forwards. 'Would you come with me for a while so that Mummy could have a break?'

Leila didn't like the sound of that at all. She turned to leave the kitchen to find her mum, only to see her being led out of the front door. 'Leila, sweetheart, it's fine. Just do as the lady says and we'll see each other soon, I promise.'

Leila ran forwards in tears, pushing everyone out of her way. 'Mummy, where are you going?'

'Just to the hospital to get my cuts looked at, nothing to worry about, and I'll see you soon. Be good, yeah?'

Claire stepped in and peeled Leila's hands from around her mum's waist. 'Do as your mum says now, and it will all be much easier.'

As Leila kicked and railed against Claire's grabbing hands, Jake appeared at the top of the garden path. 'What the fuck is going on here?' he demanded.

'Mr Turner?'

Leila saw Jake turn to run, but the police were ready for him and stopped him in his tracks. All she heard was, 'I am arresting you ...' before her attention returned to her mum. She had been moved from the doorstep to the path outside and was being placed in the back of a police car.

Hysterical, Leila screamed after her. She fought like an alley cat as the social worker tried to coax Leila into her car. In the end, she had to be physically lifted and carried into a police car, only relenting when the door slammed shut and she realised that she had no escape. Wiping her nose on her sleeve, she looked out of the car window and saw Mrs Dunn standing at her gate. She gave Leila a little wave and a smile, but Leila didn't respond. She was confused, lonely and terrified for what would happen next.

It was nearly a year before Leila heard from her mum again. Leila didn't fully understand why it had taken so long. She had asked repeatedly to be allowed home, or to meet her mum somewhere, and all she ever heard was 'soon'. Leila had spent that first year crying herself to sleep and rebelling against a system that she believed had been created solely to keep her from her mum.

Finally, she was told that her mum would be coming to see her at the children's home the following weekend. All week, Leila behaved herself. She didn't cheek the teachers or support workers. She obeyed every rule, and when Sunday came round, her house mother, Mrs Smith, had washed and pressed her best dress for her. Leila even allowed Mrs Smith to brush her hair.

Her mum was due to arrive at lunchtime, and they were to have lunch together, then walk around the grounds. Leila was pleased with this, as she could show her the gardens that Leila had had a hand in planting. Feeling nervous, but excited, Leila waited in the front living room that was used for such occasions. She waited and waited. Once in a while, Mrs Smith would pop her head around the door to make sure she was OK, give her a gentle smile, then leave.

On the fifth time, she did this, over two hours after her mum was supposed to be there, Mrs Smith came into the room and asked Leila to sit on the sofa beside her. She apologised, telling her that they couldn't get a hold of her mum, and that they didn't think she was coming. Leila was inconsolable. She ran from the room and threw herself onto her bed after ripping off her dress, tearing the sleeves and pulling off the buttons.

Later that same night, there was a tapping on her door, and Mrs Smith stood there with a tray of food and a warm drink. Leila knew something was wrong straight away. As she listened, she became fixated on Mrs Smith's mouth. She could hear words, *mum, unconscious, street, hospital, dead,* but they didn't make any sense. She just sat, staring. More words followed. *Murder. Jake. Prison.*

Eventually, Mrs Smith pulled Leila close, but she still remained silent, numb. She supposed she should cry, but she couldn't. The tears were locked inside her, and like her heart, she knew that if she let them fall, she would break in two. She couldn't allow that to happen. She would never allow that to happen.

Months passed, and Leila learnt and adapted to the rhythm of the care home, though she baulked at every turn. She never had any visitors and found it difficult to make friends. She saw everyone as a threat, and the only joy she found was in planning her escape. It wouldn't be that difficult, she reckoned to herself as she scribbled in the notebook she kept hidden under her mattress. For weeks, she watched when the main entrance doors were locked on an evening – just after tea. She had planned her route out of the bedroom window, down the drainpipe, and then, if she ran like the clappers, she would make it to the side gate and out into the housing estate that the home was hidden behind and on to her freedom. She had started running every day, and secretly laughed at the other residents and staff who thought she was trying to get fit for the upcoming sports day. She was, just not for the reasons they believed.

24

On her chosen day, Leila went to bed early, claiming not to feel very well. Not poorly enough to be checked on every thirty minutes, but enough to be left alone to sleep. Then, the next day, no one would miss her until at least lunchtime, as there were no lessons.

She went to bed in her clothes, pulled the covers up to her chin so no one would question her when checks were done at 9 p.m. She feigned sleep, and as soon as the lights went out, she crept out of bed and lifted the window latch. Lowering herself down onto the window ledge, her backpack strapped securely to her, she felt the chill of the night air nipping at her cheeks. Her fingers were cold against the metal of the drainpipe. Her feet scrambled to find the narrow ledge that she could teeter on to inch herself across. Leila was small for her age and as light as a feather, which was all to her advantage as the metal made little sound under the extra strain. Slowly but surely, she moved with the agility of an acrobat and landed on the soft ground. Ducking under the automatic light sensor, being careful not to trigger it, she scurried to the side gate and threw herself over it. Once on her feet, she started running and didn't stop until she was under the bridge alongside the Leeds and Liverpool canal.

She squatted down, opening her backpack and taking out a small bottle of water. She took a sip and regulated her breathing. She hadn't planned beyond this point, figuring she'd sleep or rest under the bridge until daylight, then head into Leeds. She was sure that if she could make her way back to her old road, she would find Mrs Dunn and stay there until she worked out a better plan. The thought of Mrs Dunn's baking made her mouth water, and her tummy rumble. She pulled out a Sherbet Fountain and relished the fizzy sensation on her tongue.

'What you got there, little one?'

Leila nearly jumped out of her skin. She had been so wrapped up in her sweets that she hadn't noticed a woman approaching. She looked at her cautiously as she sat down beside her. There wasn't much space under the bridge, but she moved over as best she could.

'Not talking, eh? Fair enough. My name's Mary, and you've nicked my sleeping spot.' Mary stuck her hand out, but she didn't look annoyed.

'I'm really sorry. I didn't know someone slept here.'

'Don't worry. Here, do you want a bit of this sleeping bag? You look half frozen.' Mary twisted round, and Leila saw that she had several bin liners and a sleeping bag, which she unzipped and placed over both their legs.

'I won't hurt you, I promise, but there are plenty out there that will. Do you want to tell me your name?'

Leila looked into Mary's eyes. They seemed kind, and Leila was cold, so she thanked her for the covers and told Mary her name, and where she had run away from.

'But I'm not going back and you can't make me.' She ended her sentence defiantly.

'Ha ha, no worries on that front, little one. I was in the care system too, so I know how you feel. But what are your plans? You're kinda young to be out on your own?'

Leila picked at a loose bit of cotton on the sleeping bag. 'Dunno. Not really thought about it. There used to be a really nice neighbour, so I thought I'd go there.'

'It was probably the nice neighbour that dobbed you in. You need a plan little one, or you'll end up back in the system.'

'I'll find a job and work really hard at it.'

Mary laughed, and Leila blushed, feeling self-conscious all of a sudden. 'Ah, my love, if it were that simple, wouldn't we all be working really hard, living in a comfortable home surrounded by family?'

'What happened to you?' Leila asked, curiously.

'Had a run of bad luck. My marriage broke down, the bastard kept the house and I found myself on friends' sofas for a few months. Then redundancies went round at work. I got laid off and with no family to speak of, here I am.'

'How do you eat?' asked Leila, feeling hungry after her sherbet.

'Depends. There are a few shelters around that run regular meals. I get by, but it's no life for a little one like you.'

'I might be little, but I am strong.'

'I can tell you are very strong, but I wonder what would have happened if you'd have bumped into a man tonight?'

Leila stared at Mary, and a knowing look passed between them that didn't need words Leila blushed and looked at the sleeping bag.

Mary adjusted herself and pulled the sleeping bag up so it covered them both more. 'Well, like I said, I'm not going to hurt you, but not everyone is like me. There are bad men out here that would take advantage of a young thing like you, if you get what I mean.'

Leila knew exactly what Mary meant, and the thought frightened her. All she had focused on was getting away. For the first time, she wondered if she had made a mistake. Had her life really been that bad? She'd had a warm bed every night, food and even the staff were mostly nice. She felt tears building, but she refused to cry. She didn't belong anywhere. She didn't have anyone who cared for her. She felt incredibly small in a very big world, and she didn't know what to do.

'Come on, everything will seem better in the morning, I promise.' Mary lifted the sleeping bag, and Leila scooted further inside, and with her back against the wall and the sleeping bag pulled up to her chin, she fell into a fitful sleep.

The next morning, hungry, cold and feeling forlorn, she agreed to let Mary walk her back to the home. She hadn't wanted to, but she was smart enough to know that without a proper plan, a long-term plan, she was opening herself up to a whole new world of unhappiness. Despite feeling constantly trapped and sad on the inside, she allowed herself to become part of the system, vowing that as soon as she was old enough, she would be out of there.

When she turned eleven, she was placed in a foster home. Bill and Irene Wood were quite nice. They reminded her of Mrs Dunn. Irene would often bake and invite Leila to join in. Bill was obsessed with his garden and his little vegetable patch. Leila helped him to plant some radish and tomatoes and he had made her promise that she would still be there when it came to harvesting them later in the year. She had nodded her head, but Bill had made her cross her heart and hope to die, which she did. Planting flowers made her think of her mum, and each one she planted with love.

With a settled home life for the first time in long time Leila made the move from junior school to the local comprehensive. She loved her new school. The science facilities were much better than any previous school, and she did an after-school science club and extra homework in biology. School had calmed Leila down considerably, and though she didn't have a huge amount of friends, she was popular and kind-hearted. Her anger issues raised their head occasionally, but her energy was mostly channelled into learning and playing football where she was the star of the boys' team.

Once a year, Irene would take her to visit her mum's grave where they would lay flowers, and Leila would have a few minutes on her own to talk to her mum. She still missed her terribly. Nothing would bring her mum back, but at least Jake had been given life in prison, so he couldn't hurt anyone else's mum.

Bill and Irene didn't have many rules, but once a week, the three of them sat around the kitchen table and shared a Sunday lunch, which had been lovingly cooked by Irene. This particular Sunday was no different from any other, so Leila was happily tucking into her Yorkshire pudding when she noticed Irene tapping the back of Bill's hand.

'What?' Bill wiped his mouth and looked across the table at Irene who nodded towards Leila. 'Oh, right, yes.' He placed his knife and fork down. 'Leila, we have something to tell you.'

Leila stopped chewing, instinctively detecting the change in atmosphere. She didn't speak, wondering what was coming next.

Bill fidgeted in his seat. 'See, the thing is ...'

'Oh, for goodness' sake, Bill,' Irene interrupted. 'Leila, we've been asked to take in another young person who has recently lost his parents in a terrible accident.'

Leila continued to look at each of them. Were they waiting for her approval? She often found in these situations it was better to stay quiet and let the adults talk.

'And we have agreed that, temporarily, and only if it works with you, we will take him.'

Silence descended on the room. Bill and Irene were staring at her.

Deciding that it was fine with her, Leila carried on with the rest of her dinner. 'No problem with me,' she said after eating a roast potato. 'I won't have much to do with him anyway.'

She sensed a huge sigh of relief in the room, as though someone had let the air out of a balloon. She smiled to herself. Adults could be really strange.

For the next two days, Irene was in an absolute tizzy. She washed everything, cleaned and tidied the spare room, and replaced the usual bedding with the red and white of Liverpool Football Club. Leila watched on and wondered if this much effort had gone into her arrival. She supposed it had, and it made her smile that this lovely couple had enough love to go round.

The day finally came when the new arrival was due, and Irene had told Leila that she had to be on her best behaviour, no matter what. Leila had rolled her eyes and agreed, though she was desperate to see who was joining the odd little family.

Leila was upstairs in her bedroom when she heard the car pull up. She peeked out of the corner of the net curtain and saw a stringy-looking lad with a floppy fringe walking hesitantly up the path with another woman, to be greeted by Bill and Irene.

'Now then, Andrew, it's lovely to meet you. I'm Irene and this is Bill. Welcome to our house, which we hope you will treat as your own home.'

Leila was hanging over the banister. The new boy didn't talk. He just followed Bill and Irene around as they showed him around the house. Leila's instructions had been to stay in her room until she was shouted. Then they would be introduced. She couldn't be bothered waiting for that, and as soon as they showed him his room and disappeared to let him 'get settled in', she made a beeline for the door.

'Hiya, I'm Leila. You must be the one they've been talking about all week.' She looked at him and reckoned she could take him in a fight. 'Hope you like your room. Bill's been at it all week, and Irene's been in a right tizzy getting everything set.'

Andrew muttered something, but Leila didn't hear him. He was unpacking things from a holdall. She peered inside it, but all she saw was football gear. She picked up a football shirt that was sitting on the top. 'Cool, I'm not a fan myself, but this is cool.' She held it in front of her and turned it over. 'Is he your favourite player, then?'

'Yeah.' Andrew took it back off her and carefully placed it in a drawer.

Leila sensed that he had nothing else exciting in his bag, so she turned and left the room. Standing at the doorway, she looked him dead in the eye. 'I think I like you.'

'Thanks.'

Deciding she wasn't about to get any more out of him, she headed downstairs. Leila reckoned it was going to be all right having Andrew around, even if he was a bit green around the gills. She'd soon change all that.

. . .

The months ticked by and the family of four fell into a settled routine. Christmas came and went, birthdays were celebrated, and Leila felt happy. As the summer months approached, Leila – who Andrew had now nicknamed 'Lolly' after a prank that went wrong – would move up a class at school, and she was excited at the prospect. She had excelled in all of her lessons. Her appetite for learning was voracious.

At fourteen, a school trip to the Natural History Museum in London ignited a spark in Lolly that was to set her on her life's path. She had always had a fascination with anatomy. When asked by teachers and the occasional friend, who found it quite morbid, she would fob them off and say that she was drawn to human composition. In truth, Lolly wanted to understand death. Why were people so afraid of it? Why was death always the villain? Why wasn't death embraced when someone was suffering, for example. Hadn't her own mother escaped Jake in her death? And what happened after death? What did the body do? Not on the outside, but on the inside? What changed, and how? Her curiosity drove her through years of study and tedious lab work until she finally accompanied her mentor to a murder scene. She had never felt more at home. Her natural aptitude and ability shone through and after qualifying, she followed her heart and worked as a forensic pathologist for the police service. Initially, she was based at where she had studied, at Kings College London, but pretty soon she followed her mentor into the Forensic Science Service in Wetherby. It didn't take long for her to establish herself and pretty soon she was in demand at most major crime scenes, and travelled all over the country.

Although her reputation and career were all in ascendence, she still had times where she felt incredibly lonely and insecure. Apart from Andrew, all her relationships were only ever surface deep. She found it hard to trust anyone. For Lolly, it was more important to save people, and though she would have loved someone to settle down with, to settle her down, she knew that the kind of love she was looking for wouldn't come her way easily.

When love did finally arrive, it wasn't in the manner she expected.

.

25

Monday, 9th September 2002

'Why can't you just leave me the fuck alone!'

Lolly tiptoed away from the door, not wanting to be accused of listening in. Frankie would tell her soon enough what was going on. No doubt her ex was playing his usual games.

Heading towards the bedroom, she dumped her work clothes in the wash basket and headed to the shower. After a full day spent in the mortuary teaching students, she was exhausted and her brain was fried. She thought about the evening ahead, which she had been looking forward to until she'd heard Frankie's raised voice. Lolly hoped whatever it was wouldn't spoil their anniversary plans. Rinsing the soap from her body, she stepped out, grabbing a towel as she did so.

Back in the bedroom, Lolly was sitting on the edge of the bed, absentmindedly rubbing her hair dry when Frankie came in.

'Hey, my love, how are you?' Lolly stood up and kissed Frankie on the cheek.

'I was fine until Dickhead rang.' They rarely referred to Frankie's ex by his actual name.

Lolly pulled Frankie into a hug, her towel momentarily forgotten and dropping to the floor. 'Come here, he's a prick. You just have to let it wash over you. Easier said than done, I know.'

Frankie pulled away. 'Don't, you're getting me all wet,' she complained. She bent to pick the towel up and passed it back to Lolly.

Taking no offence, Lolly dried herself. 'What has he done this time?'

'The house sale has fallen through. Again.' Frankie was unclipping her earrings and kicking off her heels as she spoke.

'Oh, for goodness' sake, I thought this one was nailed on?'

'Me too. It's so infuriating.'

Lolly pulled a pair of trousers out of the wardrobe, then paused. 'Do you still want to go tonight?' They had reservations at a restaurant in Leeds, the same one they had met in just over two years ago but they had both been so busy, this was the first chance they had had to celebrate.

'Oh yes. I need the distraction. I also need a glass of wine and some good food.' Frankie slipped out of her dress and headed into the bathroom. Lolly saw her shoulders drop and the dejected look as Frankie closed the en suite door.

Glad that Dickhead's phone call wasn't about to spoil the evening, but worrying about her partner, Lolly finished dressing and headed to the living room. She felt frustrated too that the house sale hadn't gone through. That was the only thing stopping them from getting a place together.

Lolly practically lived in Frankie's apartment anyway, but she wanted it to be official. Lolly was fed up with her dump of a place. She wanted to build a home, a life with Frankie. She shook her head, knowing that Ziggy would laugh if he could hear her. But it was true. Maybe it was time for Doctor Leila Turner, the free-spirited wanderer, to grow up.

Smiling, she fixed them both a gin and tonic and thought back to the first time she had met Frankie.

'Gin and tonic, please.' Lolly leant against the bar and placed her money on the counter. The bartender passed her the glass and, on turning, she immediately bumped into a woman.

She watched as, in slow motion, the liquid sloshed from the top of the glass and straight down the front of the woman's shirt. The woman reacted with a sharp intake of breath and took several steps backwards.

Mortified, Lolly garbled an apology. 'I'm so sorry! Here, let me get a napkin.' Lolly started dabbing the spilt drink from the sheer blouse. Realising that she was actually dabbing the woman's breast, she pulled her hand back, blushed an even darker shade of crimson and shook her head. She bent down and snatched her bag from the floor. 'I'll get my coat. Again, I'm so sorry.' She turned to leave, but felt a hand pulling her back.

'Whoa, slow down. It's fine, it was mostly ice, so no harm done. No need for you to leave.'

Relieved, Lolly put her bag down. 'I am really sorry. Let me buy you a drink by way of an apology.'

'If it will stop you apologising, I'll have a G and T please,' said the attractive stranger.

'I'm Lolly, by the way,' she replied as she pulled up a bar stool for each of them.

'Lolly? There's a story behind that, I'll bet. I'm Frankie.'

'Nice to meet you, Frankie. Is that short for ...?'

'Francesca, though I have no idea what Lolly might be short for?'

'I'm actually called Leila. Lolly is the nickname my best mate gave me when we were kids. I stole some lollies ... Do you know what? It's a long story, so maybe another time.'

'Another time? Planning to spill a drink down me again, are you?' said Frankie with a smile.

Lolly laughed. 'No, I'm sorry that was a bit forward of me. Gosh, I'm making a real mess of this.'

'It's fine, don't worry. I think you're funny.'

Lolly blushed again and took a sip of her drink. 'What brings you here anyway?' she said, frantically trying to change the subject.

The bartender brought Frankie's drink across, and Lolly watched, mesmerised, as Frankie took a sip before replying.

'I've just left a boring conference. Wanted a quick drink to wind down. You?' replied Frankie.

'Same. Didn't fancy going home just yet. I was just about to order food. Have you eaten?'

Lolly didn't know what it was about Frankie that made her feel a little intimidated, a rare, almost alien feeling to Lolly, but she couldn't deny there was something about her new friend. They moved over to the brasserie and chatted whilst they browsed the menu. Each chose a simple, light vegetarian supper, which arrived in no time. The conversation flowed easily, the drinks equally so, and before Lolly knew it, they were heading back to Frankie's apartment for a nightcap.

Lolly swirled the ice around her glass and took another sip. Even that wonderful first evening had ended abruptly, when Frankie's ex-husband had phoned, wanting to know where

Frankie was. She had explained to Lolly that although they were separated, he could sometimes treat her as though they were still married. Two years down the line and nothing had changed.

There was hardly a week that went by where Dickhead didn't want or expect something. Last week, it had been a meeting he had insisted on about their joint finances. It was no wonder Frankie had left him, Lolly had thought more than once. He was a control freak.

Frankie came into the living room and took her drink from the side table. Raising her glass, she proposed a toast.

'To us, and the rest of our lives together,' she said, and Lolly didn't think in that moment she could have her loved her any more than she did.

The evening had flown by, but Lolly still noticed that Frankie had been distracted, often looking around the restaurant instead of at Lolly when she spoke. Frankie barely touched her food, just pushed it around the plate, and Lolly noticed that she was constantly chewing the skin on the inside of her cheek. Lolly hadn't mentioned it at the time, not wanting to draw attention to it, but this morning she couldn't help but feel helpless to ease Frankie's evident distress. Not for the first time, Lolly wondered what she could do to help. The whole thing was playing on Lolly's mind as she headed into work. She had a day of lectures at the university with trainee pathologists, and was feeling a little woolly-headed. Her sleep had been broken, and she had an uneasy feeling in the pit of her stomach.

Pushing open the door to the staffroom, she greeted several of her colleagues and headed to the coffee machine.

'Morning, Lol, how are you?' asked Joe, a fellow lecturer.

'I'm good, you?'

'Not bad. Back-to-back lectures all day, God help me.'

Lolly laughed. Though she enjoyed lecturing, she would much rather have been in the mortuary. 'You know you love it really.' She felt her phone vibrate in the back pocket of her jeans.

'Excuse me, I need to take this,' she said, seeing Frankie's name on the screen. 'Hey my love, everything OK?'

'No.'

She could hear Frankie was crying, which was completely out of character. Closing her eyes, she braced herself. 'What has he done now?'

'He's been a bastard again and I don't know what to do.'

Lolly left the staff room and found a quiet corner. 'Tell me what he's done.'

'You won't believe it. My car has been repossessed.'

'What? I thought he'd bought that for you years ago? It was a present, wasn't it?'

'Oh Lolly, I don't know what to do. Two men came to the door and ... and now it's gone.'

Lolly heard a fresh bout of tears. 'Sweetheart, I'm so sorry. He's a prick. Have you called him?'

'Yes, he just laughed at me. Told me I was stupid and naive if I thought he was going to keep paying finance on a car he didn't own.'

Lolly had only ever had clapped-out bangers that had cost her five hundred pounds at the most. Frankie drove a Mercedes CLK. 'I don't know what to say. I have a full-on day here. Will you be OK?'

She heard Frankie blow her nose. 'I don't want you to come home. I just didn't know who to call. I'll have to work from home today and figure something out.'

'I'm in lectures again for most of the day, but I will leave my phone on silent. Call if you need me. And remember, try not to let him get under your skin. That's what he wants.'

With promises that she would call, they said their good-byes, and despite the advice she had given Frankie, Lolly was fuming. Who the hell did Dickhead think he was? How dare he try to control Frankie's life?

'Selfish prick,' she muttered, heading for her first class-room. 'It's about time someone called him out.'

26

Lolly struggled to concentrate for the rest of the day. At her first break between lectures, she phoned Frankie. 'How are you, my love?'

'I'm so fed up. Why can't he just move on?' Lolly could hear the desperation in Frankie's voice, and it broke her heart. 'It's not even about the car, really. I just want to be happy. Why can't he let me be happy?'

'Because he's selfish and a narcissist. We have to show him that it doesn't affect us.'

'But it does, Leila. We can't move on. We can't get a place together, we can't get married, or even think of having kids until he lets go.'

These were all things they had talked about, but every time they tried to take a step forwards, there he was, like a spectre, holding them back.

Lolly wasn't sure what Dickhead had done to acquire his wealth, but she knew from Frankie that he was wealthy. Frankie had never explicitly said, but piecing together what she had gleaned, he held a lot of authority in financial circles. He had a team that worked for him, a driver and one or two people that managed his day-to-day business whilst he played golf or holidayed in his Spanish villa.

Lolly hated him, and she never used that word any more. She had met him completely by accident when she'd arrived back at Frankie's early from work one day. He had just been leaving the apartment. They hadn't even spoken. He had just barged past her, knocking her shoulder. She remembered how much it had hurt, and how he'd nearly knocked her tiny frame off her feet. He was a big man, a mountain of muscle. What little hair he had left was silver and slicked back. He was so tanned he looked almost orange. Lolly had also fleetingly taken in the diamond pinkie ring and the heavy gold chain. All flash, all for show, Lolly had thought at the time. Frankie had since admitted that she couldn't remember what had attracted her to him in the first place, blaming her infatuation on youth and naivety.

As the final bell rang for the day, Lolly decided that she had stayed in the background for too long. She was tired of watching Frankie suffer. She had carried this sense of impotence for too long. She had had enough. He was a bully, and she wouldn't stand for it in any other area of her life, so why should she continue to let him get away with it? She could feel her anger rising as she headed to her car. She made a decision. It was time she took charge, protected Frankie.

Frankie had mentioned a few times where he played golf and if Lolly took a slight detour, she could more or less pass the front door on her way home. Reversing out of the car park, her mind was made up.

South Leeds Golf Club lay on the outer edges of the thriving industrial area of the city. Lolly pulled into the car park and looked at the clubhouse ahead of her. It didn't look much from the outside, she thought, though, she had never played golf, or even been to a golf club before so she had nothing really to compare it to. Paint was peeling from the pebble-dashed clubhouse walls, and the outside seating looked like it needed updating. She deftly negotiated the potholes in the car park as she parked up. From what Frankie had told her, she had been expecting something a lot more upmarket.

Despite the appearance of the building, though, she realised the car park itself looked like an expensive car showroom. BMWs, Mercedes, even Porsches were all lined up, as though on display, each one of them spotless. Lolly's poor Fiat stood out like a sore thumb. Her confidence wavered momentarily as she questioned what she was about to do, but she reasoned with herself that as long as they were in public, what was the worst that could happen? He could tell her to piss off, she supposed, but at least she would have tried.

Lolly knew he drove a Range Rover and, thankfully, glancing around, there was only one. Who Lolly assumed to be Dickhead's driver was casually leaning against the driver's door. He was dressed in a black suit with a white shirt and black tie. As he straightened up, Lolly could see the seams of his jacket were struggling to hold him in, whether it was fat or muscle – she couldn't tell. Before she could change her mind, and whilst her confidence was relatively high, she exited her own car, slammed the door, and marched over.

'Hi, hello,' she said, hoping to catch his attention. His eyes were a piercing blue, and he screwed his face up, clearly trying to place Lolly.

He continued to stare, instantly alert. 'All right.' He tilted his chin in a challenge.

Heart thudding, Lolly swallowed and carried on, trying

to sound as casual as she could. 'What time are you expecting Dic— him to finish his game?' She had to stop herself from using his nickname.

'Now, why do you want to know?'

Determined not to be bullied, she stood her ground and dug her heels in as the driver approached her. She was getting ready to deliver a well-placed kick when a voice boomed behind her.

'Looking for me?' The deep baritone reverberated through her bones. Gulping, Lolly temporarily lost her nerve and turned around. 'Well ... I, erm.'

'You what? What do you want?'

Lolly shook herself, pulled her shoulders back. She would not to be intimidated. 'I'd like to talk to you about your ex, Frankie.'

'Would you indeed?' he said, condescendingly.

Lolly was certain she felt the ground shake as he strode past her. She flinched slightly as his driver stepped forwards to open the rear door. He climbed inside.

'If you want to talk, you will have to ride with me. I have somewhere to be.'

She faltered and gulped. *Shit.* As sweat broke out on her palms, she had the sense of a sliding-doors moment.

Something took over her stubbornness – her strong will or complete lunacy, she wasn't sure which – but she grabbed hold of the car door and hauled herself in. Her senses were immediately assaulted by the overpowering smell of polished leather. It took her a moment to adjust to the low-level lighting. Not quite believing what she was doing, she tried to position herself so that she was half turned towards the door in case she needed a quick exit, whilst also keeping an eye on Dickhead. There was a heavy silence for a minute before either of them spoke.

'Well? What can I do for you?' he snapped.

Now she was here, Lolly seemed to have lost the ability to speak a coherent sentence. She faltered a few times before she finally got the words out. 'I don't know if you remember me, but...'

'You're Francesca's latest craze. Yeah, I remember you.'

'I'm hardly a craze.'

A loud booming laugh came from the man mountain. 'Don't make me laugh. You're her latest muse, Doctor Turner, her pet project. Don't let her fool you into believing anything else.'

Lolly was indignant and felt a fire of rage through her as he continued his belittling laughter.

'You can say and think what you like. You won't bully me like you have her.'

'Is that right?' He continued to laugh as the driver took off around the inner ring road. 'And what is it that brings you running to her defence?'

Lolly shifted uncomfortably in her seat again, adjusting her seat belt so she could turn and face him more. She was determined to be heard. 'I just wanted to make a few things clear.'

He slowly turned his head and stared at her. 'Really? And what would they be?' A condescending smile danced across his lips, infuriating Lolly even more.

'For one, Frankie doesn't need to play your mind games.' She swallowed, willing her voice to remain steady. 'Stop messing her around with the whole house-sold, not-sold thing. It's messing with her head and if you had any feelings at all, you wouldn't keep lying to her. The latest stint with her car is, well, it's beyond childish.'

He didn't speak, but continued to stare intently at Lolly.

She pushed on. 'And secondly, you need to accept that

Frankie is with me now. She's moved on. We want to be together and you won't change that.'

Silence filled the SUV. Lolly couldn't think of anything else to say, so stayed silent, desperately fighting to get her heartbeat under control. She was shaking on the inside, her stomach turning to jelly.

After a few minutes, he spoke. 'What do I get in return?'

Lolly looked at his face, genuinely confused. 'What do you mean?'

'If I give Frankie what she wants, what do I get in return?'

Lolly was momentarily stunned. Bewildered and feeling out of her depth, she shrugged her shoulders. 'This isn't a negotiation.'

'Would seem that way to me, Doctor Turner. I'm a businessman. I do deals. I give you something, I get something in return.'

Lolly was floored. She hadn't expected that. She was frantically trying to think of something. 'I don't have any money,' she said, which sounded lame, even to her.

'I don't want money. I have more than enough. I want something that only you can give me.'

'Wait, what?' She pulled a face of disgust. 'I'm not sleeping with you ...'

Dickhead let out a deep belly laugh. 'Sleep with me? That's hilarious.' He clapped his hands. 'Did you hear that?' He banged on the headrest in front of him to catch the driver's attention. 'She thinks I want to have sex with her.'

The driver joined in the laughter, and Lolly felt her cheeks burn. She kept silent, not wanting to embarrass herself any further.

Once the laughter had died down, he turned to face her.

Lolly shrank back in her seat as he leant closer to her. She could smell whisky and cigarettes on his breath.

Snarling, he said, 'You silly little bitch. I don't want to sleep with you. I can't bear to be sitting this fucking close to you, but I *will* have something in return.'

His tone was dark and threatening. Lolly remained still, stunned into silence. 'You travel with work, yes?'

Lolly hesitantly nodded. 'Yes, sometimes.'

'You use your own vehicle?'

'Yes.' *Where was this going?*

'Perfect.'

'Why? What do you want from me?'

He sat back in his seat, looking pleased with himself. 'Deliveries. You can make deliveries for me.'

Confused, Lolly asked. 'Deliveries? What kind of deliveries?'

'Whatever I want you to deliver. It's simple really.' He crossed one leg over the other and turned to her, a pinkie ring catching the single interior light. 'You get an address. The goods will be in your car. You deliver, then leave.'

Lolly's heart was beating out of her chest. Was this real? 'I can't.'

'Then we carry on as we are.'

'You're not being fair.'

'Fair? My wife of twenty years left me for *you*. And you want me to be *fair*?' he roared.

She couldn't believe how purple his face had turned. She momentarily worried he would have a heart attack. Trying to regain some control, she said, 'Then take it out on me, leave her out of it.'

'And this is what I'm offering. Work with me.'

Lolly shuddered to her core and despite all her misgivings, for Frankie's sake, she knew she would.

27

Wednesday, 11th September 2002

Leila didn't give in easily. She had argued at every point, but ultimately, she reluctantly agreed. She scolded herself for being so naive, stupid even. She should have known it wouldn't be that easy, but then she hadn't expected to meet a low-level gangster type. All that night and the following day, the conversation replayed in her head.

Still annoyed with herself, and now exhausted after a full day in the mortuary, Lolly stripped off the Tyvek coveralls and slipped out of the wellington boots. She washed her hands thoroughly and headed to her locker to change her T-shirt. It had been a particularly long and complex post-mortem of a young male victim. There had been several areas of blunt force trauma and multiple knife wounds that all needed to be carefully measured and accurately documented. In all, she'd been in theatre for just over five hours.

As she pulled her clean T-shirt out of her locker, she felt something clunk on the floor. Bending down, she saw a small Nokia mobile phone. She picked it up. It didn't belong to her. Her heart fell to her odd-socked feet. *Is this it? Is this how he is going to play it?* Her hands were shaking as she looked at the screen.

Unknown Number flashed up.

Should she answer or ignore it? Would he go away as easily as that? She doubted it. Hesitantly, she pressed the green button and raised it tentatively to her ear.

'Hello?'

'Dr Turner. You have a delivery to make. Details will be sent to you.'

'Wait. What? I ...'

The line went dead before she had time to recognise the voice, but it hadn't been Dickhead. The phone beeped and vibrated in her already trembling hand. An address in Harrogate appeared in the received messages. But what was she supposed to deliver? How would he get it to her? With her heart racing, she quickly ran her fingers through her messy hair and grabbed her bag, throwing the Nokia on top of the junk she carried around with her on a daily basis.

Hurrying out of the building, she headed straight for her car. As she approached her Fiat, she saw a piece of paper trapped under her windscreen wiper. She glanced around; none of the other cars had one. Checking no one was looking, she retrieved it and hurriedly climbed into her car. Locking the doors, she sat with her head in her hands, desperately trying to calm down. 'What the hell have I started?' she muttered. She felt tears building, but deciding that this wasn't the time for hysteria, she looked at the ominous paper in her hand. Fumbling to open it, it simply contained one word, stark and handwritten in black marker pen: *BOOT.*

Unsure whether to get back out of the car and look, she decided it would be less conspicuous if she did so somewhere other than work. With her legs shaking, she pulled out of the entrance, headed to the nearest supermarket and pulled into an isolated space at the back of the car park. Again, she sat in shock for several minutes, trying to gather her thoughts. What the hell was in the boot of her car? Trying to calm herself, she took a few deep breaths and closed her eyes.

It's fine. You're fine. Whatever it is, just do as he asks and then it will be over. It's all for the greater good. It releases Frankie from his grip.

Internal pep talk over, and acting more courageous than she felt, she stepped out of her car and walked round to the back, all the time checking there was no one watching.

She clicked open the boot and saw a number of black shrink-wrapped packages tucked inside a seemingly normal bag for life. How the fuck had that got in there when it was locked? Then she remembered who she was dealing with.

At least it's not a body.

She wasn't sure she was supposed to touch them, and ingrained procedure saw her pulling on a pair of nitrile gloves before she took one of the bundles out. She was surprised at how heavy it was. She didn't dare open it, so she gave it a good feel. It was oblong, about the size of a house brick. The edges were uneven, and somewhat flexible. As she ran her thumb down the short side, she could feel ridges. It wasn't solid, like a brick, and it had some movement to it. She knew it wasn't drugs; the numerous drug awareness courses she had been on told her that a block of cocaine or crack would be solid. There was only one thing this could be. Money. Stacks of notes. God knows how much. The bag that she had lifted it from was stacked to the hilt. She quickly closed the boot and slipped back into the driver's seat. She took several minutes to slow her heart rate down before starting the car.

Thousands of thoughts were flashing through her mind. Was she expected to head to Harrogate now? What would happen when she reached her destination? Who would be there? What would they do? Was this entire thing a set-up, designed to catch her out? She rested her head against the steering wheel. She felt physically sick. What had she agreed to?

The little Nokia started to ring, making her jump. She reached into the passenger footwell and fumbled around to reach it from her bag.

'Hello?'

'Dr Turner, you received the package, I see?' It was Dickhead.

She straightened up in her seat and turned the engine off. 'Yes, it's in the boot.'

'So what are you waiting for? You have the address.'

'I just needed a minute ...'

'What for? You agreed to—'

Lolly snapped. 'I didn't agree to anything, you piece of shit. I said I wanted you to leave Frankie alone.'

'And I said I would, if you gave something in return.'

'I will not be a money mule for you and your sordid dealings.' Lolly was seething and could hardly contain her anger.

There was silence on the other end of the phone.

'Are you still there?' she snapped, momentarily confused.

'Oh, I'm still here. I was waiting until you had finished your tantrum.'

She was so outraged she could barely speak. 'You ...'

'What? Piece of shit?' Laughter. 'I've been called worse, so I take no offence. It's your choice, Doctor Turner. Make the delivery and I leave Frankie alone. Don't and ... well, you really don't want to find out. If you think life has been made hard for Francesca now, wait until you see what I can really do.'

The line went dead. Lolly collapsed over her steering wheel in floods of tears. Angry, frustrated, feeling humiliated and stupid, she threw the phone across the car.

'Bastard!' she screamed.

She angrily wiped the tears away and yanked the car into first gear.

'Wait until you see what I can really do.'

Oh, God, what had she signed up to? All she wanted to do was make Frankie happy, build a life together. How had it come to this? It went against everything she believed in. But so did bullying, and that's what Dickhead was. A bully. And now he had Lolly caught up in his grimy underworld. She could go straight to Ziggy. Yes, why hadn't she thought of that? Would that cause Frankie even more grief, though? How far did Dickhead's reach go? The driver had looked like a nasty piece of work. There were probably more of them. And what would she say to Ziggy?

'I wanted to protect my girlfriend but ended up becoming a money mule. Please go arrest him.' She laughed out loud. Even to her, who was actually living it, it sounded ridiculous, implausible. She could see the news headlines.

Prominent Home Office pathologist turned into money mule to save girlfriend, jailed for twenty years.

The thought of prison actually shocked her back into full awareness. 'Shit, shit, shit.' She indicated and took the exit onto the Harrogate road.

How the fuck had she managed to get herself so tangled up in all of this? She felt very much out of her depth and that everything was out of her control. It was a feeling she wasn't used to, and most definitely didn't like.

28

Lolly pulled into the car park of the Crown pub, just off the Royal Parade in Harrogate. Still schooling herself in staying calm, she retrieved the discarded mobile phone, once again, from the passenger footwell. Opening the message she had received earlier, she double checked she was in the right place. However, after confirming she was, she had no idea what she was supposed to do next. She pushed her car seat back, stretching her legs as far as she could, and took a look around. Taking in the Victorian buildings and monoliths that Harrogate was known for, and apart from the obvious tourists, there was no one person that stood out to her.

I don't even know who or what I'm looking for, she thought. She reached to unlock the car door, scanning around her constantly. Then, from nowhere, came a sharp tapping on the passenger window that scared the living daylights out of her, making her physically jump in her seat. She made an attempt to compose herself and looked at the face staring at her. He was pointing at the window, indicating she should roll it down, her finger hovered over the window button, all the while playing terrifying scenarios in her head. A gun being drawn. A knife being pulled. Another threat. This was next-level fear. Nervously, she pushed the button and watched as the window slowly descended, flinching as it did so before slumping down in her seat. Gripping the steering wheel, she hardly dared breathe. The neck of her T-shirt suddenly felt too tight, and she pulled it away from her neck.

The face, what she could see of it in between the gap of the baseball cap and zipped-up sports jacket, spoke to her. 'Open your boot,' he said, making it clear she had no other option.

'It's ... it's open,' she stammered.

The face disappeared momentarily, then reappeared in her rear-view mirror for a second before the light blue of the Fiat's boot filled the screen. Lolly felt the car rock slightly as he removed the bag. Then a slam that again made her jump. When she looked again, he was gone.

Shocked, dazed and feeling overemotional, she had to get out of the car before she exploded with anxiety. With one hand against the roof, and the other on her waist, she leant forwards and let out a long held breath.

'Fuuuuck,' she exhaled, before immediately apologising to the elderly couple who were staring at her.

Feeling wired, still shaking, nerves shot to hell, she climbed back into her car. She had to wait several minutes before she could operate the clutch, her legs were trembling so much.

As she started the engine, she heard the ping of a mobile phone. The colour drained from her face. Hadn't she done enough? Grappling with her bag, she found the Nokia, but it wasn't coming from there. Digging further in, she found her own Samsung mobile and saw she had several missed calls and text messages from the coroner's office in Wakefield. As she wasn't on call, she wondered why they had tried her repeatedly. *They didn't know already, did they?*

She turned the engine off again, composed herself and returned the call.

'Leila, we need you to come into the office.'

What? She had been expecting to go through to Rita on the switchboard, but instead she had reached Doctor Callaghan direct, the senior coroner and who she ultimately answered to. Flustered with the abruptness of his greeting, she couldn't think of what to say. 'Why?' was all she could come up with. It was getting on for 7 p.m., and she was already drained from the day.

'It would be better if you could come in. Can you be here at 9 a.m. tomorrow?'

'Yes, sure. Is everything OK?'

'See you tomorrow at 9 a.m.'

The call ended. She sat with the phone in her hand, nervously tapping it against her chin, replaying the short conversation. If she wasn't already shaken enough with the events of the day, the tone and abruptness of Doctor Callaghan had unnerved her. It could be nothing, she tried to reason with herself. But why so many calls? And why first thing in the morning? The next day was supposed to be her day off. She had made plans with Frankie. How was she going to explain it to her?

Was it about the delivery? Did they know already?

Starting the car, she set off for home. She just wanted to climb into bed, pull the covers over her head and ignore the world.

Closing the door of her flat behind her, Lolly leant

against it and slid to the floor. Relieved to be in familiar surroundings, but feeling a huge amount of guilt –she knew it wouldn't be long before Frankie rang. Lolly had yet to think of excuses for her absence.

Kicking off her shoes, she grabbed a beer from the fridge and threw herself down on the battered sofa. Lolly's small, one-bedroomed flat was a far cry from the luxury she had at Frankie's, but she just couldn't face her right now. It was one thing to lie over the phone, but she didn't think she could do it face to face without giving anything away. She was over-wrought with emotion and needed some time to recalibrate herself. She replayed the day in her head, feeling increas-ingly gullible. She finished her beer and, deciding that beating herself up wouldn't solve anything, she took a shower and headed into her bedroom. After flicking through endless TV channels, unable to concentrate, she pulled her mobile phone out of her bag, took a deep breath and dialled Frankie's number. It seemed to take ages to connect, and Lolly was about to hang up when she heard Frankie's voice.

'Hello?' She sounded sleepy. 'I'm sorry, did I wake you?'

'No. Yes. I've taken a sleeping tablet.'

A part of Lolly felt relieved that Frankie hadn't been sitting there waiting for her, but she also knew that Frankie only took pills when she was in a dark place. 'I'm sorry I'm not there. I've just had one hell of a day.'

'It's fine. I guessed you weren't coming over when I hadn't heard from you.'

Frankie sounded so desolate, Lolly felt a rush of love mingled with guilt. 'I could head over now if you want me to?'

'No, it's fine. I'll see you tomorrow.'

'I've been called into the office tomorrow morning. I'll ring you when I'm done.'

'Fine.'

'OK, get some sleep and I'll see you tomorrow. Love you.' Lolly ended the call and laid back on the bed.

'What a fucked-up day.' She closed her eyes and prayed that she would get a good night's sleep.

29

Thursday, 12th September 2002

No such luck. Lolly had been awake on and off for most of the night, and had given up the ghost at 5 a.m. She sat at her kitchen table, nursing her third cup of coffee, replaying yesterday and wondering what today would bring. Time seemed to be passing so slowly. She was glad that the little Nokia hadn't rung or received any messages. She considered taking the battery out and throwing it down the toilet, but what would that achieve? He'd only find a way of getting to her, probably via Frankie. The whole situation was fucked up, and Lolly couldn't see her way out of it.

As she locked the flat, she dialled Frankie's number. She'd already tried twice, but there had been no answer, which was unsettling, but knowing that Frankie had taken a sleeping tablet, she wasn't overly surprised.

Driving into Wakefield, she tried to put thoughts of Dickhead temporarily to one side as she pondered on what Doctor Callaghan could want her for. Quite sure that it wasn't the deliveries (It was too soon, surely?), she figured it could be about an inquest, but she hadn't been required to give evidence recently, so possible but unlikely. Although she was classed as freelance, she still answered to the General Medical Council and the Wakefield coroner's office was her point of contact. If she had any problems, Doctor Callaghan was her first port of call. She parked in the public car park opposite, paid at the meter and crossed the road.

Pushing open the heavy swing doors, she signed in with Rita at reception and made her way upstairs. The building had once been the registry office for births, deaths and marriages in Wakefield and the surrounding district. Whilst it still retained some of the Georgian opulence of sweeping staircases, it had faded over the years and the Grade II building was in need of some restoration work.

Reaching Dr Callaghan's office, she took a deep breath and knocked on the door, before following the command to enter.

'Good morning, Leila. Thank you for coming in,' said Dr Callaghan, standing to shake Lolly's hand. He was a tall man, over six feet, so he towered over Lolly. She always thought he had a bit of a Dickensian look about him, with a curled moustache and unruly, wispy grey hair with long sideburns. He wore small circular glasses that sat halfway down his nose, so he had to raise his head when he spoke to you. Lolly liked him. He had always been fair with her, and it was his recommendation that had secured her the part-time lecturing job at the university.

Lolly returned the greeting warmly and sat in the allocated chair. 'I'm a bit surprised to say the least. What's this about?' Her left leg bounced up and down frenetically.

'I'll get to that in a moment and I'm sure it's nothing to worry about, just a mix-up. Would you like a drink?'

His voice was calm and even-tempered, which made

Lolly feel a little easier, though she had already had several cups of coffee, so she politely declined. 'Just a glass of water, please. Can we just get on with whatever this is?'

Callaghan nodded at her, pressed a buzzer for his assistant to bring the glass of water, and continued. 'I understand you're on edge. I'll get straight to the point and forgive me for being direct, Leila, but I think it's sometimes better to deal with these things head on.'

'Yes, absolutely. Go ahead.' Lolly frowned, willing him to hurry up. If it was about yesterday's deliveries, she would confess all and face the consequences, she silently decided in a rush of panic.

Callaghan shuffled some papers around on his desk and flipped through a brown folder before pulling out a sheet of paper. 'There's no easy way of saying this, but there's been a complaint made against you, I'm afraid.' He tilted his head up to look at her.

Lolly stared at him in disbelief. The colour drained from her face. An electric shot jolted through her body as the words sank in. It was several moments before she spoke.

'What?'

'I know. I can assure you, I am as surprised as you.' He removed his glasses, and she thought he genuinely did look concerned.

'Complaint? I don't understand?' she asked, frantically searching her memory for something, or someone that she might have upset, whilst secretly relieved it wasn't Dickhead.

'It's from the family of a man whose post-mortem you conducted a couple of weeks ago. You interpreted the findings as suicide, but they are convinced it was murder. They've asked for a second opinion.'

Families disputing the result of a post-mortem was

unusual, but not unheard of. A second opinion, again, sometimes happened. Lolly was used to having her work scrutinised. It was standard practice, but from a member of the deceased's family? That hadn't happened to her before.

'And has that taken place?' If it hadn't, then Lolly had every right to be there and justify her initial findings. But again, it wasn't a requirement.

'Not as yet.'

'What happens now?'

'The second post-mortem will take place, and depending on the findings, you'll be asked to make a statement regarding your initial report and we'll take it from there.'

Lolly's head was spinning. She gripped the arms of the chair to ground herself and closed her eyes for a second. 'Can you tell me the name of the complainant?'

'Just that it's a family member. All communication is being done through their lawyers. I can tell you the victim had been a prisoner in HMP Leeds, about to be transferred to a category D open prison.' Callaghan passed Lolly's original report to her.

Casting her mind back, she remembered that day now. She'd stood in for a colleague who had phoned in sick. She skipped to the conclusion she had written and paraphrased her findings.

'It was a straightforward, low-level hanging. The victim had tied a sheet to his bed frame, knelt down, leant forwards and asphyxiation occurred. There was petechial haemorrhaging on his face and eyelids, as well as a clavicle contusion and fractures in the neck.'

Lolly knew he had been a prisoner at the time, and she wondered why the family thought it had been murder. She recalled it seeming quite straightforward. The hyoid bone had also been broken and the ligature marks around his neck had quite apparently been made by the torn sheet that had been found around his neck. Where had she gone wrong? She felt sick.

'Why do they think it was murder? I can't believe this.'

'Apparently, one of the other inmates has been heard bragging about how he did it and how he'd got away with it. It's taken this long for the police to action anything. The prison service thought they could handle it internally, but the family took it up with the GMC when they weren't getting a satisfactory response.'

The office door opened, and a glass of water appeared. Lolly accepted it with shaking hands and took a sip. 'When will you know about the second post-mortem?'

'It's taking place tomorrow. I'm unsure of the time, but I will find out for you. You do, of course, have every right to be there, and to be honest, Leila, I think you should be. You won't be able to discuss it, but you can observe from the gallery.'

Tears built as the enormity of what was happening hit her. 'This is my career, my reputation.'

'And I'm sure everything will work in your favour. Take the rest of today and I'll be in touch in due course.'

Lolly stumbled out of the Georgian building and found her way back to her car. She sat for a few minutes, running the conversation over in her mind. It didn't make sense to her. From what she remembered, it was a pretty straightforward case, and she had been as thorough as she usually was, so what had she missed? She felt so upset. Her work was everything to her, and she took the responsibility of providing families closure at a traumatic time very seriously.

She was so wrapped up in her thoughts that when the Nokia started its tinny ringing tone, she wondered what it was. Realising, she pulled it from her bag and looked at the screen. She groaned inwardly.

'What?' she snapped into the receiver.

'Now that's not a nice way to greet a friend, is it?'

'We are anything but friends. What is it you want?' She hated his leering tone and creepy manner. She had wondered more than once just what Frankie had seen in him.

'I need you to make a special delivery for me.'

'I can't do it today.'

'Oh, you can, and you will.'

Lolly was adamant. 'No, absolutely not. I've got a lot on my mind right now. I won't do it.'

'Oh, the post-mortem, you mean?'

Lolly nearly dropped the phone. 'What the actual? How do you know about that?'

'I have my ways. So, are you going to make this delivery for me?'

'How do you know about the post-mortem?' Lolly was almost shouting into the phone.

'I've told you, I have my ways. It's not important. I'll get the details of the delivery sent through.'

'No, I've told you I'm not doing it.'

'Let me spell it out for you, Doctor Turner. Make the delivery and the result will go in your favour. Don't make the delivery, and well, do you really want to find out?'

Lolly was dumbfounded. Her frazzled brain couldn't make the connection. What was he saying exactly? That he was behind the complaint? How could that be? Even though she was acutely aware that he was waiting for a response, she struggled for something to say.

'I'll take your silence as a yes,' he said, before her thoughts could order themselves. 'Details will be sent to you.'

She was still processing everything when the line went dead. The phone immediately beeped again with a text message. Whilst she fumbled with the keypad, she felt the boot of her car open and felt the rear suspension drop slightly as something heavy was loaded in. She didn't dare to look behind her. Instead, she just stared at the address on the phone screen. Liverpool. Sefton Park in Liverpool, to be precise. Resigning herself to the long drive ahead, she waited until the boot was slammed shut and slipped the car into gear.

30

It took Lolly until mid-afternoon to do the Liverpool delivery. It had been exactly the same process. She'd sat in her car, anxiety ridden, whilst the inconspicuous bags were retrieved from the boot of her car. Once the receiver had walked away, she simply drove off. She wanted to say it was easy, but her conscience was telling her otherwise. She had told an outright lie to Frankie to explain her absence, telling her that she had been mistakenly included on the rota to work the weekend. The guilt was all-consuming, and she despised herself for being so weak. There were only so many times she could convince herself that it was 'for the greater good'.

Lolly had broken every speed limit on her way back up the M62. On the one hand, she wanted to see Frankie, to assuage herself that she believed her, but conversely, Lolly wanted to run far away where no one could find her. Conflicted, she had considered ringing Ziggy, or just dropping by his house, but she knew he would see through her fragile exterior and her pride couldn't bear the thought of him finding out what she was involved in.

No, this was her mess. There was no one else that could get her out of it. She would have to push through, whatever the cost. She kept checking her personal phone, but there had been no word from Dr Callaghan. She longed for him to call and tell her it had all been a huge mistake, but no luck. Her tummy dived at the thought of the outcome. She'd done the delivery.

She just had to trust that Dickhead would keep to his word. At that thought, she huffed. Could she trust him? She had to. He held her future in the palm of his hands. Her life with Frankie, her career, her future prospects, her reputation. Everything.

Shuddering at the thought of what she may be forced to sacrifice, she slowed down and took the exit into Leeds city centre. As she pulled into the courtyard of Frankie's flat, her heart skipped several beats when she saw that Dickhead's Range Rover parked there.

Pulling into a space, she watched for a minute, wondering what the hell he was doing there. She couldn't see his driver and the rear windows were tinted, so she had no idea if Dickhead was watching her. She had no choice but to get out of her car. She cautiously opened her door and stepped out. She grabbed her bag from the passenger seat and walked behind the Range Rover towards the door. As she punched Frankie's access code into the door panel, she saw the driver from the other day coming down the stairs. He pushed the door open, nodded his head, winked at Lolly and walked off. Not sure why he would be there, she grabbed the swinging door with sweating palms and headed upstairs. On opening the apartment door, she could hear the TV playing in the living room.

'Hey, I'm here,' she shouted.

Lolly took her coat off and hung it on the coat rack along

with her bag. She took her shoes off, replaced them with slippers and headed to the living room. Frankie was laid out on the sofa, still in her pyjamas with a quilt tucked in around her. Lolly was immediately concerned.

'My love, are you OK?' She dashed in, and dropped to Frankie's eye level, stroking hair away from Frankie's face.

'I'm fine, just feeling a bit under the weather. I wasn't sure what time you would be here, so I thought I'd have a lazy day.' She turned the TV off as she spoke and pulled herself up into a seated position.

'Can I get you anything?' asked Lolly.

'A cup of camomile tea would be nice.' Frankie looked at Lolly and reached her hand up. 'You look tired too.'

Not wanting to have to explain more than necessary, she gave Frankie a weak smile and headed into the kitchen. She returned shortly afterwards with two mugs of camomile tea. Sitting next to Frankie, she blew the heat from the top of her mug and took a sip.

'How did this morning go?' asked Frankie.

'Fine, I told them they had made a mistake, and it was all sorted out.'

'How come you're so late getting here, if it was all sorted out?'

Lolly blushed and pulled her mug closer to her, resting the rim on her bottom lip, hoping Frankie wouldn't look at her too closely. 'Oh, there was some paperwork that they needed me to sign off. Boring admin stuff.' Eager to change the subject and remove the spotlight from her, she tried to turn the tables. 'How about you? What has your morning been like?'

'What paperwork did you have to sign?' persisted Frankie.

'Just some reports, nothing significant.' She tried to sound nonchalant.

'Doesn't sound like you, to forget to sign something?'

'I didn't forget, it's just some new regulation. You know what it's like.' She wished Frankie would move on. She tried again to change the subject. 'Shall we get a curry tonight? And open a bottle of wine? Something to lift your spirits?"

'Huh, there's nothing wrong with my "spirit", as you call it. My problem is my ex.' Frankie folded her arms across herself. 'I've just had one of his minions here issuing orders.'

Lolly held her breath, not trusting her voice to sound normal. Thankfully, Frankie carried on.

'Can you believe he had the cheek to ask for the logbook back for the car?'

Lolly shook her head. 'No way?'

'Yep. I didn't give it to him. Fuck him. If he wants it, he'll have to get it himself. Why would he send one of his little lackeys for it, anyway?'

Lolly shrugged her shoulders, realisation dawning on her. She felt an army of spiders crawling over her skin as each hair on her body stood on end. He hadn't been sent to pick up a logbook. *He'd been sent to make sure I was back.*

'I just need the loo. Back in a second.' She calmly walked from the living room, heading to the bathroom. Once in there, she quietly closed the door, leant over the bowl and brought up what little she had digested that day. Wiping her mouth with a toilet roll, she splashed her face with cold water and sat on the closed lid, not yet flushing.

'Oh God, oh God, oh God, what have I done?' She ran her hands through her hair, scrunching and pulling it as she did so. She had to leave, she had to get out. She couldn't hide it from Frankie any longer. She'd make an excuse. She'd say that work had phoned her. She'd say that little

Ben was poorly and Ziggy was working. She'd say she didn't feel well. No, she couldn't say any of that. She started silently crying when she heard footsteps in the hallway.

'Lolly, are you OK?'

Sniffing, coughing in an attempt to disguise it, Lolly wiped her nose and eyes. 'Fine, love, I'll be out in a minute.'

'I can hear a phone ringing. Is it you?'

Lolly nearly swallowed her tongue. She listened carefully and she could hear a phone going too. Flushing the toilet and checking herself in the mirror, she slowly opened the door. Frankie was standing right outside.

'Have you been crying?' she asked, her voice full of concern.

'No, I had a coughing fit. I'm fine now.' She reached behind Frankie to the coat rack for her bag. The mobile stopped ringing as she rooted around for it. She had been fairly certain it was her Samsung, but there was every chance it had been the Nokia, they had the same ring tone. She'd thrown both phones in her bag. Lolly could feel Frankie's eyes staring at her, waiting for her to produce a phone. Similar in shape and size, her hand fell on one, and she pulled it out. It was her work phone. Lolly let go of her breath.

'Ha, bloody thing.' She waved in front of her, in Frankie's direction.

'Is that work again?'

'It will be a mistake. I had it out with them this morning. Rita couldn't organise her way out of a paper bag, honestly.' *Sorry, Rita.* She was conscious of the fact that not only was she waffling, but the armpits of her T-shirt were showing the sweat that had broken out all over her. She pushed her phone into the back pocket of her jeans.

'What are we both stood in here for? Come on, let's go sit

down.' Lolly turned and headed towards the living room, praying that Frankie would follow. She tried desperately to inject some joviality into her voice. 'Come on, let's catch up on last week's *Silent Witness* so I can shout at the TV.' She grabbed Frankie's hand and dragged her into the room.

Once Frankie was comfortable, Lolly insisted on opening a bottle of wine. As she poured two glasses in the kitchen, she slipped the phone out of her pocket and redialled the office.

'Dr Callaghan, it's Lolly,' she said in a whisper.

'Hello there, yes. Just heard that the PM will happen at 9 a.m.' She nearly dropped her phone.

'9 a.m.?'

'Yes. As I said, I really think you should be there.'

Lolly's brain tried to process the information. Tomorrow? What was she doing tomorrow?

Callaghan continued. 'I'm sure you've nothing to worry about, and as soon as I have the results, I will let you know.'

'Lolly? Who are you talking to?' Frankie popped her head round the kitchen door.

Shocked, Lolly jumped and almost dropped the phone. She caught it just in time and tucked it back into her pocket.

'Oh, just work. Nothing to worry about.' She passed Frankie her glass of wine with shaking hands.

'You're acting very strange, Lolly. Is everything OK?'

'Yes,' said Lolly, dismissively. 'I'm fine. Just work stuff. I'm fine, honestly.'

After once more settling on the sofa, Lolly was aware of the TV playing but couldn't process any of the pictures or sounds. She was at her wit's end. As the evening progressed, she drank far too much wine and passed out on the sofa long before Frankie tried to wake her to go to bed. She hadn't slept so much, rather more unconscious, and now, as daylight peeked between the blinds in the living room, her tongue felt like it was Velcroed to the roof her mouth, and she had the beginnings of a thumping headache. Groaning, she rolled over, almost falling off the sofa, putting her hand on the floor just in time.

'Ah, nice to see you awake,' said Frankie snarkily as she walked into the room carrying two mugs. She passed one to Lolly and opened the blinds.

Lolly winced as daylight flooded in, covered her eyes and slunk back on the sofa. 'Morning.'

'It's nearly noon.'

Lolly sat bolt upright. 'What? Why didn't you wake me?'

'You didn't seem to be up for a walk around Roundhay Park when I tried to stir you at ten.'

'Fuck, fuck, fuck!' She placed her mug on the coffee table and jumped up. Pulling her phone from the back pocket of the jeans she was still wearing, she glanced at the screen. Two missed calls from Callaghan.

'Lolly, what on earth is wrong with you? Will you please tell what's going on?'

Lolly sat back down. 'I can't. I mean it's just work stuff.'

'You work with students and dead bodies. What on earth could have gone so wrong? You were very secretive when you finally arrived yesterday, and I might as well have been on my own last night. You drank far more than you usually do, and now you're as jumpy as fuck. What the hell is going on?'

Lolly closed her eyes. She owed Frankie some kind of explanation for her behaviour. 'Someone has made a complaint against me.'

Frankie sat next to Lolly. 'A complaint? What do you mean? A student?'

Lolly sighed. 'No. A post-mortem result.' She quickly ran

through the facts. 'And I'm sure it will all be fine, but it was due to take place at nine, and I wanted to be there, but now I've missed it.'

Frankie took Lolly in her arms. 'Poor you, you should have said something.'

'I didn't know what to say. I think I was still in shock.'

From the hallway came the sound of a mobile phone ringing. Frankie glanced at the phone in Lolly's hand, pushed her away, and looked at her face questioningly.

'If that's your mobile phone' – she jabbed her finger at the screen – 'what the fuck is that ringing in your bag?'

31

Friday, 13th September 2002

Lolly wanted the ground to swallow her whole. Silently cursing Frankie's ex-husband, Lolly dashed from the living room into the hallway and fished the Nokia out of her bag, Dickhead's name was lighting up the screen. She rejected the call and turned the phone completely off, gripping it in her hand.

'Well?' demanded Frankie, who was standing outside the living-room door, hands on her hips.

'I ... it's ...' A wave of sickness washed over her, so she ducked into the bathroom.

Frankie followed and stood at the open door, watching with a look of complete disgust on her face.

'I'll make some coffee,' she spat, turning away as Lolly heaved over the toilet bowl.

When there was nothing left in her stomach, Lolly flushed, washed her face and brushed her teeth, buying herself some time. *What the fuck do I say?* She knew without a doubt that if she told Frankie the truth, she would absolutely blow a fuse. Frankie was as stubborn as Lolly herself was at times. She would perceive Lolly's help as an attack on her capabilities. In truth, all Lolly had wanted to do was create a way for them to be able to move forwards with their lives.

Instead, she'd created a web of lies that she couldn't explain.

She timidly opened the bathroom door, quashing down fear, flashbacks from her childhood creeping into her mind. Nervously, she tiptoed into the kitchen.

'My love, I need to explain ...'

Frankie was standing with her back to Lolly, pushing the plunger down on the cafetière. She whipped round, and Lolly was astonished to see that she was smiling.

'You don't have to explain, I know.' Lolly's heart stopped. 'You know?'

Frankie seemed as pleased as punch with herself. 'Yes, I *know*.' She exaggerated the word so that it seemed to go on forever.

'You do?'

'Yes. It's so obvious I don't know why I didn't put it together when you arrived here late yesterday.'

The smile had changed to a snarl, and Frankie had an unusual look on her face. One that told Lolly she knew the truth, whilst also wanting to throw the boiling hot coffee over her. Lolly took a step back.

'I did it for us, Frankie.'

Frankie laughed maniacally whilst pouring coffee into mugs, with most of it missing and splashing onto the work-top. 'For us? That's a new one.'

'I want us to move on, to build our lives.'

'Build our lives?' Frankie screwed her face up. 'Build our

lives?' She repeated as though Lolly had spoken another language.

'Yes. Do the things we want, get married, have kids ...'

Frankie looked shocked, and Lolly had a sudden realisation that they were talking about different things.

'You think I'm having an affair?'

'Aren't you?' Frankie slammed the mugs onto the worktop.

Lolly jumped back, just missing being splashed. 'An affair?' Part of her did think that would be an easier option right now. 'No, I'm not having an affair.'

'But the second phone, the strange absences. I've seen it before.'

Lolly took a step forwards and reached for Frankie's hands. 'My love, I am not having an affair.' She felt almost relieved that Frankie hadn't worked out the truth, and she couldn't bear to open up to her now. 'The second phone isn't mine. It's for Ziggy.'

'Ziggy?' Frankie looked incredulous.

Mentally scrabbling around, she tried desperately to give a plausible reason as to why she would have a phone for her best friend.

'Yes. It was his fault I was late yesterday. He needed my help with something. I guess he must have dropped his phone into my bag by mistake.' Laughing, the words tumbled out of her mouth before she had time to engage her brain. 'I'm returning it today. That's why it was ringing. It will have been him trying to find it.'

There wasn't a pore in Lolly's body that wasn't sweating, and her earlier headache had developed into something akin to a migraine. She picked up her mug, hoping Frankie wouldn't see her hand shaking, and took a sip. It was awful, bitter and cold. It took some swallowing. She turned her back to Frankie and headed into the bedroom. When Frankie didn't follow, she shouted, 'I'm jumping in the shower.'

Lolly stripped off and turned on the shower jets. She stepped into the cubicle and let the water run cold in an attempt to clear her head. She had lied. She had told lies. She had lied to the one person she loved most in the world. She felt dreadful. Slowly turning the heat up, she lifted her face into the water stream and held her breath as it washed over her, wanting to wash away the guilt, the regret, the mistakes. She was in way over her head, and she knew it.

Saturday, 14 September 2002

After Lolly had entrenched herself with further lies and having no choice but to leave her relationship with Frankie in a precarious state whilst she tried to sort out the mess, she had headed home, and spent the night with a bottle of Sauvignon and a biscuit jar, ignoring the waiting messages on the burner phone.

The next morning, knowing she couldn't ignore Dickhead any longer, she headed out to her car and drove to the Calls, where she pulled into a parking bay. Taking the Nokia out of her bag, she saw she had several missed calls and numerous text messages with demands for her to return the calls immediately.

Reluctantly, she dialled his number. 'Where have you been?'

'Oh, don't start. What do you want?'

'You sound stressed, Doctor Turner. Something wrong?'

'Everything is wrong, everything.'

'Ah, shame, I hope it won't keep you from the next job I have for you.'

'I can't. I need to go to work.'

'Oh yes, the post-mortem result.'

Chills ran down her spine. 'Do you know what it is?'

'Now, how would I know that?'

'Stop pissing me about.'

He laughed, that short bitter laugh that Lolly had grown to hate. 'I don't know, but I would have thought you would have been there.'

'I couldn't. I was with Frankie.'

There was an ominous silence. 'Oh. You haven't told her, have you?'

'About the complaint? Yes, I had to tell her something. She knew something was wrong. This morning she accused me of having an affair.'

'And are you?'

'Oh, fuck off. I've had enough of your bullshit. I need to go.'

'Details of the next job will be sent to you.'

'This is the last time.'

'We'll see.'

Furious, knowing she should have handled that better, she pulled out her personal mobile and rang Callaghan. She braced herself as she waited for him to answer. After what felt like an age, the call was finally answered.

'Dr Callaghan, it's Leila, I'm so sorry I missed your calls.'

'I must say, Leila, I was very surprised to hear you didn't attend the PM yesterday.'

'I know, I'm sorry. I just couldn't face being there. Do you know the outcome?'

'I need you to come into the office.'

Shit, that didn't sound good.

Lolly arrived at the offices thirty minutes later. During her car journey, she had tried to collect her thoughts and pull herself together, but to no avail. He wouldn't call her into the office if it wasn't bad news, would he?

But Dickhead had promised. She should have known better. Hadn't life already shown her that she couldn't trust anyone?

Pulling into the car park, she forced herself to calm down and concentrated on breathing as she walked across the road to the office. The outside door was locked, it being Saturday, so she rang the buzzer. Dr Callaghan was waiting in reception. He gave her a weak smile that set Lolly's nerves on edge and unlocked the door.

Walking into the usually bustling office on a Saturday was a very different experience from the one she was used to. The old building looked tired, and she randomly noticed that the once vibrant red carpet was badly worn in places.

'Morning,' he said, heading up the staircase to his office.

'Morning, again,' she said, following him. 'I'm sorry I didn't attend. It's just been a bit crazy.'

'It's fine, Lolly, though I would have thought you'd have been keen to hear the outcome.'

'I was, I mean, I am. God, I'm sorry it's just, well, it can't be good news. Sorry, I'm waffling.'

'Stop apologising. What's done is done. Let's just see what we can salvage from the situation, shall we?'

Lolly didn't like the use of the word *salvage*. What was that supposed to mean?

Callaghan stopped in front of the public vending machine and ordered two coffees without consulting Lolly if she wanted one. She did, and her headache from earlier came surging back.

Callaghan passed her a polystyrene cup, and she took a sip. Her mouth was so dry; she wished she had water instead. Or even better, a gin.

Taking seats opposite each other in Dr Callaghan's office, he began.

He coughed, placed his glasses on his nose and tilted his head, reading from the report in front of him. 'As you know, a second post-mortem was conducted on one of your cases where the outcome is being disputed by the family. There will be an official investigation, but initial stages would indicate that the family was right and that the death was, in fact, a homicide. I'm afraid to say their complaint is being upheld.'

Lolly sat, aghast at the news. Had she heard that wrong? Upheld? What did that mean? What the hell? How could that be? She needed to hear it again.

'I'm sorry, what? Can you repeat that?' She ran her fingers through her hair whilst her brain worked through all the connotations of his words. She felt numb.

'I know, I had to read it a few times to believe it too, but there are indications that the victim was murdered and didn't commit suicide, as your report indicated.'

'What the fuck? How can that be?' She felt her face flush, then drain of colour. 'That's impossible.' She leant forwards, and reached for the report in Callaghan's hands, but he pulled it away.

'Please, Doctor Turner, let me finish. I understand you're upset, but let me explain.'

Lolly sat back down in disbelief. She felt empty.

'It would appear that there were defence wounds on the arms of the victim, as well as bruising to the ribs, which are consistent with being repeatedly kicked.'

Lolly was gobsmacked. 'But, I don't understand? That can't be right. I was thorough – I would have seen something as obvious as that. There must be some mistake ...'

Callaghan closed the file and placed his hands on the

desk. 'I'm sorry, Leila. I know this is hard to take. For now, or at least until the official investigation is over, I'm going to have to ask you to stand down from your duties as a pathologist, I'm afraid.'

'No. I can't do that. I won't.' She was shaking from head to toe. Callaghan left his seat and came round to her side.

'I am sorry, Leila. I understand this is hard to take in. Go home, take a couple of days to process everything.'

She stared at him as he squatted down in front of her, glasses balanced precariously on his nose.

'I'm ruined,' she whispered, tears forming. She stood up and walked in a daze back to her car. If Callaghan said anything else to her, she didn't hear it. She sat in her car, feeling lost, knowing she needed to sleep, but her head was such a mess she wasn't sure she would ever sleep again. She collapsed against the steering wheel and let the tears fall. She felt utterly bereft and had no idea how to dig herself out of the mess – the mess she alone had created.

Not sure of what else to do, she headed to Frankie's, hoping to put the day behind her and find some comfort in her arms. Frankie had started on at her the minute she walked through the door, and was still relentless hours later.

'I've told you. I was working on a job in Liverpool. I left my phone in the car and that's why I missed your calls.' Lolly had had to raise her voice to get herself heard over the music that Frankie was blasting. She'd never seen her like this before. They had been arguing on and off for the last four hours and Lolly was exhausted. Frankie had accused her of everything, including having an affair.

Frankie was sitting in the living room on the sofa. Lolly

had been standing in front of the TV. She now threw herself down next to Frankie and grabbed hold of her hand.

'I don't know what else to say to you, Frankie. I haven't been cheating on you. Why would I? What we have is epic. It's so important to me. I love you.' She leant over and tried to kiss Frankie's cheek, but she moved her head. Lolly sat back, not knowing what else she could do or say. 'Please Frankie, just listen to me,' she tried one more time.

'Just go, Leila. I think we've both said enough for one night.' Frankie continued staring ahead at the music channel on TV that was playing in the background.

'But I can't leave us like this. Just tell me you believe me, that we're OK?'

'Have some self-respect. Just go and leave me alone. I need to think.'

'There's nothing to think about. I love you, Frankie. Please.'

Lolly watched as Frankie stood up and headed to the kitchen. She saw her grab a wine glass from the draining board and a half-empty bottle of Chablis from the fridge. Pouring herself a glass, she headed back into the living room and took up her place again on the sofa, without saying a word.

Lolly felt lost. She needed to sleep. Her head was a mess. Realising that she wasn't going to get anywhere with Frankie, she turned and headed to the bedroom, feeling utterly bereft.

PART III

32

Tuesday, 24th September 2002

Leaving Sadie to tut and sigh her way through the briefing with Whitmore, Ziggy made a few decisions. As much as he would have given his right arm to be in the briefing, he had to prioritise the elements of the investigation that he *could* do. And right now, his priority was to ensure Ben and Rachel were safe.

He was quietly seething with Witless Whitmore by the time he had reached his car. He'd legitimately – well, not entirely legitimately – turned up new leads and connections for them to be ignored. There was a link between the note delivered to Chrystal Mack and the one left in Ben's school bag, if only he'd been given a chance to explain.

He'd thrown the copy emails onto Sadie's desk on his way out – let them work it out for themselves. If he couldn't do it via the usual channels, then he'd go rogue and damn the consequences. In the meantime, he dialled Rachel's number.

'Rachel, I need you to take Ben and go to your mums.'

'What? Now?'

'Yes, as soon as possible.'

'Why, Ziggy, what's happened?'

'I'll tell you later, but please do as I ask.'

'OK, I will. Are you all right?'

'I'm fine – well, I might be out of a job, but I'll worry about that later. Please, Rachel, can you take him now?'

'I'll give her a call. Yes, yes, I'm sure it will be fine.'

Ziggy rang off before Rachel could say anything else. With Chrystal Mack missing, he wasn't about to run the risk of his son disappearing. He should have done this right from the start.

Ziggy took the M621, to join the M1 motorway before exiting onto the Denby Dale road towards Holmfirth. The weather had taken a turn, and freezing fog had descended from seemingly nowhere. He crawled along local country roads to his destination, and it took him over an hour to do a forty-minute journey. He finally pulled off the road close to the barn conversion where Frankie lived. When he'd read H and F Cohen on the foot of the letterhead that Freddie had handed to him, it had triggered something, but he hadn't been able to work out what at the time. As with most things, the answer had popped into his head midway through his rant at Whitmore.

Ziggy abandoned his car a few hundred metres from the sweeping driveway, partly because of the condition of the road, but also, he wanted the element of surprise. He had made the decision not to call ahead, but none of the anger he had felt had dissipated on his drive over. When he knocked on the door, it was with full force. He called her name several times.

'I know you're in, Frankie – your car is here.' In fact, there were two cars, a supposedly repossessed Mercedes CLK and a Range Rover. Judging from the amount of leaves that had gathered around the wheels, both had been there for some time.

The door was eventually thrown open, and a harassed-looking Frankie stared at him. 'What the fuck, Ziggy?'

He pushed her to one side and entered the hallway.

'Where do you think you're going?' she called after him as he headed into the kitchen.

'Who else is here?'

'No one. Ziggy, what the hell is going on?'

'What haven't you told me?' He turned and looked at her.

'What?' Frankie looked shocked, completely taken aback.

'When I was last here. Why didn't you tell me who your ex-husband is?' Frankie looked at him, eyes wide open.

'What difference would that make?'

'Your ex-husband is Howard Cohen. Howard Cohen, the crook, the gangster wannabe. And you're still in touch with him?'

'What? I'm not sure what you're getting at?'

'You gave me the impression that you had had nothing to do with him.'

'That's what you took away from the conversation. I didn't say that.'

'How do you know the O'Connors?'

'Who?'

'Don't give me that shit. Stephen O'Connor. Esso. How do you know him?'

Frankie ignored the question and walked past Ziggy, filled the kettle with water and turned it on to boil. 'I think we need to take a minute here. I have no idea where any of this is coming from, or why you're so angry, but can we at least sit down and talk? I can't stand all the shouting, and I really don't do anger.'

Ziggy was breathing heavily. He closed his eyes, took a few deep breaths and gripped the worktop he was leaning against. This hadn't gone the way he had planned. Frankie was right; he needed to calm down.

'Now, what would you like to drink? I have camomile tea?'

Ziggy shrugged his shoulders, he had no preference what they drank. 'Sure,' he said.

'Shall we sit down and start again?' She gestured to the sofa. Ziggy took a seat whilst Frankie finished the tea. She brought it over on a tray, stirring as she sat down, making sure to release the full flavour of the leaves. She passed Ziggy a huge mug and sat down on the opposite sofa.

'Now, do you want to tell me where all this has come from?' she said, as they sipped.

Ziggy closed his eyes as he took a drink. The smell and flavour took him back to a memory of himself and Lolly discussing the state of the world around his kitchen table. It wasn't a flavour he relished, but he drank it nonetheless.

After a few minutes of silence and a chance to catch his breath, he was able to get his emotions under control, somewhat. Taking a deep breath, he explained the fresh evidence, namely the emails, the letterhead, and why he thought that Frankie had been holding out on him. 'I just want the truth. Are you mixed up in all this, and how does it involve Lolly?'

Frankie was silent for a minute, then stood up, walking around Ziggy with her cup in her hand. 'You are right. Howard Cohen is my ex-husband. I have no idea why Lolly hadn't told you that. We have some shared business interests, but that's all.' She paused and placed her cup on the draining board behind him. 'Stephen O'Connor, as far as I'm aware, drives for Howard, and looks after his business interests when Howard is out of the country.' She sat down opposite Ziggy, leaning forwards and staring into his face. 'What else would you like to know?'

Ziggy shifted on the sofa and moved into a more comfortable position. His eyes suddenly started flitting from side to side and felt weighed down. He reached forwards, trying to place the cup he was holding onto the table in front of him, but his depth perception seemed to be off. Scrabbling around, he put a hand down at the side of him to steady himself, but everything seemed to be made of water. He vaguely wondered if he was having a stroke and tried to call out to Frankie for help, but he couldn't get his lips to move.

The last thing he remembered before blackness took over, was the sound of the cup smashing into a thousand pieces.

33

Wednesday, 25th September 2002

Sadie was still trying to contact Ziggy. She had left message after message on both his personal and home phone. She'd even called round to his house on her way home, but there had been no answer. At a loss, she had tried calling Rachel but had had no joy there either.

She knew – hell, everyone knew – that Ziggy always sailed close to the wind, but she feared he had really blown it this time. Giving her head a shake and taking a few deep breaths, she pushed open the main door to the Major Investigations' office. There was a buzz around the room, a low hum as each officer went about their work. Every enquiry generated a huge amount of paperwork, most of it tedious but absolutely necessary. Sadie headed over to the corner workstations where the close-knit team worked. Nick was already at his desk.

'What's the latest?' she asked as she placed her bag in the bottom drawer of her desk and hung up her coat.

'We've got Freddie O'Connor in custody. I picked him up

yesterday, holding him initially on blackmail charges based on the emails he passed to Ziggy. Interview room booked, was hoping you'd join me.' said Nick. 'Whitmore is about to give a briefing and has asked Peter and myself to join you. I have no idea where Ziggy is or what is even happening with that.' Nick sounded exasperated.

'Sounds like you need a brew.'

'If that brew contains vodka, then I'm in.'

Sadie laughed. 'Ha ha, just milk and sugar.' She headed off to the kitchen, greeting colleagues as she went. More than one asked if she'd heard from Ziggy. Some were genuinely concerned, most were interested in the gossip.

Across the office, she could see Peter heading her way. She sighed inwardly and silently prayed that he wouldn't see her.

'Sadie, hi, how are you feeling?' He placed a hand on her shoulder, which she politely shrugged off.

'Hi, Peter, I'm good thanks.' She'd finished making the brews and turned to head back to Nick. Peter followed her.

She passed Nick his coffee just as Whitmore entered the room, and everyone repositioned themselves to focus their attention on him. Sadie had handed everything to the incident team before she had left late last night, but she still had a notebook full of actions, all fighting for attention.

Whitmore shuffled uncomfortably at the front, and, as she was deputy SIO, he beckoned Sadie to join him.

He cleared his throat and greeted the room.

He looks like a man under pressure, thought Sadie, opening her notebook to a clean page.

'I'm not even sure where to start, in all honesty.' Whitmore coughed, as all eyes turned to him. 'By fair means or foul, Detective Inspector Thornes has uncovered new evidence. After some outstanding work by officers overnight, it would seem valid and needs following up as soon as possible.' He glanced around the room, and Sadie took the chance to speak up.

'Sir, I believe Freddie O'Connor was brought in last night. Nick and I have an interview scheduled with him for later this morning.'

Whitmore turned to her, nodding, 'Good stuff.'

'Any news on the second lot of carpet fibres?' asked one of the uniforms from the rear of the room who was supporting the door-to-door carpet enquiries.

Angela jumped in, 'Ah, you're referring to those that were found on the glove left in Ben Thornes school bag? Only just had this back but,' she consulted the forensic report that had just landed in her inbox. 'They are a match for the colour found at the murder scene of Doctor Leila Turner.'

Sadie shot round and stared at her colleague. 'Bloody hell, really? When did we find that out?'

'It's literally just landed in the inbox,' said Angela, heading to the printer so she could pass the report to Sadie.

With her hand shaking, Sadie read through it. 'Ochre seventies polyester acrylic – damn. It is the same.' She turned to Whitmore. 'We have to search all known locations for the O'Connors, as a matter of urgency.'

'We have a warrant in place at the mother's house. She lives in Middleton,' said Whitmore. 'Stephen O'Connor, Esso – or E. Soh to give him his "street" name – has an apartment by Leeds Dock, so we're coordinating search teams. Both brothers need to be taken into custody, and there will be a team briefing following this update.' Whitmore paused and turned to Nick and Peter. 'It's evident now that the money-laundering case you have been working on is tied in with the murder enquiry. Can you update the team on everything you learnt at the interview with the student?'

Nick stayed seated, clearly happy for Inspector Stiles to take this one. Sadie noticed Stiles adjust his jacket sleeves and run a finger around his collar as he stood up. She felt certain if there was a mirror nearby, he would have looked in it.

'In conclusion,' he said, as he wrapped up the team's findings, 'whilst DI Thornes may have made several assumptions, he was, in fact, correct about the two cases being linked.'

'Thank you Stiles. Finally, but of no less importance this morning, Chrystal Mack, the reporter from the *Yorkshire Press*, was officially declared missing. Due to the threat against her, the search for her whereabouts has taken high priority. A team has been allocated and enquiries are ongoing. Needless to say, we have considerable media interest, but the PR team will deal with it. We have no further comment to make if approached.'

He looked around the room. 'Right, you all know what you're supposed to be doing. Let's get to it.'

Sadie, Nick, Peter and Angela waited until the room had cleared, then gathered their chairs around DCS Whitmore.

'Sadie, what's your strategy for interviewing Freddie O'Connor?' asked Whitmore as soon as the rest of the officers had dispersed.

'Very much exploratory at this stage. We know he is a CHIS for DI Thornes, hence getting the email info and the letterhead – albeit I'd had it from Ziggy first. At that stage, we had no idea – or should I say Ziggy had no idea – who had sent them.'

'Good, good,' said Whitmore. 'Nick, I think you should be in on the interviews too.'

Nick nodded in agreement.

'Stiles, I really need you to firm up any evidence you

have on the money laundering. How exactly does it tie in? What role had the Cohens played in all this?' Whitmore said.

'Sir, since that name came to light, I've done some digging. Howard Cohen has an arrest record. Nothing recently, and nothing that we've been able to pin on him but suspected cheque and credit-card fraud ten years ago. He's connected to the pawnshops that Stephen O'Connor runs. He's down as a shareholder but not a director, possibly to lessen his tax liabilities. A look at his financials tells me he is very rich, which might stem from the alarmingly high-interest rates that the pawnshops charge on their loans.'

'Great, stay on that. Find him, bring him in.'

Whitmore wrapped everything up, and they all set about their duties. The tension in the air was palpable as Sadie felt all the strands were finally coming together. She pulled a chair round the quadrant of desks, Nick, Peter and Angela joining her.

'Have any of you heard from Ziggy?' she asked, fearing she already knew the answer.

It was confirmed when all three shook their heads in unison.

'He's either gone AWOL, or the wrong people have caught up with him,' said Peter very matter-of-factly, and the others were inclined to agree with him.

'Let's all keep trying his mobile when we can,' suggested Sadie, though she was more concerned than she let on, especially with not being able get a hold of Rachel either. She'd made Whitmore aware, and he was sending uniform to the house. She turned to Nick. 'Custody is about to get busy, so shall we crack on and interview Freddie ?'

Nick nodded in agreement, and the two huddled together to go over the strategy whilst Angela and Stiles headed to the money-laundering incident room to update the boards.

Once they'd left, Sadie sighed. 'This is just an unholy mess, isn't it?'

Nick looked up from where he'd been making notes. 'Weird how it all connects.'

'What's your theory? If you have one.'

'I can't understand what Frankie Cohen has to do with any of it, if I'm honest. Lolly was dating Francesca Cohen. So what? If Howard Cohen was up to something dodgy, it didn't mean his ex-wife was.'

'Hmm. I'll give Frankie a call, see if she's seen or heard anything from him. Right, let's go say hello to young O'Connor.'

34

'What cell is he in?' asked Sadie.

'Twelve,' replied the custody sergeant. 'He's been well-behaved so far.'

Sadie walked down to the cell whilst Nick set up the interview room. She peered through the viewing panel and saw that Freddie was curled up in the foetal position, facing the wall. She slammed the viewing panel shut and opened the door.

'Mr O'Connor. Nice snooze, was it?'

'Fuck off,' came the surly reply.

'Now then, that's not a great start, is it?'

'I'm not saying owt.'

'Of course, that's your prerogative, but we will ask you all the same.'

She knew that would illicit a response. Freddie bolted upright and swung his legs round, planting his feet firmly on the cold concrete floor. 'Aww man, can't you leave me alone?'

Sadie laughed. 'No can do, I'm afraid. Come on, grab your blanket if you want. It's time for a quick chat.'

Despite his continued protests, Freddie went along with Sadie, muttering profanities all the way. She showed him into the interview room and took the seat opposite, next to Nick. The necessary introductions and legal statements were made as he pressed record on the machine.

'Freddie, are you comfortable there? Is there anything I can get you. A drink, perhaps?'

'Nah, it's all good.'

'You have been told that you have the right to solicitor, but you have declined that. Are you happy to carry on answering our questions without representation?'

'Yeah, whatever, innit.'

Sadie looked at the young man opposite her and couldn't help but feel sorry for him. He was wearing a thin tracksuit top that was zipped up to his chin, and he was sucking on the collar.

'Freddie, on or around the twenty-fourth of September 2002, you handed copies of an email that contained threats against a newspaper reporter to Detective Inspector Thornes. What can you tell me about that?' Sadie pulled the relevant sheet of paper out of the folder Nick had placed on the desk in front of them.

Freddie leant forwards, squinting. 'No comment,' he said after a cursory glance.

Sadie heard Nick sigh. She felt much the same.

'Can you tell us how you came across these documents?'

'No comment.'

'Are these documents yours?'

'No comment.'

'It's just that, if they are yours, you have a much bigger case to answer. One that we're currently investigating as a high priority.'

Freddie lifted his head up. 'Like what?' Sadie saw a flash of panic in his eyes.

'The subject of this email, Chrystal Mack, has gone missing.'

Freddie's eyes went as wide as two saucepans. She watched as he swallowed. 'Can I have some water, please?'

Nick obliged by pouring water from the jug in front of them. Freddie drank a cup full, like he'd been in the desert for months.

'So, what can you tell me about this email, Freddie?'

'I don't know owt about that woman.'

Sadie noticed sweat was pouring off him, making the already stale odour emanating from him ten times worse. Wishing they were in a room with windows that would open, she continued. 'Let's start again. The email, Freddie. What do you know about it?'

'I found 'em di'nt I.' He folded his arms around himself and leant forwards. 'They're nowt to do wi' me.'

Sadie smiled reassuringly and softened her tone, hoping to put him at ease somewhat. 'Where did you find it?'

Freddie looked up, his face a nasty shade of crimson. Nick, an expert in body language, watched as he swallowed again and his foot started tapping loudly on the floor. The unconscious behaviour of a person that wanted to run.

'Nothing to say for yourself, Freddie?' asked Sadie.

'I want my brief. Nah, sod that. I want that other detective bloke.'

'What other detective bloke?' asked Nick, jumping in, momentarily thrown.

'Always hanging round Cross Green, 'arassing me. I should report 'im.' Freddie folded his arms defiantly.

Sadie and Nick exchanged confused looks. Nick shifted

in his seat, and Sadie leant forwards. 'Tell us what you know, Freddie. It will help you in the long run.'

'That other fella, the one who's been 'arassing me. He wanted some information as well.'

'I'm well aware that you're a source of information for Detective Inspector Thornes,' said Sadie.

'Yeah well, he wanted some info. Mr Forns or whatever his name is wanted some stuff on our kid.'

'Our kid meaning your brothers? Stephen and Robbie?'

'Yeah.'

'What did he want?'

'Anything. I told him that they'd had a falling out and he wanted to know why.'

'OK, go on.'

'Anyways, I found them papers and handed them to Mr Forns. I swear down that's all I did. He promised me a shed load of cash if I found out anythin'. I'm not gonna get owt now, am I?' He kicked his legs out underneath the table, huffing.

Sadie sat back and looked at Nick. 'You know, you could make this a lot easier for yourself. Right now, we have a missing woman and you're the only person who seems to know anything about it. Let's try this again. DI Thornes asked you to find out why your brothers had fallen out and you turned up an email. Why do I get the feeling that you're not telling us something?'

Freddie glanced between Nick and Sadie. 'You can't say it came from me, right?'

'Go on.'

'Ste were mad at our Robbie cos he threatened some kid called Ben.'

Sadie frowned. 'Ben?'

'Yeah, some school kid or summat.'

Sadie's heart was thudding, and she could feel the tension pouring off Nick. 'What else?' she persisted.

'Ste said he thought it was bang out of order, and that he didn't care what Howard thought. Kids shouldn't be threatened like that, and not at school. Anyways, shit really started flying when Ste found out Rob had dropped his glove when he'd tucked the note in that kid's school bag.'

Sadie had to take a minute to digest Freddie's bombshell. 'Robbie placed a note in Ben's school bag and left a glove behind?'

''Swhat I 'eard.'

Sadie glanced briefly at Nick and made a note.

Not sure which point to pick up on first, she started with the easy one. 'Freddie, you mentioned Howard. Who's he?'

'Aww fuck, I'm going down for this, aren't I? God, I should have kept me mouth shut.' The detectives watched as Freddie huffed and swore, stood up and sat down.

'Calm down, Freddie, we can sort this out,' said Nick. 'Sit back down and let's just talk, yeah?'

Freddie did as he was told and reluctantly took his seat again. 'We work for Howard. Well, I don't, but Ste and Robbie do. He's not around all the time, but I know when he is cos our kid is always right twitchy. The bloke has him jumping through hoops.' He took another drink of water. 'More Ste than Rob. Rob just does as he's told. It's Ste that does most of the work, in the pawnshops and that.'

Sadie just sat back, taking notes, and let Freddie talk. It was like the floodgates had opened and there was no stopping him. She interrupted occasionally to clarify a couple of points, but in the space of twenty minutes, she reckoned they could close at least three open enquiries, and had firm leads for others. Nick's hand flew across his notebook as he too made a copious amount of notes.

When she sensed Freddie was running out of steam, she picked up her questions again. 'You've certainly given us a lot to work with, Freddie, and we'll make sure the relevant people are aware of how helpful you've been should any charges be brought further down the line.'

Freddie let out a long sigh and started sucking the top of his tracksuit again.

'One final question, Freddie. Where are your brothers?'

35

As Freddie was taken back to his cell, Sadie and Nick headed upstairs to the MIT office. Bursting through the doors, they headed to Whitmore's office to share the updates.

'The O'Connor brothers are at an industrial unit they rent on Cross Green,' said Sadie, breathlessly. 'He reckons they're waiting for some kind of delivery.'

Whitmore picked up the phone and called the head of the search unit, notifying him to have the team ready to go. He also contacted Armed Response as a precaution. Once the appropriate teams were in place, he briefed the remaining officers and made sure everyone knew what their role would be.

As Sadie strapped herself into her Kevlar vest and pulled on her high-vis jacket, she turned to Nick.

'Do you think we might find Chrystal Mack there?'

'Got to be honest, Sadie, I think at this stage, I'm just hoping we'll find Ziggy.'

They had both been trying him on and off, with no luck. Uniform hadn't been able to find Rachel and Ben, so units were also out searching for them.

Three police vans and the Armed Response unit had parked around the corner from the industrial unit, aiming for the element of surprise.

Sadie's radio crackled into life. She heard Firearms issuing orders, and she hung back at the rear with Nick and Whitmore in case any shots were discharged. She heard the 'Go, go, go' command, and what looked like organised chaos ensued.

Firearms officers ran straight into the unit, weapons drawn, red dots shining everywhere. Shouts of 'Clear!' came from the various rooms until one officer shouted, 'Armed police, do not move!'

Sadie followed the voice, and in a small back room, she saw Stephen and Robbie O'Connor. Stephen looked as if he was about to run, but with nowhere to go, and several semi-automatic weapons trained on him, he seemed to realise the futility. Both brothers reluctantly stood with their hands in the air. Stacks and stacks of cash were all around them. Notes of varying denominations were scattered around, strewn all over desks, and on the ochre-carpeted floor. Several banknote counters sat on desks, some still reeling through cash, some standing idle. Sadie stepped forwards, taking the handcuffs from her belt and snapping them around Stephen O'Connor's wrists whilst Nick did the same with Robbie, simultaneously reading them their rights.

Once the brothers were safely ensconced in the custody van, the team returned inside to search for the missing *Yorkshire Press* reporter, but there seemed to be no trace. Exiting and handing the scene over to Forensics, they headed back to the station.

Elated with the outcome of the arrests and the incredible amount of evidence they had seen, celebrations were somewhat tempered. They were well aware that a woman was still missing, and that somehow Chrystal Mack was tied up in all of it. Whitmore walked into the office, and they all headed into a conference room for the debrief.

As Sadie was about to sit down, her mobile phone rang and Rachel Thornes flashed on the screen. Excusing herself, she answered whilst walking through the office to the stairwell where it was quieter.

'Rachel, hi. How are you? Where are you?'

'Hey, Sadie, I heard you'd been looking for me. I'm sorry, I thought Ziggy would have told you.'

'He might if I knew where he was. Is he with you?'

'No. What do you mean? You don't know where he is?'

Sadie heard Ben chattering away in the background. 'Rachel, I haven't seen Ziggy for nearly twenty-four hours. We're right in the middle of a big case, a couple actually, and he's gone AWOL.'

She heard Rachel ask Ben to be quiet, then a huge sigh. 'I'm at my mum's. Ziggy asked me to bring Ben here.'

'Do you have any idea where he might be?'

The line went quiet. When Rachel spoke again, Sadie heard the uncertainty in her voice.

'Have you tried Frankie's?'

'Not as yet, but that's our next stop. Do you think he might be there?'

'Oh, I don't know, Sadie. His head has been all over the place recently, and I'm worried about him. He hasn't been the same since ... since we lost Lolly.'

'I know. He's been a bit unpredictable at work, too. Look,

as long as you and Ben are safe, that's one thing. I'm just about to go into a briefing, so I'll make sure you're kept up to date with what's happening. I'm sure Ziggy will be fine. Try not to worry.'

They said their goodbyes and ended the call. Sadie wished she felt the confidence she feigned in her voice to Rachel. Heading back into the conference room, all kinds of scenarios as to where he might be ran through her head.

'This had better be good, Ziggy, or so help me,' she muttered under her breath.

36

Ziggy flinched as he struggled to open his eyes, then recoiled as light seeped under his eyelids. His head felt thick and groggy, like a hangover but ten times worse. He tried to shake his head, but that only aggravated it more. Instinctively, he tried to move his arms, only to find them somehow pinned behind him. He tried his legs next, but they too refused to budge, held in place by something. He could feel the stickiness around his mouth and knew immediately it had been taped shut. He shook his head again, more gently this time, but the pounding restricted him from anything but the smallest of movements. The inside of his mouth felt like the bottom of a proverbial bird cage. He fought against his bindings and saw that the ones holding his legs weren't anything special, just everyday packaging tape. Certainly not enough to hold him. His hands were a different matter. They were fastened behind him, and he could feel the plastic digging into his skin – a cable tie of some sort?

If only he could shake the groggy, hungover feeling. He stopped struggling for a second to gather his breath and his thoughts. Inhaling deeply, he resettled his nervous system, allowing him to function from a place of measured control rather than out-and-out panic. He mentally assessed his situation.

He was in Frankie's house – or at least that's where he had been.

He was strapped to a chair.

He had been drugged by Frankie.

He needed to let someone know where he was.

He guessed that Frankie would have taken his phone, so he needed to break free and look for a landline or an escape route. She couldn't possibly have moved him on her own, which meant there was someone else in the house that he had yet to meet.

With a sharp kick of his left leg, he heard and felt some of the binding split. Kicking out again, he felt more movement until it finally snapped. He repeated the same with his right leg, kicking harder this time knowing how much force to use. Standing and unhooking his arms from the back of the chair, he took a closer look at his surroundings.

The light that had blinded him earlier was streaming in through a small window. He figured he must be at basement level somewhere. He did a full 360 look to take in his surroundings. There was a flight of stairs to his right. He ventured up to them and used his shoulder to shove the door, but it didn't move. He banged his shoulder against it again, harder this time, as best he could with his hands still behind him and whilst balancing on the narrow top step.

With the tape still around his mouth, his shouts came out as a mumbled noise, neither loud enough nor long enough to attract attention.

Heading back down, he saw a washing machine, a separate tumble dryer, and a small sink in the far corner. He stood in front of them, looking for something sharp that might help him release his hands, but found nothing.

On the far wall was what looked like house-move boxes with *kitchen*, *bedroom*, *lounge* scrawled on them in black felt tip. He closed his eyes as he realised that it was Lolly's hand-writing. A memory flashed back to him of storing some boxes for Lolly one time whilst she was away overnight with work. The familiarity of the spider-like handwriting filled him with same sadness that had settled within him on the day of her death. Stalling for a moment, he was filled with something else. An urge for justice so powerful it almost took his breath away. He had to see this through. For Lolly. For Bill and Irene. For Ben. For everyone who had loved her. With a renewed sense of determination, he looked more closely at the boxes.

They were definitely the same ones he had stored for her, the ones she had packed, ready to move in with Frankie. Turning round, so he had his back to the boxes, he used his cuffed hands to flip open one of the flaps that hadn't been sealed. The box labelled *kitchen* was primarily full of crockery, but tucked into one corner was a steak knife. He turned again and felt around, flinching slightly as his hand landed on it. He returned to the chair and, after much fiddling around, which involved dropping the knife a few times, he finally held it in a position that would hopefully cut through the plastic. Slowly, very slowly, he started carving.

37

Everyone gathered around as Whitmore began updating the wider team with the developments in both cases, the entire department having now been brought together to pool resources on the ground.

'We are currently trying to locate Howard Cohen, along with his ex-wife Francesca. Thanks to the rather unorthodox approach taken by DI Thornes, we can connect this case to the death of Doctor Leila Turner through forensic evidence, namely the carpet fibres. As luck would have it, when the O'Connor brothers were arrested, the search team recovered a sample of carpet from the room where the cash was being held. This has been sent away for more extensive testing, but preliminary findings are that it is the same colour as that identified on the glove connected to the threat to young Ben Thornes, as well as those found at the murder scene.'

There were nods and murmurs of understanding from around the table.

'More compelling evidence has come to light with regard to the CCTV around Doctor Turner's apartment leading up to her death, which also ties the brothers in. Angela, I believe you have the details?'

Angela blushed, as she found public speaking uncomfortable, but she pushed through. 'The team has uncovered CCTV footage of what we believe to be the car that the student victim, Daniel Kimble , was driven around in. The same car that was also seen outside Doctor Turner's apartment in the days leading up to her death. We've had the backup footage from Francesca Cohen's building, which is now being trawled. Updates to follow.' There were more murmurings around the room as she passed the report over to Whitmore.

'Excellent work, thank you, DC Dove.' Whitmore shifted his focus across the room. 'Peter, what's the latest with the money laundering?'

Inspector Stiles coughed and pulled out his notebook. 'Sir, I have images of the O'Connor brothers that I am going to show to our witness, Daniel, so we can get a positive identification.'

'Good stuff. Sadie, what are your next steps?'

'Locating Howard and Frankie Cohen, sir. I believe a team is about to head over to Francesca Cohen's address in Holmfirth, so I will join them whilst Nick and Peter interview the O'Connors.'

'Excellent. Let's not forget we still have a missing woman who is tied up in all this, somehow. Whilst search teams are doing all they can, remain vigilant.' Whitmore looked around the room, sardonically. 'And if you happen to see your colleague, DI Thornes, please do let me know.' No one could mistake the bitterness in his tone.

Everyone dispersed and broke into smaller groups or left to go about their actions.

'Daniel, I'm going to show you a picture of two men. I'd like to know if you can identify either of them. Is that OK?'

Peter and Nick were back in the conference room, chatting to the student who had fallen for the squaring scam.

'Sure.'

The officer that was sitting next to Daniel showed him the photographs.

'That's Arroh,' he said, pointing to the first photograph of Robbie O'Connor. He pulled the second one of Stephen O'Connor's closer. 'That's Esso, the dude that drove me round Leeds – the one with the long leather coat.'

'Thank you, Daniel, you've been extremely helpful.'

Peter ended the connection and turned to Nick. 'Got 'em. Let's go chase up Forensics.'

Nick was already a step ahead of him, heading for the door. As they entered the MIT office, Angela turned to them.

'Just the pair,' she said.

'What have you got?'

'I've just been having a chat with your pals in ECU.' She looked at Peter. 'Turns out that the company registration number on that letterhead is being investigated for corporate camouflage, raising fake invoices and the like. We believe the fake bank account details tie in with the bigger scheme your team has been tailing, and guess who is one of the trustees? Howard Cohen. I'm just on my way to update DCS Whitmore.'

Peter could hardly control his excitement. He turned to Nick. 'Excellent news. It's all coming together, isn't it?'

'We're getting there, that's for sure. Let's go see what these two reprobates have to say for themselves.'

Peter and Nick opened the door to the interview room and introduced themselves to Robbie O'Connor. The room itself was small, just wide enough for a desk and four chairs with very little space around it. The furniture, like most things in the room, was battered and had seen better days. The walls were painted a dark blue with an emergency buzzer situated on the wall near the door. The paint was scratched and wearing thin, scuffed and pitted. The desk faired a little better, and the chairs were plastic moulded, not ideally suited for sitting in for long periods of time. The recording equipment was next to the wall, and Peter sat next to it in order to operate it. They'd agreed that Nick would lead, and Peter would observe.

Once all the introductions were made, Nick fired up his laptop , adjusted his notebook and straightened the brown file he had brought with him, taking his time, putting the suspect on edge.

'Robbie, you have declined your right to have a solicitor present, is that correct?' asked Nick.

Robbie O'Connor shrugged his shoulders.

'I need you to speak up for the tape, Robbie.'

He slowly pushed himself into an upright position and confirmed the lack of legal representation. 'Nowt to hide,' he concluded.

Robbie was the tallest of the three brothers, but they all had the same stringy, lanky build with closely cropped hair and very ordinary looks. He had clearly suffered from acne as a teen, and his skin was as pockmarked as the table he was leaning on.

Nick watched as Robbie rolled his eyes, looking thoroughly bored. Nick knew silence was a powerful interview weapon, so he let it descend upon the room as everyone waited.

After a heavy sigh, Robbie finally spoke. 'What do you wanna know?'

'I'd like to know where you were on the following dates.' Nick consulted the file in front of him and reeled off the dates related to the night of Lolly's murder, and also when the witness had identified Robbie in the potential money-laundering case.

'How am I supposed to know?'

Robbie had walked straight into their game plan. Nick turned the laptop and showed the screen to Robbie. He proceeded to play the various footage they had of Robbie's car driving in and around the Library pub in Leeds, of Daniel climbing into the car and at various points as it drove around Leeds.

'Doesn't mean I was driving though, does it?' came his flippant reply.

'Are you saying it isn't you?'

The final piece of footage was clearer. As the car pulled over to the McDonald's at the Oakwood, the side profile of the driver could be made out. With absolutely no attempt to hide his face, Robbie's troubled skin stood out like a beacon.

Not so cocky now, thought Nick, watching Robbie's reaction closely. He looked extremely uncomfortable.

'Do you agree that this is you, Robbie?'

'No comment.'

'This is your car, isn't it?' Nick pressed.

'No comment.'

'What were you doing in Roundhay at that time of night, Robbie?'

'No comment.' He huffed and blew out his cheeks whilst folding his arms across his chest. 'Are we done yet?'

'No, we're not. Robbie. Let's focus on the first video footage we saw,' Nick spoke whilst Peter played the footage again. 'Are you familiar with the Merchant Quay apartments, Robbie?'

'No comment.'

'Do you know this area of Leeds?'

'No comment.'

'Your brother, Stephen, also lives in apartments not dissimilar to these, isn't that right?'

'No comment.'

'There are clearly two people in this car, of similar build with one taller than the other. Does that match the description of you and your brother?'

'No comment.'

Deciding to change tack, Nick let the silence descend for a minute or two and shuffled his notes. 'Do you know a Francesca Cohen, Robbie?'

Robbie's head snapped up. 'Why?'

'Do you know her? Your reaction tells me you do.'

'Why do you want to know?'

'Do you know a Doctor Leila Turner, or you may have known her as Lolly?' Nick watched the colour drain from Robbie's face.

'No.'

'But you do know Francesca Cohen, and her husband Howard Cohen?'

'Ex-husband,' said Robbie, and immediately realised his mistake.

Nick had to force himself not to smile. He made no sign of having heard the slip-up. He carried on. 'Were you working for Howard Cohen when you were driving past the apartment building?'

'No comment.'

'We know that your brother Stephen works for Howard, so perhaps you were helping on these occasions too?'

When they received a further 'no comment' responses, Peter wound up the interview, both detectives hoping they would get more from his brother.

'How do you know Howard Cohen, Stephen?'

'No comment.'

'Do you work for him?'

'No comment.'

'Does he own the pawnshop that you work in?'

'No comment.'

'Do you act as his driver?'

'No comment.'

Peter tried not to let his frustration show, but he and Nick had been sitting with Stephen O'Connor for close to ninety minutes, and they were getting nowhere. He, too, had refused a solicitor, even a duty solicitor, but he had also refused to answer any questions other than to confirm his name. The custody clock was ticking, and they only had a limited amount of time. Pausing the recording, Peter instructed the custody officer to return Stephen to the cell whilst he and Nick assessed their strategy.

'It's obvious it's him outside Frankie Cohen's flat. The black leather coat gives it away. How can he continue to deny it?'

'He hasn't though, has he? He's said "no comment",' said Nick as he punched the vending machine for a cup of tea. He passed one to Peter and started one for himself.

'Why go "no comment" if you've nothing to hide?'

'It's frustrating, I know, but you can't let it get to you.

Stephen O'Connor is the smartest of the three brothers. We have to play him at his own game.'

They headed to a side office and sat down at a spare desk.

'What do you suggest then?' asked Peter, burning his lip on the hot liquid and almost spilling it down him. 'This is awful, by the way,' he said, pushing the cup away from him.

Nick chuckled. 'It's not Yorkshire Tea, that's why.' He flicked open his notebook. 'It's obvious that he's not going to give us anything. We need to up the ante, really drill into what role he played. The money-laundering stuff just segues into it all, I think. The crux of the remaining interview time has to be focused on the murder.'

Agreeing that strategy, this time with Nick leading, they headed back into the interview, tea cups thrown away en route.

'Stephen, what can you tell us about your movements on the night of fourteenth September 2002?'

The suspect stared at them both, glassy-eyed. 'No comment.'

Nick carried on as though Stephen hadn't spoken. 'We have evidence that on that night, the fourteenth, when Doctor Leila Turner was brutally murdered, you were in the vicinity of the apartment that she shared with her partner, Francesca Cohen.'

Stephen crossed and uncrossed his legs. He leant forwards in his seat and repeated, 'No comment.'

Again Nick continued as if he hadn't spoken. 'We have quite a bit of solid evidence that places you at the scene of a murder, Stephen. Do you have anything to say to that?'

Silence.

'As you've chosen not to have legal representation at this time, I can disclose that we have found carpet fibres that connect you to the murder victim, to the money-laundering operation and also to threats of violence being made against a minor and a newspaper reporter, who is also missing.' Nick looked up from his notes and saw Stephen's face pale.

'Do you have any comment to make now?'

'Yeah, I want my brief.'

38

Wednesday, 25th September 2002

Ziggy saw light streaming into the basement from under the door as it opened. He had retaken his seat on the kitchen chair to which he'd been bound, still diligently cutting away at the plastic ties that held his hands together. He stopped and remained completely still as a commotion erupted, led by a female voice screeching. He couldn't be sure as it was so high pitched and it was distorted, but he thought it was Frankie.

'Get down those stairs, you little bitch!'

A yelp, followed by several thuds and a body appeared at Ziggy's feet. What the hell was happening? He was disoriented and confused. It couldn't possibly be Frankie, the love of Lolly's life, the softly spoken woman who was now screeching like a banshee?

He didn't dare reveal that he had broken loose from his bindings as Frankie flew down the stairs after the body. She marched over to the prone figure on the floor and delivered a swift kick to the head with her pointed shoes.

'And you can stay here!'

Shock must have been written all over Ziggy's face, as she caught him staring at her.

'Ah, we're awake now, are we?' She walked towards him, and he flinched as she reached out to remove the tape from his mouth. 'Make a noise and it goes back on.' She unceremoniously ripped the adhesive, causing Ziggy to let out an involuntary yelp as it ripped his skin.

Frankie stepped back and kicked the figure on the floor again, rolling it onto its back with the heel of her shoe. Ziggy did a double take as the head fell towards him. Chrystal Mack. *What the fuck?* She looked to be in a bad way, with a black eye and cuts and bruises all over her face.

Frankie saw him looking. 'Oh, don't worry about her. She's had enough diazepam to knock out an elephant. She'll be asleep for a long time.' Frankie walked round the basement, touching the boxes and eventually came to rest on the washing machine. Ziggy could see she was still agitated by the erratic rubbing of her hands and the tightly clenched muscles of her jaw, but some of the anger seemed to have worn off. He watched as she paused in her movements, then began pacing backwards and forwards furiously.

'It didn't need to be like this,' she whined, her voice full of self-pity. 'This is all your fault.' She turned and glared at Ziggy. 'You always got in the way. Did you know that?'

Ziggy didn't respond. She was erratic, unpredictable, but more than that, she was volatile. He was struggling to equate the unhinged persona in front of him to the image he had of Frankie. He continued to remain silent, tensed, ready to move out of her way or defend himself if needed. He was equally aware of the woman lying unconscious in front of him. He could see she was still breathing, but blood was trickling from her ear, which was never a good sign.

He listened as Frankie rambled, though he didn't fully understand every word as she spoke so quickly.

'I did love her, you know? Maybe not at first. At first she was just a means to an end, but over time, I fell in love with her, I think.' Frankie walked over and leant against the washing machine, lost in her own memories. 'She was special. I could see why you were best friends. She was very loyal. Once you were part of Lolly's circle, that was that, she rarely dropped anyone. We couldn't have a night out in Leeds without bumping into people who knew her. She was like a local celebrity.' She took a breath. 'I remember one time, someone she used to go to uni with approached her. A mutual friend had fallen on hard times, started using drugs and was in a bad way, homeless. Lolly found them on the street and took them to St George's Crypt. Made sure they had food, clothes and support to come off the drugs. Takes a special kind of person to do that. To save someone else.' Frankie sighed, her anger replaced by a wistfulness. 'Is that why you loved her? Did she save you?'

Ziggy shrugged his shoulders, but didn't answer.

'Why did you love her?' she asked again.

Ziggy stretched his mouth and tried to generate saliva. His lips were clinging to his teeth, so he licked them. Frankie saw what he was trying to do. He panicked slightly when she reached into one of the boxes, but she took a teacup out and filled it with water for him. She held it to his lips, and the temptation he felt to just stab her in the neck with the steak knife was overpowering. He had to remember the bigger picture, so he fought the urge and sipped the water, gratefully.

'Yes, she saved me. More than once,' he said. He'd never admitted that to anyone before, not even Rachel.

'How, Ziggy? How did she save you?'

'The first time was when I arrived at our foster home with Bill and Irene. I was lost, my parents had both been killed, my brother and sister had their own families, and I felt abandoned. She swept in like a sister and made me her cause. She watched out for me throughout school, and I like to think I helped her too.'

'You did. She told me that. You were her steadying hand. She had to set an example for you. That's what drove her. You were all that mattered.' Frankie let out a deep sigh. 'It wasn't supposed to end this way.'

'In what way, Frankie?'

'In this mess. It was all going so well. Howard was pleased with me, Lolly was none the wiser, but you had to spoil it, didn't you?'

'What did I spoil?'

Frankie hitched herself up, so she was sitting on top of the washing machine. She stared off into space, clearly lost in her own thoughts. When she spoke, it was with a wistful air, almost a longing in her voice.

'For an academic, she was charmingly naive. I blamed you and told her so.' Ziggy didn't interrupt. He was scared she might lose her train of thought. 'You shielded her, didn't you? Always one step ahead, making sure she got the summer job she was looking for, that her dorm room was on campus and not some dump somewhere. She genuinely believed that she had breezed through later life with no stress. Hell, she didn't even know you fenced stolen goods to top up her monthly allowance.' Frankie laughed maniacally.

'How the hell do you know all that?'

'Is that all you've got to say? Don't you want to know how we pulled her in? Why she did what she did?'

Ziggy stayed silent, but his heart was pounding and he had a feeling of being on the precipice of something explosive. He hardly dared breathe when the figure of Chrystal Mack groaned and tried to move. Frankie was immediately on her.

'Get back to sleep, bitch. You're not innocent in all this.'

Chrystal moaned again and made a feeble attempt to lift her head, but the drugs were too powerful and kept her in their grip.

Ziggy looked at Frankie, willing her to pick up where she left off.

'Howie would take all the credit if I let him, but it was all me, really. We'd trialled a few others first, but we fell lucky with Lolly. She was so easy to reel in. Admittedly, I didn't expect to be with her for so long but needs must.' She jumped down from the washing machine and walked over to the packing boxes. 'We would never have moved in together, you know? It was all a front, and I was having too much fun playing her. I kind of miss that.' She flipped opened a box and lifted out pictures that she flicked through, discarding them as she went. 'For the plan to work we had to be particular. Lolly wasn't the first person we looked at. White-van man was getting too much attention, and was too obvious really, so I told Howie we needed to think outside the box if we wanted to grow. That's when I started to look at professionals who legitimately travelled for work. Postal workers, service engineers, that kind of thing. When Lolly signed up for the conference I was attending, I saw that she was a pathologist. Perfect, she'd travel all over the country and no one would suspect such an upstanding member of the community to be a money mule.'

Ziggy was blindsided. *What the fuck?*

39

'Lolly? A money mule? I don't understand,' stuttered Ziggy. 'You're lying. Why? Why would she do that?'

Frankie looked incredulous. 'Why? Because she loved me! She loved me, and she trusted me. She fell for me quickly, but then I had done my homework before meeting her.'

'Homework?'

'Of course, do you take me for some kind of amateur? She'd had a shocking childhood before she met you at your foster home. Drink-addled mother murdered by alcoholic stepfather, left abandoned, unloved. I just needed to play to her unmet needs – something that not even the saintly Ziggy could do.'

'You evil bitch,' said Ziggy through gritted teeth. Now he saw Frankie for what she was, it was taking every ounce of self-control to not jump from the chair and smash her teeth in.

'Hmm, maybe.' Frankie moved onto another box. Ziggy saw it was the kitchen box that he'd taken the knife from. He sent silent prayers to whoever might be listening that she wouldn't notice, though he needn't have bothered. Frankie was in another world entirely.

'She loved me completely. And yes, she trusted me. It was amazingly quick, actually. She must have been crying out for some kind of affection for a long time. Some sense of security. How does that make you feel, Saint Ziggy? Her best friend, but deep down, she was, in fact, incredibly lonely.'

Ziggy didn't know how he felt, other than punched in the solar plexus. His scrambled brain was trying to make sense of what Frankie was saying. Trying to put the pieces together, he asked. 'Where does Howard fit in with all this?'

'Oh, he played his part well. The threatening calls he made to me, the fake letters from solicitors, even the fake house sale. Of course, I needed to play my role of bullied ex for it to be really convincing. He can't take all the glory, but yes, he did his bit.'

'And because Lolly wanted to make you happy, she agreed to what exactly?'

'I lost a little weight, cut a few chunks out of my hair, made sure I looked a little pale. She couldn't bear to see me "suffering" so just as I suspected, she sought Howie out and bargained with him.'

Knowing Lolly as he did, he could see she would want to save Frankie. *'Oh, Lolly.'* A deep sadness washed over him. Why hadn't she told him?

'Bit late for that now. She was so innocent. It was sweet, in a way. I don't think I've ever had anyone defend me quite so fiercely. Of course, in the end, at the end, she had to defend herself.'

Ziggy noticed tears in Frankie's eyes. 'I'd never seen her so angry.'

. . .

Sitting on the bed, Lolly tried to get her head around everything that had happened. How had she got herself into this unholy mess? She thought back to where it had all started. All she had tried to do was protect Frankie. Why would Frankie turn on her so suddenly? Why would she accuse her of having an affair? Surely she knew Lolly well enough to know that would never happen? If she couldn't see after all this time the lengths that she would go to for her, then did Frankie really even love her? Lolly flinched at the thought, feeling the potential hurt and knowing it would be too much to bear. She had sacrificed everything for Frankie. Why couldn't she see that? With tears falling and her heart breaking, she slowly ventured out of the bedroom and back towards the living room to see what she could salvage from the situation. There was that word again.

Thankfully, Frankie had turned off the TV and was on her phone. Lolly hovered at the doorway, wondering who she was speaking to at this time of night. It was past midnight.

'Silly little bitch – "But I love you, Frankie". Honestly, Howard, I'm not sure I can keep this up for much longer. Problem we have is, would she go to her detective friend and reveal all? It's a risk we can't afford to take.'

Silence. Then Frankie spoke again, clearly annoyed by whatever Howard's response had been. 'Oh, you always have to be right, don't you? I've told you I'll sort it.'

Lolly couldn't hold herself back any longer. 'What the fuck is going on?'

Frankie jumped, dropped the phone and turned. 'Oh, I thought you were asleep,' she said in a very matter-of-fact tone.

'What can't you keep up? What's going on, Frankie? Why were you talking to Howard?' Lolly was bewildered, replaying the overheard conversation in her head, trying to put the pieces together whilst Frankie refilled her wine glass and floated about the room with a look of pure hatred on her face.

'Frankie, what's going on? This isn't like you.'

'How the fuck would you know?'

There was so much venom in Frankie's tone that Lolly took a physical step back. Was this the real Frankie she was seeing? Then, with a clarity she had never possessed before, she could see everything for what it was. She felt physically sick. How could she have been so stupid? Wiping her eyes, she turned and started to walk out of the room. 'I need to get out of here.'

Hearing a noise, she turned round to face Frankie and took a step back when she saw she had a knife in her hand.

'I don't think so. Sit down.'

Lolly felt her knees go weak, and she had to reach out her arm to support herself on the doorjamb. She felt the colour drain from her face. She stared at her. 'What the fuck, Frankie? Put the knife down.'

'Oh seriously, enough with the whiney voice.'

Something inside Lolly snapped. She had had enough. She'd been taken for a fool. Frankie and Howard had played her, that much was obvious now. Rage built from her stomach and she exploded forwards, reaching for the knife.

Frankie reacted quickly and brought the blade down in one slicing move. Lolly dodged to the left, but the knife caught her shoulder and tore through her jacket. Before she had a chance to recover, she caught a glimpse of silver in the corner of her eye as the blade came down again.

Realising she had nothing to defend herself with, she tried to make her escape. She ran out of the living room and headed towards the kitchen door, trying desperately to not turn her back on Frankie, but it was impossible and Frankie was relentless. She felt a cold, sharp scratch down her back and screamed out as the sensation hit her brain.

She fell forwards through the open door and lay on her stomach, survival being the only thought in her head. She tried to

heave herself along the parquet flooring, but her hands kept slip-
ping. She fought to get to her feet, but something was crushing
the centre of her back. Suddenly, she felt her arms being pulled in
front of her, and she was being dragged across the floor. Her
mobile phone was digging into her hip in her front pocket – if
only she could wrestle an arm free. She looked up as best she
could, just in time to see Frankie bringing the knife down one final
time.

'It was you,' gasped Ziggy, tears streaming down his face as
he heard of Lolly's last moments. His heart shattered, and
his grief took his breath away. 'You killed her.' Lolly, his
Lolly, killed so needlessly, so savagely, by someone who was
supposed to love her.

'Yes! Who did you think it was?'

'Why? Why now?'

'She knew too much. I could see she'd worked it out and
I couldn't risk her telling you everything. No, that would
never do. We couldn't have that, so Howie fixed it for me and
did an excellent cleaning job. I'm sure you'll agree.'

Ziggy was gobsmacked, but he couldn't drop his guard
for a minute in front of this psychopath.

'What happens now then, Frankie, now that I know
everything?'

'Oh, I could kill you. That is an option, but it's messy and
I don't have time. Besides, it's my word against yours, if it
comes to it.'

There was a sudden movement from the floor.

'No, it's our word against yours,' said Chrystal, sitting up.

Frankie and Ziggy stared at her in equal measures of
wonder and bafflement.

Chrystal moved stiffly, but seemed quite coherent.

Seeing the shock on both of their faces, she let out a little laugh. 'I've been conscious long enough to hear your little monologue, Frankie. So it's two against one, plus you seem to be forgetting why you drugged me in the first place.' Chrystal turned to Ziggy. 'I'd worked it out. I wasn't a hundred per cent certain, but I had found out enough to be able to bring you evidence. There's always a paper trail. It's all in my notebook.'

Frankie cut in, a look of utter contempt on her face. 'Ha, I think you'll find that has been destroyed,' she said triumphantly.

'Not that one, the one that is currently being scrutinised by my colleagues at the *Yorkshire Press*, ready to hand over to the po—'

Chrystal didn't get a chance to finish her sentence before Frankie delivered a heavy backhand to the side of her face. It sent Chrystal reeling, and Ziggy was off his feet in no time. Frankie looked shocked that Ziggy wasn't tied to his chair, but she bolted for the stairs. Ziggy reached out to catch Chrystal. But he was too late, and her head bounced off the corner of the bottom step. Frankie jumped over her and pounded up the steps. Ziggy heard the door locking before he had even had a chance to reach the top step.

Breathlessly, he ran down to Chrystal and checked her for a pulse. Thankfully, it was there, but she already had a massive contusion on her head where it had collided with concrete. He dashed back to the chair he had been sitting on and looked at the floor behind it. Letting go of a breath of relief, he reached forwards and pressed stop on the Dicta-phone he had held behind his back. He had all the evidence he needed, silently thanking Lolly for being terrible at packing boxes.

40

Howard was waiting when Frankie reappeared at the top of the basement steps. 'Are you ready to leave?' she asked.

'Leave? With you? Honestly, Francesca, at times you're as naive and stupid as your fake girlfriend.'

'What's that supposed to mean?'

Howard walked towards Frankie, shaking his head. He'd really had enough of playing games. He had been more than ready to move on for a long time, but had been waiting for the right moment. He deeply regretted getting involved with Frankie's insane plans in the first place. They had seemed a good idea at the time, a good way to keep the money moving, but between her and those idiot O'Connor brothers, he was more than ready to start his new life. Bigger, better opportunities had been placed in his way, and he was never one to turn down a good deal.

'How do you think all of this has been paid for?' He waved his hands at the plush surroundings and decor, not waiting for an answer. 'Do you really think a few dodgy invoices and petty student accounts would keep you in the lap of luxury?' He laughed. 'Did it never occur to you that you were living a life beyond your means? Did you never once think where the money was coming from?'

Frankie looked bemused. 'I don't understand. It's from the money laundering, the pawnshops...'

'No, you're too stuck up your own arse to see the truth of what's been going on around you. That's small change. It's a handy cover story. Whilst you and those idiot brothers have been playing small, I've been busy building an empire. A vast, glorious, ludicrously wealthy empire, and I'm about to cash in my chips.'

Frankie stepped forwards and reached over to touch Howard's chest. 'But we're in this together.'

He sneered down at her. 'No, we're not. We haven't been for a long time.'

'You need to explain yourself, Howard, you're not making any sense.'

'I'm tired of playing with bottom feeders, Frankie. My business interests are about to go global, and I don't have the time or inclination to deal with plankton any more. Whilst you've been keeping your "lover" sweet, I've been broadening my horizons.'

Frankie did a double take. She couldn't believe what she was hearing. 'You've gone behind my back?' She reached forwards and grabbed his arm.

Howard shrugged her off as though she were a piece of dirt. 'Don't you dare lay your hands on me. You are nothing to me.'

Howard walked off and headed into the downstairs office. When he came back, he was holding a Glock 0.9 mm, aiming right at Frankie's head.

'Penny dropping now is it, my love?' Howard turned the endearment into a threat.

'You wouldn't dare,' gasped Frankie.

'Wouldn't I?' He walked slowly towards her, keeping the gun perfectly still. 'I have nothing to lose here. My flight leaves Heathrow tomorrow morning, by which time you will have been either arrested, or be on the run. Your little plan will have fallen down around you and you'll be scrambling in the dirt of a police cell, wondering how all this happened.' He walked around her and placed the barrel of the gun at the back of her head. 'Meanwhile, I'll be flying first class to the Dominican Republic to start my new life.' He pushed the muzzle further into Frankie's skull, forcing her head forwards. As she righted herself, he raised the gun and pistol-whipped her around the back of her head. She fell forwards onto her knees, and Howard stood in front of her, sneering, and leant close to her ear. 'Don't ever try to contact me, you evil little bitch, I am done with you.' He shoved the gun in the waistband of his trousers, grabbed his flight bag from the counter and slammed the front door.

Dazed and confused, it slowly dawned on Frankie that she'd been as much of a victim of Howard's as Lolly had been. She lay in the foetal position on the cold kitchen floor, trying to reconcile her husband of twenty-something years with the monster who had left her to fend for herself. As she gathered her senses and pulled herself back from the self-pitying hole she had been about to step into, she sat up. She felt her head and winced at the lump starting, but there was no blood on her hand when she pulled it away. She had a headache, the mother of all headaches, but she couldn't dwell on that now. She had to act fast; she had to get away.

Her bags had already been packed, and her passport was

in her bag upstairs. She dashed up into the bedroom, retrieved her hand luggage and made for the front door. With only a cursory glance at the basement door, she headed outside and climbed into her car. With any luck, if she put her foot down, she would still be able to make Leeds Bradford Airport in time for her scheduled flight, only this time it would be solo.

Sadie had broken every speed limit on her way over to Holmfirth. Firearms and the supporting search teams were not far behind her, but she had used her own car, not wanting to wait for the cumbersome police vehicles to weave their way along Denby Dale road and the M62. She was convinced Frankie held all the remaining pieces of the jigsaw and she wanted to be there when it all came together.

The first thing she spotted was Ziggy's car parked along the lane leading to Frankie's address. The hairs on the back of her neck stood up.

So this is where you've been hiding, she thought, though something didn't feel right. She drove into the sweeping driveway and parked up. The house was impressive. Where would the funds to buy such a place have come from? She walked round the perimeter of the building, peering through windows as she went. She had just returned to the front of the property when backup arrived.

She made herself known to the Firearms commander, and updated him; intel was vitally important at this stage. 'I've had a quick look around the outside, but nothing seems to be obviously out of place. DI Thornes's car is over there, so he's here somewhere, potentially being held hostage, as I don't know who the other car belongs to. I'll get the plates checked. I'll follow your lead.'

They set off to the entrance, with a team of officers going around the rear. When they were all in place, Sadie knocked loudly and shouted, 'Police!' No answer, so she tried the handle. Locked. The 'red key' or battering ram was passed along, and within seconds the door was flattened, and officers burst into the entrance. Sadie followed the team, checking rooms as she went, careful not to get in the way. She headed towards the kitchen, but still nothing.

Fearing the worst, she shouted again, and waited. This time, she heard a noise coming from behind a closed door in the corner of the kitchen.

'Ziggy?' she shouted, dashing over to the door. It was locked, and she looked around frantically for a key.

'Sadie?' the muffled response came through the door. 'Thank God, get me out of here.'

'I'm trying. Do you know where she kept the key?'

'No, use the red key.'

'Hold on.' She turned to the uniformed officers who had followed her lead. 'Do either of you have a crowbar or something we can use to get this door open?'

One of them took off on his heels and returned with a crowbar moments later. 'Ziggy, step away from the door. We're going to prise it open.'

Ten minutes and much sweating later, they were in. Ziggy hurtled up the steps, closely followed by a battered and bruised Chrystal Mack.

Ignoring Sadie's look of shock at seeing Chrystal, Ziggy grabbed Sadie by the shoulders.

'It was Frankie.'

'What was? Slow down. Are you OK, first of all? I'll call

an ambulance for Ms Mack. Here take a seat.' Sadie pulled out a kitchen stool as Chrystal stumbled over, holding her head. Ziggy and Sadie helped her to sit down as one of the uniformed officers called for medical assistance.

The Firearms commander confirmed there was no one else on the premises and called his team outside for a debrief before departing back to the station. The search team entered, suited and booted to stop scene contamination. They asked Sadie, Ziggy and Chrystal to relocate outside. Sadie unlocked her car, and then carefully helped Chrystal into the back.

Her pallor was growing paler by the minute, and Sadie willed the ambulance to arrive. She retrieved a foil blanket from her boot and wrapped it around Chrystal's shoulders. Ziggy sat in the front, where Sadie joined him.

'What the hell happened?' she asked.

Haltingly, pausing for breath and occasionally shutting his eyes as he recalled the scene, Ziggy recalled the events of the last twenty-four hours. He recounted the story Frankie had told him in the basement, and as he reached the end, he pulled the Dictaphone out of his jacket pocket.

'I have everything recorded,' he said.

Sadie noted that far from sounding triumphant, he sounded defeated and broken. 'And I heard everything too,' said Chrystal drowsily from the back seat. 'I can back it all up.'

Grateful that they were both still alive, but crucially aware that they both needed to be thoroughly checked by paramedics, Sadie's heart flipped with gratitude when she heard the sirens and saw the blue flashing lights.

As the pair were helped into the back of the ambulance, she leant against the side of her car, hands on hips, eyes skywards, blinking away tears. She thanked Lolly for watching over their friend. She couldn't even begin to imagine how he must feel after hearing the brutal details, but she hoped that in time he would find peace.

For now, they had a deranged psychopath and her ex-husband to catch.

41

Thursday, 26th September 2002

'I appreciate we're all tired, and I thank you for your dedication. We are almost there.' Whitmore looked around at the weary eyes in front of him at the morning briefing. 'Sadie, updates please.'

Equally exhausted and running on caffeine and adrenaline, Sadie ran through the events of the early hours that had led to the safe recovery of Ziggy and Chrystal Mack.

'Our priority now has to be catching Howard and Francesca Cohen. We have intel that Frankie has a reservation on a flight out of Leeds Bradford to Malaga, which is precisely where I'm heading after this briefing. Howard Cohen is headed to the Dominican Republic and we have a team at Heathrow Airport awaiting his arrival.'

Impatient to get away, she stood, rattling her car keys until Whitmore dismissed her with a nod of his head.

Moving as quickly as she could, she almost knocked over someone as equally impatient to get up the stairs as she was to get down them.

'Whoa,' she called out. She pulled herself back when she saw it was Ziggy. 'Oh, it's you. I thought you were at the hospital.'

He was looking a little battered and bruised, so Sadie reached out a hand to help Ziggy right himself. She took a step up so they were level with each other.

'All checked out. No serious harm done. Where are you headed?'

'Airport. Frankie.' Sadie had already started moving down the steps, so Ziggy followed her.

As they dashed out into the car park, Sadie raised her voice over the road-traffic noise. 'Is there any point saying no to you, or that you should perhaps check in with Whitmore first?'

'Nope,' replied Ziggy as he opened the passenger door to Sadie's car.

'I mean, I'm not sure if you're suspended, if you've quit, or are on leave.' She started the blue flashing light on her dashboard and switched the sirens on.

'Me neither,' said Ziggy, fastening his seat belt.

Sadie tore out of the car park and negotiated her way through the early-morning traffic onto the A65 through Kirkstall, swinging a right through Horsforth, taking back roads and shortcuts to avoid the worst of the traffic.

Finally reaching the airport, she pulled straight into the pickup/drop-off zone. Abandoning the car, both detectives raced to the check-in desks, searching the boards to see which gate the Malaga flight was due to depart from.

'Gate ten,' yelled Ziggy, shooting off in the direction of Departures. Waving their warrant cards at security, before finally arriving at the gate, Sadie hot on Ziggy's heels, they flashed their warrant cards once more.

'We're looking for a passenger,' he said breathlessly, to the young man on the desk.

'They won't be boarding for another ten minutes. I'm ground crew, but if you can give me a name, I can tell you if they have checked in.'

'Francesca Cohen, Mrs Francesca Cohen.'

Crucial minutes passed, with Ziggy impatiently tapping his foot.

'Yes, Mrs Cohen has checked in, so she must be somewhere in the terminal.'

Ziggy and Sadie looked round. Had it been high summer, they wouldn't have stood a chance of spotting her, but as it was late September and term time, the airport was relatively quiet. They scoured the seats, but there was no sign of her.

'Can you put a call out for her?'

'You would need to go to the check-in desk for that.'

'This is urgent,' stressed Ziggy, amazed that fact wasn't obvious even to bystanders. 'We don't have time. Can you *please* put a call out to her?'

Tutting, as if there was all the time in the world, the young man picked up his tannoy and asked for Mrs Cohen to make herself known to any member of the airport staff.

Whilst they waited, Sadie and Ziggy scanned the other passengers. 'She must be here somewhere,' said Sadie.

'Think, think, think. Where would you go if you were about to catch a flight and didn't want to be seen?'

'I wouldn't sit in public view for a start,' replied Sadie.

'Could she be in the toilets?' Ziggy was prepared to try anything at this point.

'She might be in the first-class lounge?' offered the ground crew.

Looking at each other, they silently agreed that that was

exactly where she would be. 'Which direction?' asked Ziggy, bouncing on his toes.

The young man thrust his arm out, and they set off. They had just reached the swing doors when Francesca Cohen came through in the opposite direction. Seeing Ziggy, she bolted, hurling the bag she had been carrying into Ziggy's path. She ran towards the lifts, pushing people out of her way as she went, but she was too slow. Ziggy had recovered and threw himself, rugby style, at Frankie's legs, bringing her crashing down.

Sadie caught up and quickly wrestled Frankie's arms behind her back.

Breathless, Ziggy slapped handcuffs on her wrists. 'Francesca Cohen, I am arresting you on suspicion of the murder of Doctor Leila Turner. You do not have to say anything, but anything you do say may be used in evidence.'

Dragging her to her feet, Ziggy pulled Frankie's face close to his own. 'Got ya.'

As they left the terminal, each with an arm looped through one of Frankie's, they were greeted with a custody van and the rest of the arrest team.

'About time,' Sadie scoffed, as Ziggy pushed Frankie into the back of the waiting van.

'Any news on Howard?' Ziggy asked, taking great pleasure in slamming the door shut on a face he had grown to detest.

Whitmore appeared, seemingly from nowhere. 'Yes, he's in custody and being transported back to Leeds.'

The relief was overwhelming, and for a second, Ziggy felt his knees go weak.

He closed his eyes for a moment, letting the emotions wash over him until he felt steady enough to continue.

'Thornes, get back to the station. We need to talk.'

Ah, back to reality, he thought. 'Yes, sir.'

Ziggy hardly spoke on the way back to HQ. He was battling so many emotions: relief that the pair had been caught, frustration that it had taken him so long to see what had been happening, but most of all an incredible amount of guilt that had dogged him throughout the whole investigation. What had stopped Lolly from telling him what was going on? He would have protected her. He would have helped her.

What had she been afraid of? That he wouldn't believe her? Thousands more questions on a similar theme ran through his head, and he knew it would take years, and possibly a considerable amount of counselling, to reconcile his head with his heart. In the meantime, he had Whitmore to face and his job to save.

They pulled up outside, and as Ziggy unclicked his seat belt, Sadie put her hand on his.

'I know you're not in a great place, Ziggy, but please try and stay calm when you're in front of Whitmore this time. I may be deputy SIO on this case, but I want you back as my boss, but more importantly, as my friend.'

Ziggy nodded, touched by Sadie's gesture. 'I will, I promise, and I appreciate your support.'

Together, they headed upstairs into the MIT office. Nick, Peter and Angela greeted them with a round of applause and claps on the back.

Ziggy laughed. 'Thank you, but I need to find out if I still have a job before I celebrate anything.'

Whitmore walked into the office just at that point. 'My office, Thornes. Now.'

Grimacing, Ziggy followed him in, choosing not to take a seat. Instead, he stood with his hands behind his back, heart pounding furiously.

'Sir, I would just like to—'

'Oh, no, Thornes, you don't talk your way out of this one.' Whitmore pulled his chair from under his desk and slammed his hands down on the Formica surface. 'You have deliberately, *repeatedly* ignored any orders that I have issued. You have wilfully gone behind my back throughout this investigation, and I have warned you more than once that I would not be able to keep this at my level. The assistant chief constable has been made aware of your actions and has recommended that you be placed on restricted duty whilst a full investigation takes place.'

Ziggy looked down at the floor. He felt gutted that his professional conduct was being questioned, but he knew it was the least he deserved. As long as Lolly's killers were brought to justice, he would stand by his actions and decisions any day. He'd done what he had to do, and could look Ben, Bill, Irene in the eye – and more importantly, himself in the mirror – and know that he had done what was needed to deliver the justice that his best friend deserved.

42

Friday, 27th September 2002

The custody clock was ticking once more after an earlier extension for the O'Connor brothers. As the team frantically pulled together all the latest evidence against Howard and Francesca, ready to present to the CPS, Nick, Sadie, Peter and Ziggy talked over the next steps.

'I think Nick and Sadie should take the interviews,' suggested Peter. 'I still have a few loose ends to tie up, then I'm headed back down south.'

Ziggy couldn't help but notice that he looked a little bit disappointed. 'Aww, will you miss us?' he goaded the Met detective, good-naturedly.

'Not you, that's for sure, you're a loose cannon,' he retorted.

'Just as we were beginning to like you as well,' said Sadie.

'Take a box of Yorkshire Tea with you,' suggested Nick.

'Don't think I won't,' he laughed, heading off to a meeting.

Ziggy turned to the rest of the team. 'He turned out all right in the end, didn't he?'

Sadie laughed. 'I think once he realised he didn't have a point to prove, and he climbed down from his high horse, he wasn't too bad.'

The others agreed as they grabbed their notebooks and headed into the conference room for an interview briefing. Whilst Ziggy was somewhat restricted in what he could and couldn't be included in, his years of interview experience and in-depth knowledge of the situation had been recognised and he was allowed to advise and oversee the interview strategy. He was quite glad that he couldn't take part. It would give him the chance to observe and offer feedback, and that was enough for him, for now.

'Mr Cohen, we would like to talk to you initially about your role in relation to a suspected money-laundering operation and the murder of Doctor Leila Turner. You should know that as well as your arrest, we are searching your home address, several pawnshop premises that you have a significant interest in, as well as any vehicles and computer equipment on the various premises.' Nick moved several pieces of paper around as he mentally lined up the questions they had all agreed on.

Howard Cohen shifted his considerable weight in the plastic chair that he was wedged into, and crossed and uncrossed his legs. Considering the early-morning arrest, Howard was dressed somewhat formerly in tailored suit trousers and an open-neck shirt. He was deeply tanned and had the demeanour of someone who had lived a comfortable life. Nick wasn't surprised that he had his brief alongside him – he just hoped it wouldn't be a no-comment interview.

Silence filled the interview room. Nick pressed on. 'What do you think we'll find in those searches?'

'Depends what you're looking for I guess,' replied Howard.

'The parameters are quite narrow at the moment, Howard. We'll be looking for anything that links you to money laundering and murder.'

Howard sighed and picked up a pen that his solicitor had left lying on the desk and started tapping the end against the table. 'Is that all you've got?'

'I'd say that's quite a lot,' said Nick. 'Tell me, how does it work, Howard?'

'How does what work?'

'We know about the false emails and the fake bank details that are currently being investigated,' said Nick. When there was no reply, he pressed on. 'Will we find details that lead back to you?'

'You tell me, you seem to have all the answers.'

'It's a complex operation, isn't it? I suppose you targeted the bigger businesses, as invoices get paid as part of a process and go almost unnoticed. Is that right?'

Howard laughed. 'You're clutching at straws here, aren't you?'

Nick ignored the jibe and the self-assured, cocky attitude. 'Talk me through how it works. What happens once the money hits the account?'

No answer.

'Who withdraws the cash?'

Again, no answer. Nick refused to let it frustrate him, and he removed a photograph from the folder in front of him. It was the crime scene photograph of Lolly lying in the

bloody bath water. He turned it round to face Howard and
watched as he visibly recoiled. Howard reached out and
turned it over, only for Nick to turn it back.

'Upsetting, isn't it?' said Nick. 'That's how we found her,
but you know that, don't you?'

'No comment.'

'You cleaned up the scene, didn't you?' pressed Nick.

'No comment.'

'To cover up Francesca's actions, you went to the scene,
cleaned up and helped your wife build an alibi.'

'Don't refer to that bitch as my wife.'

'But you covered for her, didn't you? You were angry
with her for creating such unnecessary drama and drawing
attention to you, but you still did it, didn't you?'

Nick looked at Howard's face and could see he was
increasingly getting wound up. Sweat had broken out on his
forehead, and he fingered the neck of his shirt.

'It must have taken a while. That's a lot of blood.' Nick
pulled out more photographs and laid them out. 'What did
you do with the murder weapon – kitchen knife, wasn't it?'

Nick kept applying the pressure and asking leading
question after leading question, sensing that the pressure-
cooker atmosphere he had created was about to blow.

'Did you do it on your own? Was your wife, Frankie,
there?'

'SHE IS NOT MY FUCKING WIFE!' Howard shot up
out of his seat and threw his chair backwards. Spittle flew
from his mouth. 'You should be asking her all this. All I did
was tidy up after her. That's all I've ever fucking done –
clean up after her shit.'

Nick and Sadie were both on their feet, ready to apply
the handcuffs to Howard if needed.

Howard's solicitor was cowering in a corner. He

nervously spoke up. 'Right, I think we need a break so I can consult with my client.'

'Excellent work, Sergeant Wilkinson,' Ziggy slapped Nick on the back. 'You really got to him.'

Nick looked quite pleased with himself, but there was no time to gloat. 'We need to talk to Frankie whilst Howard consults with his solicitor,' he said, addressing Sadie, though Ziggy still hovered nearby, like a bird with clipped wings.

'Yes, we do. I'll take this one,' she said. 'Any advice, boss?' she asked Ziggy.

'Make her feel clever, like she is superior, important, special. When we were in the basement, she took great pride in telling me how it had all been her idea.'

Sadie nodded. 'Sure, let's do this then.'

She pushed open the door to Interview Room 3 and saw Frankie sat there in a custody-issue grey tracksuit and white slip-on shoes. Sadie hazarded a guess that Frankie had never worn a tracksuit in her life.

Sitting down heavily and dropping the various folders on the table, Nick started the recording whilst Sadie made the introductions. Once everyone had declared themselves, she began.

'Mrs Cohen, you are being questioned today with regard to the murder of Doctor Leila Turner. You have legal representation and you should have been informed of the evidence we have disclosed to your solicitor.'

Sadie pulled out the same photograph that Nick had used with Howard. Pushing it across the table, it didn't surprise Sadie in the slightest that Frankie neither looked away nor turned the photo over. She just stared at it with a blank expression on her face.

'Before we go any further, Sergeant, I must make you aware that my client has a prepared statement and will be giving a no-comment interview, as is her right.'

Sadie looked at Nick, neither of them surprised but equally frustrated.

'No, I won't,' broke in Frankie. 'Ask away.'

'Mrs Cohen, I strongly advise you to give a no-comment interview,' the solicitor urged.

'To hell with that. If I'm going down, the whole sorry lot can come down with me. What do you want to know?'

Vindictive to the end, Francesca Cohen proceeded to repeat, more or less verbatim, everything she had confessed to in the basement with Ziggy, this time with no emotion at all.

It's like she's reading a script, thought Ziggy, as he watched from the viewing room.

He listened as she shared the clean-up role that the two older O'Connor brothers had played, and how it had been her idea to issue the threats against the reporter and Ben.

'Course, that idiot brother managed to leave behind more than the note. Fuckwit that he is.'

Ziggy flinched, remembering the bollocking Sadie had given him for chasing evidence behind her back. The glove had been critical in connecting the dots, but with all the forensic evidence that had been found in the warehouse, thankfully they now had enough additional evidence to put the O'Connors away for a long time.

She boasted how she had plied Chrystal Mack with gin until she revealed everything she knew about the money-laundering operation, and the squaring scam, but it had been the revelation about the investigation into Howard's bogus business that had triggered her anger.

'I just diluted the diazepam with copious amounts of gin, and hey presto, one unconscious reporter.' Frankie took a sip of water. 'I couldn't resist a few swift kicks whilst she was down. I mean no one likes the media, do they?' She laughed and sat back.

Ziggy felt sick to his stomach with disgust. Unable to watch any more, he left the room and reached for his mobile phone. He'd already spoken with Rachel, and she and Ben were once again back home, but he needed the reassurance that they were both OK, so he rang again.

'Hey, just checking in,' he said on hearing Rachel's voice.

'Hey, we're still fine,' she said gently.

He was grateful for her patience with him. 'Is Ben there?'

He listened as she shouted their son and heard his clumsy footsteps as he bounced downstairs and crossed the landing to the phone.

'Hiya, Dad.'

Ziggy felt a surge of love for his boy. 'Hey, son, you OK?'

'I'm good, thanks. Are you coming for tea?'

'Yeah, I can do if it's OK with your mum?'

'Mum said to ask you. She said you had something to tell me.'

He smiled, knowing exactly what Rachel meant. 'She's right, I do.' He paused, the words catching in his throat. 'I did it, mate. I caught the bad guys.'

EPILOGUE

Six weeks later

Ziggy kicked the ground beneath his feet and adjusted his position on the wooden bench. 'I just wish you had come to me. I would have helped. We would have found a way.'

He could hear Lolly's voice in his head responding with a laugh that was full of love. He had done the best he could, what he had set out to do. He'd provided justice for his best friend.

Standing and touching the headstone, he bid his best friend goodbye and headed to his next meeting.

'Wait, you're not recording this, are you?'

'No, what do you take me for?'

Ziggy raised his eyebrows and looked at Chrystal over his coffee cup. 'That's a joke, right?'

Chrystal smiled as she stirred her latte. 'No, I'm not recording. This is just two friends chatting. I will be writing up the trial for tomorrow's paper, though.'

That didn't surprise Ziggy at all. After everything Chrystal had been through, he secretly felt she had earned the right to tell the story from the 'inside', as she insisted on saying.

'Go on then, give me an overview of the article.'

'Well, it starts where it was always going to, sharing Lolly's upbringing with the reader so they get an insight into her early childhood trauma, which would go some way to explaining why she did what she did, that unfortunately resulted in the loss of her life.'

A respectful silence fell between them until Ziggy broke it. 'What will you say about the Cohens?'

'Twisted, money-grabbing, small-time gangsters.'

'Oh, that will infuriate Frankie. From everything she said at the trial, she has an even higher opinion of herself than even I believed.'

'Typical narcissistic behaviour. She presented herself to Lolly as a pleaser, an excellent listener, honest, a high level of integrity. Spoilt her in the early stages with expensive dinners, flowers and gifts. Then, when Frankie was sure she had her under her spell, she started the manipulation. It's a long game, for seemingly little reward, but for Frankie, it was worth it. It was always about the game, not the reward. Howard saw her as just another money mule.'

'I was surprised her defence team let her take the stand. If I'm honest, she was a liability to herself.'

'I imagine she will have insisted – plays to her ego.'

A tinkling bell showed someone else had entered the coffee shop. Ziggy looked over to see Sadie and Nick shaking the rain from their umbrella's as they came in out of the cold. Ziggy waved, and the pair joined them after ordering their own drinks.

'Bloody weather,' Nick grumbled, as he warmed his hands on the wall heater.

'What are you two talking about?' said Sadie. 'Like I need to ask.'

'Chrystal has just been giving me her insights into Frankie's personality.'

'Absolute nut job,' said Nick as he took his coffee from the waiter. 'No, not you,' he quickly corrected himself after seeing the waiter's face.

The other three laughed.

'Howard's on trial next, isn't he? What charges did the CPS agree to?' asked Chrystal.

Sadie ticked them off her fingers. 'Accessory to murder, seventeen charges of corporate money laundering and a further nineteen charges relating to the student squaring scam, plus a load more offshore activity that's too long to go into.'

Ziggy sighed. None of this was new information. He'd helped the team build the case, after all, but he still couldn't believe that Lolly had somehow managed to get herself tied up in it all.

'What about the O'Connors?'

Nick answered Chrystal's question. 'Freddie was released without charge, but the other two are charged with malicious threats, accessory to murder for cleaning the scene and Stephen O'Connor is also facing numerous charges for money laundering.'

'Even without Ziggy's evidence, we had enough to tie them all into Lolly's murder with Frankie's confession,' Sadie chimed in.

Silence fell around the table as they each relived the part they had played in securing justice for their friend.

'What next for the great DI Thornes, then?' Chrystal asked, after a moment.

Sadie and Nick stared at him. 'We'd like to know that too,' Nick said.

Ziggy scratched the back of his head and smiled. 'Do you know what? I'm not sure.'

Sadie sat back. 'That was not the answer I was expecting.'

Ziggy nodded and fiddled with the spoon on the table. 'I know, I would usually be keen to get on with the next case, but I'll admit, this has pushed me to my limits.' He raised his hand as Sadie was about to jump in. 'Before you say anything, I have a meeting with professional standards in a couple of weeks, so until then, I'm taking some time out. I'll spend it quietly with Ben and Rachel—'

The force of the blast smashed the glass and threw all the cafe-goers towards the rear of the coffee shop. Glass, pottery, cutlery, condiments, chairs, tables all collided to create a cacophony of noise that pierced ear drums and ripped off limbs.

Then silence. An eerie silence, with no movement or sound. A stillness that was out of place in the usually bustling high street.

Sadie groaned and removed an object from across her chest. She tried several times to open her eyes but debris caused her eyelashes to flutter and close until she lifted her hand and wiped the dirt from her face. She lifted her head and looked to the left, seeing a familiar but distorted face with wide, staring eyes.

'Ziggy?'

WANT TO READ MORE?

FREE EBOOKS TO DOWNLOAD

Download behind the scenes insights on the following link
https://catherineyaffe.co.uk/behindthescenes

Download Little Girl, Lost (Lolly's Story)
Download Feel The Fear (Ziggy's Story)

All available on my website www.catherineyaffe.co.uk

ALSO BY CATHERINE YAFFE

Book 1 – The Lie She Told

Book 2 – The Web They Wove

Novella – Feel The Fear, Ziggy's Story

Novella – Little Girl, Lost, Lolly's Story

ACKNOWLEDGMENTS

Thank you so much for reading When We Deceive, and I do hope you've enjoyed Ziggy and Lolly's story.

I have referred to this book as the 'book-that-refused-to-write-itself' as it feels as though it has been a part of my life for so long, when in reality it's been about 18 months (not bad when you consider my first book took me ten years!). It has been a labour of love, and I hope you've enjoyed reading it as much as I enjoyed writing it.

No book is written in isolation, and the list of people who helped with this one is long! But first and foremost, my dad. He's been on my shoulder with every word I wrote, and I could hear him clearly telling me I could do better, it was too predictable or too flowery – 'change it, you'll thank me later'. I made the changes, Pops and I hope you like the ending!

My amazing, patient and incredibly supportive editor Rebecca Miller. It has taken some doing but we got there, and thanks to your encouragement in my ability, I don't think we've done too bad a job! Onto the next one, if you'll have me.

Sam Brownley, proof-reader extraordinaire and fabulous interviewer over on UK Crime Book Club on Facebook. How have we not actually met yet? (Any errors were inadvertently added by me!)

For the police procedures, I have taken some small liberties that I needed to make the story work, but my thanks go to Graham Bartlett, and Carol and Bob Bridgestock for their guiding hands and words of encouragement.

Kate Bendelow, my wonderful CSI contact and friend, thank you from stopping me from making an almighty blooper – credibility saved (mine, yours was never in question!)

Jim Fraser (Murder Under The Microscope), thank you for your insights into the life of a Forensic Investigator. Any mistakes are all my own.

To my incredible advanced readers, beta team and the mailing list gang aka #TeamZiggy. You are all amazing and I am so grateful for everything you do, for me and the whole writing community. Never stop emailing me your anecdotes, they really do make the hard days easier!

My online friends, and fellow writers – the most supportive community I have ever worked with. You lift me up when the going gets tough and I will always return the favour. Bookshops, libraries – thank you for all you do.

Finally, but by no means least my family. Daniel, Mark, Sadie, Milo, Mary; the best bunch of cheerleaders any girl could ask for. Thank you all for being there for me – I love you.

Did you know that every time you leave a review, an author somewhere does a happy dance?

Please consider leaving a review! 😊

- Goodreads
- Amazon
- Facebook

Printed in Great Britain
by Amazon

40902820R00165